G000152916

Before You Grow Up

Before you grow up

Poems by Finola Akister

Illustrated by Colin West

VIKING KESTREL

VIKING KESTREL

Penguin Books Ltd, Harmondsworth, Middlesex, England
Viking Penguin Inc., 40 West 23rd Street, New York, New York 10010, U.S.A.
Penguin Books Australia Ltd, Ringwood, Victoria, Australia
Penguin Books Canada Ltd, 2801 John Street, Markham, Ontario, Canada L3R 1B4
Penguin Books (N.Z.) Ltd, 182–190 Wairau Road, Auckland 10, New Zealand

First published 1987

Text copyright © Finola Akister, 1987

Illustrations copyright © Colin West, 1987

All rights reserved. Without limiting the rights under copyright
reserved above, no part of this publication may be reproduced,
stored in or introduced into a retrieval system, or transmitted,
in any form or by any means (electronic, mechanical, photocopying,
recording or otherwise), without the prior written permission
of both the copyright owner and the above publisher of this book.

British Library Cataloguing in Publication Data

ISBN 0–670– 81712–0

Printed in Great Britain by
Butler and Tanner Ltd,
Frome and London

A butterfly just fluttered by
And settled on a rose.
Where it came from I don't know,
I cannot say where it will go,
For suddenly it flew away.
But still, I'm glad it came today.

Always it amazes me
How slippery the soap can be.
I pick it up and start to rub,
When WHOOSH – it jumps into the tub.
I search and search and search around:
That bar of soap just can't be found.
Instead of lying in the dish,
It's swimming round, just like a fish.
I cannot catch it – golly gosh,
I think I'll go without a wash.

It was early in the morning,
Just as the day was dawning,
That Fido packed his bone and ran away.
But, realizing what he'd done,
He thought it wasn't much like fun,
So he turned about and hurried home next day.

Cats like milk.

Mice like cheese.

Little dogs like sausagees.

Crabs always walk sideways, and so
Spare a thought for this unhappy plight.
If a left-handed crab always walked to the left,
And his true love was geared to the right,

They would pass by like ships in the night.
Just a wave as they hove into view,
Destined never to walk side by side, or to talk
Claw in claw, like the other crabs do.

The solution is not hard to find,
And matters could be so much worse —
There's the chance they could meet on the
  strand or the street.
If one of them walked in reverse.

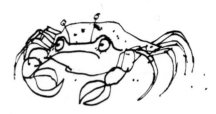

Zanzibar was a very large lion,
With a beautiful lion-like mane.
He looked very fierce, ferocious and wild,
Though, in fact, he was terribly tame.

His grandad was born in the jungle,
Where the weather was sultry and hot.
But Zanzibar knew, as he gazed round the zoo,
That, in England, the weather was not.

He thought, with his lion-like thinking,
As he lazily gazed round the zoo,
How happy he'd be, if he only were free.
He was bored. There was nothing to do.

He longed, with his lion-like longing,
To go for a stroll round about.
His cage was too small – there was no room at
 all –
But his keeper would not let him out.

Zanzibar scowled at the keeper,
In his lion-like sort of way.
Should I eat him? he thought. But he'd have to
  be caught.
And the keeper kept out of his way.

So Zanzibar lay there and brooded,
Till one day – it was just getting dark –
They hustled him into a lorry
And drove him away to a park.

Now Zanzibar gazes about him.
He is pleased with this lovely new place.
He lies on the grass with a lion-type lass
And a smile on his lion-like face.

There is one thing I cannot do
Because, you see, I'm only two.
No matter how I try and try,
It nearly always makes me cry.
I don't know when it all began,
Or why some very clever man
Thought that buttons could be fun –
I simply can't get mine undone.
My mother comes and helps me out,
But, really, what's it all about?
Although I try, it's all in vain.
I just can't do them up again.

14

He was small and white,
With eyes so bright,
But he wandered away from the house.
He was small and sweet,
So if you should meet,
Please bring me back my mouse.

I'll polish up the teapot, thought Sarah Jane
  one night.
Mummy will be so surprised to see it shining
  bright.
She found the cloth for polishing, and then, with
  might and main,
She rubbed it once, and just for luck she rubbed
  it once again.

Sarah Jane was worried that she hadn't done it
  right,
For as she rubbed, with might and main, there
  came a blinding light.
And standing there before her was a giant, ten
  feet tall.
He was smiling down upon her, which made her
  feel so small.

16

His mighty arms were folded on his very mighty
  chest.
He wore a turban on his head and jewels on his
  vest.
His shoes were just like gravy boats, and
  everybody knows

That shoes like that are always made with
  funny curled-up toes.

Sarah Jane was speechless, so great was her
  surprise.
She gazed upon the giant – she could not believe
  her eyes.
His arms unfolded slowly, then he waved one
  mighty hand:
'I am the Teapot Genie, and I wait for your
  command.'

Sarah Jane had heard about the Genie of the
  Ring.
She had heard about the Genie of the Lamp and
  everything.
But she had never thought that teapots had a
  genie too –
She'd heard of 'instant', 'quick' and 'fine' but not
  of 'genie' brew.

'Please, could I have a teddy bear?' asked little
  Sarah J.
At once, with just a puff of smoke, the Genie
  went away.
Sarah Jane woke up and found that she was still
  in bed.
It must have been a dream – but what was this
  beside her head?

It was a lovely teddy bear and just exactly
  right.
She wondered where it came from 'cause it
  wasn't there last night.
It's very, very strange, and Sarah Jane cannot
  explain.
She isn't even sure herself from where her teddy
  came.

It came down from the ceiling
On a silken, single thread.
I screamed out loud
Because I don't
Like spiders in my bed.

Lots of spots

Are polka dots.

An elephant, they said, had come to see me in
the morning.
I thought it very odd that this should be.
I was surprised – no, even more, I was certain, I
was *sure*
That I didn't know an elephant, so how could
one know me?

I didn't like to tell them that I didn't know an
elephant,
So I pretended that it wasn't strange to me,
And I made it very plain that, should he ever
call again,
I'd be obliged if they would ask him in for tea.

It's very odd, they said, that I was friendly with
an elephant.
It might seem odd to them, but not to me.
They hinted I was lying and remarked, 'Perhaps
a lion
Or a hippopotamus might come along and want
some tea.'

'I am not,' I said, 'acquainted with a single
  hippopotamus,
And a lion is an animal with whom I disagree.
The monkeys that I knew are really very, very
  few,
But an elephant is different and should be asked
  to tea.'

Still I couldn't make them see that elephants
  were different.
Perhaps it's just as well, you will agree,
For I really do not know a single elephant,
  and so
They will never be obliged to ask my elephant
  to tea.

The tortoise moves, but slowly,
As he goes from A to B.
He takes his time along the way,
But what he thinks, I cannot say
Because (it's very sad to tell)
He never comes out of his shell.

He never rushes, I am told,
Or runs on recklessly.
What his pace is I don't know,
But I am certain it is slow.
Why he lingers I can't say –
It must be 'cause he's made that way.

The tortoise moves, but slowly.
It is obvious that he
Has got a heavy load to bear.
He takes it with him everywhere.
The house he carries on his back
Must be a heavy handicap.

The tortoise moves, but slowly,
As he plods from A to B.
He crawls along from day to day,
Slowly but surely on his way.
He stops – I don't know what he thinks.
Perhaps he's having forty winks.

Yes, the tortoise moves so slowly:
He seems to lack the pace.
I asked him, was he good or bad,
Was he happy, was he sad?
He said he didn't want to tell,
And disappeared inside his shell.

The tortoise does not move at all
From A or B or C.
It's winter, and the snow came down.
He didn't laugh or smile or frown
But, slow and steady, he did creep
Into his shell, and fell asleep.

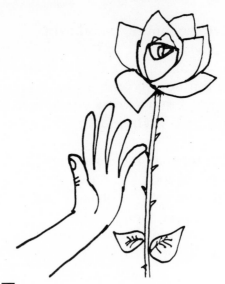

I saw a lovely rose one day,
As I was passing on my way,
But when I tried to pick it, oh,
It pricked my little finger so.
I will not pick a rose again.
Instead I'll make a daisy chain.

My bedroom gets into a mess.
I tidy up and then
The next day it is just as bad,
So I tidy up again.

If I could choose
What I would be,
I'd like to be a bumble bee.
I'd bumble in and out of flowers,
But only during sunny hours,
For if it rained hard, you can bet
I'd bumble off and not get wet.

When I was just a foal,
My mother said to me,
'Always do as you are told,
And never disagree.'
I'd like to do just as she said –
There isn't any doubt –
But whenever I open my mouth to say, 'Yes,'
It's always a 'Neigh' that comes out.

Neigh!

If, walking down a busy street,
It happens that you chance to meet
A tiger,
You must be discreet.
But
If it is a pussy cat,
By all means stop and have a chat.

A camel can race through the desert
Because everyone knows
He doesn't get hot,
Or bothered a lot,
By sand between his toes.

You have heard of the ugly duckling
Who turned into a beautiful swan.
But have you heard
Of the ugly swan
Who had rotten luck
And didn't turn into
A beautiful duck?

They look like little baskets,
Hanging up there in the tree.
I know that they are birds' nests,
But I think you will agree
That if their owners spent more time
And built a little roof,
Nests really would be warmer
And much more weather-proof.

The mule is a beast of burden.
He is strong, but he's obstinate too.
If he's bearing a grudge,
And unwilling to budge,
There is nothing at all you can do.

Just when I thought I had made it,
And it really was looking so grand,
I picked up my model kit aeroplane –
Then it all fell apart in my hand.

I wash my face – that's easy –
Though sometimes I have fears:
Mum says she could grow potatoes
In the space behind my ears.

I've thought and thought about it,.
And it might be just as well,
If I took some care, while the soap is there,
To wash that space as well.

When we go on a trip to the seaside,
My mum and dad take my hand.
Because it's in reach, we go down to the beach
And make castles with buckets of sand.

Mum takes a case to this heavenly place.
It is packed tight with goodies to eat.
Dad digs a hole, with the zest of a mole,
Then the tide comes and tickles my feet.

But when we get home to the garden,
Dad's fervour for digging is slack.
He puts down the spade, goes and sits in the
 shade
And explains that he's got a bad back.

The tide comes in
Upon the shore.
It turns about.
The tide goes out.

I have a lovely car, you know.
I get in it and go, go, go.
Near and far, up and down,
I travel all around the town.
I toot my horn (it's only fair
To let the people know I'm there).
Even on hills I do not shirk,
Though pedalling up hills is hard work.

I try not to paddle in puddles,
And I try to eat cabbage as well.
I try to be good 'cause I know that I should,
So why I am bad I can't tell.

It's just that a puddle is tempting,
And cabbage, I think, is a mess.
I'll have to start walking round puddles
And swallow the cabbage, I guess.

They tell me an elephant never forgets,
And, of course, what they say may be so.
That's all very well, but how can they tell?
I mean, how can they possibly know?

The extraordinary thing about daisies –
I must make this abundantly plain –
Is they're mowed with the lawn
(You can't see one at all),
But the next day they're all back again.

The barn owl looked out through his spectacled
  eyes,
And he gazed at the farmyard below.
The sun was beginning to rise in the east,
And the cock was beginning to crow.
It is time, thought the owl, I was going to sleep.
He was old, he was wise and he knew
That for him it was right. He'd been up half the
  night
Serenading that girl owl with two things in
  sight,
Namely, to-whit and to-woo.

Dog was a stray with nowhere to stay.
He just wandered about in the street.
He spent every day in the usual way,
Just looking for something to eat.

He wasn't to blame 'cause he hadn't a name,
Though he desperately wished that he had.
He never had known a name of his own.
He was lonely and hungry and sad.

One day, without warning, at ten in the
 morning,
He walked up to a cottage and found
Something really appalling – a lady had fallen
And lay in a heap on the ground.

The lady was old and she seemed very cold.
Dog had to get help, that was plain.
Without waiting to stop, he ran to the shop
And barked loudly, again and again.

44

'It's that black-and-white stray. I will chase him
  away,'
Said a tall man who looked very grand.
But a woman said, 'Stay, he is trying to say
Something we don't understand.'

'I think that I know,' said the man. 'Let us go.'
Then they followed Dog out of the door.
The old lady they found. She was still on the
  ground –
She was lying there, just as before.

There was a bump on her head, so they put her
  to bed,
And soon she recovered and cried,
'How lucky am I that you chanced to pass by.
But for you I would surely have died.'

'It was not just by chance,' said the man, with a
  glance
At the lady who lay in the bed.

' 'Twas the stray dog that cried, brought us here
   to your side,
So you really should thank him instead.'

Then the old lady knew what she wanted to do,
And she smiled. It was lovely to see.
'If the dog is a stray, don't send him away.
Bring him in. He shall live here with me.'

Dog has got his desire as he lies by the fire,
For the days of his hardship are past.
He is pleased to claim that he now has a name:
It is Ben, and he's happy at last.

Humpty Dumpty sat on a wall.
He fell, so now I can see
Why all the king's horses
And all the king's men
Had scrambled egg for tea.

Jack and Jill walked up the hill,
Then they had to stop.
There was nowhere else for them to go –
They had reached the very top.

49

They take me here,
They take me there,
They take me almost everywhere.
But wherever they take me,
Wherever I roam,
I'm just a homing pigeon,
So I am going home.

50

If you should see a little dog
(He's sort of black, but here and there,
Just mixed amongst the black,
You'll find odd spots of brownish hair),

Perhaps he isn't really lost.
He just strayed off the other day.
I'm certain that he would come home
If only he could find his way.

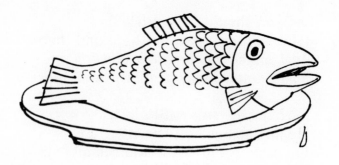

I do not wish to be a fish.
I might end up upon a dish.
But, worse than that, if I should linger,
I might become a fried fish finger.

The good things are bad,
If you see what I mean,
Like chocolates and toffees
And cakes full of cream.
They are bad for your teeth,
And they make you grow fat,
Then they spoil your complexion.
Just think about that.

The Vikings sailed across the sea.
Each man pulled upon his oar.
Without a doubt they were all tired out
When they reached the foreign shore.

After a rest they fought with zest.
They won but, alas and alack,
They had to stay – there was no other way.
They were all too tired to row back.

They said that there were fairies at the bottom
of the garden,
And I thought I'd go along so I could see
Just what a fairy looked like, 'cause I'd never
come across one,
And I really longed to see just how a fairy ought
to be.

Though I didn't see a fairy at the bottom of the
garden
(So what a fairy looks like I really cannot say),
I think perhaps they do live at the bottom of the
garden
But now, because it's summer, they've gone off
on holiday.

I'm looking out the window.
I'm feeling kind of blue.
I've played at trains and lots of games,
Now I don't know what to do.
The cat's gone out. Without a doubt,
She's catching mice again.
The puppy dog has gone to sleep.
I wish it would not rain.

I've read the jolly comic book
I got from Auntie Kit.
I've tried to do the jigsaw,
But the pieces will not fit.
I've been and asked my mother
If she'd like to come and play,
But she says she's much too busy.
And the rain won't go away.

I've chatted to the goldfish,
But it doesn't make a sound.
It really doesn't do a thing
Except swim round and round.
Oh, how I wish that somebody
Would come along and play,
And how I want the sun to shine
And chase the rain away.

When it was my birthday,
Daddy asked what I would choose
For a special birthday present,
So I answered, 'Dancing shoes.'

We went to town to buy some,
But they cost an awful lot.
'Have you any cheaper?' Daddy asked,
But that was all they'd got.

So Daddy had to pay the price,
Though he made an awful fuss.
'I'm glad you're a little girl,' he said,
'And not an octopus.'

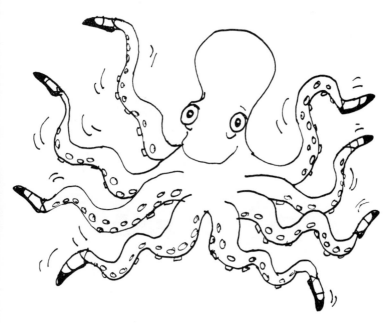

An eagle flew out of his eyrie,
And soared over mountains and plain,
Then when he was feeling quite weary,
He turned round and flew back again.

My roller skates won't ever do
The simple things I want them to.
I put them on and try my best,
But one goes East and the other goes West.

I often fall upon the floor,
Then, full of pluck, I try once more.
But my roller skates think they know best:
One still goes East and the other goes West.

Should you wish to see a crocodile,
You'll find one swiming in the Nile.
But think before you seek one out –
Their manners leave much room for doubt.
They're slinky creatures, full of guile,
And have a most preposterous smile.
I've heard it said, and think it's true,
There are some dreadful things they do.
They care not what or who you are
And are not too particular
About the menu for their tea –
They eat up anything they see.

So if, by chance, it happens you
Are wondering what is best to do,
Don't paddle near this carnivore
But safely stay upon the shore.
Throw him a bun or two and say,
'Good morning, how are you today?'
But take my warning. Do not forget:
Never keep one as a pet.

A mother bird sat in the nest
And said to her fledglings, 'Cheep, cheep.'
Roughly translated, her words meant this:
You must look before you leap.

Rings go round,
Squares are square,

But whirlygigs
Go everywhere.

 If you stumble and tumble,

And you're not very tall,

You won't have very far to fall.

Will you give me a clue
As to what I should do
When I'm sent up to bed without tea?
Do I sit there and cry?
Or look out at the sky?
Oh why does this happen to me?
It's no good being haughty –
I really was naughty.
I should never have eaten that jam.
And I have to confess,
I made rather a mess
When I carved up the rest of the ham.
But when all's done and said
I sit here on my bed . . .
I'll be better tomorrow I vow.
But consider my plight:
I get no tea tonight,
And I'm ever so hungry right now.

If I was a cat,
I'd sit on the mat
And chat
To the mouse
Who lived in the house.
But
If I was the mouse
Who lived in the house,
I doubt if I'd feel
Like having
A chat
With the cat
Who sat on the mat.

If you should go to the Isle of Man,
And you should see a cat
Without a tail, don't be surprised,
Manx cats are made like that.

I know I have to go to bed.
I do not want to sleep,
For Santa Claus comes here tonight,
And I want to have a peep.

If I was very rich,
I'd walk into a shop.
I'd buy myself potato crisps
And then a lollipop.

I'd buy some pink ice-cream for you
And then some sweets for me.
But, alas, I am not very rich —
I've only got ten p.

Hey diddle diddle, the cat had a fiddle
And played it all day and all night.
Then, before very long, he burst into song,
Which, of course, gave the neighbours a fright.

The loud caterwauling was really appalling.
The noise rent the air like a knife.
The neighbours would hoot him. They
  threatened to shoot him.
So the cat had to run for his life.

69

I travel slowly, but I go
From here to there, and though I'm slow,
I always, always leave a trail.
I have to 'cause I am a snail.

I said I'd do my homework
(There was an awful lot),
But I forgot.
I said I'd write a thank-you note
For the present from Auntie Dot,
But I forgot.

I should have been quite sorry,
And I was, but not a lot,
'Cause I forgot.

Now I'm being good as gold,
So Mum won't be upset.
Tomorrow is my birthday.
I do hope she won't forget.

The camel has a funny lump,
Which everybody calls a hump.
He carries it upon his back.
It's like a sort of storage pack.
So he can live a long, long time
Without the need to stop and dine.
In deserts, if you stop to think,
There's nowhere he can get a drink,
And as the sun is very hot,
He's happy with the hump he's got.

He is just a fluffy chicken.
He is only one day old.
His beak is sort of yellow.
The rest of him is gold.
'Cheep, cheep,' is all he says.
It doesn't mean a lot.
But it's all that he can utter.
It's all the speech he's got.

He said his name was Walter.
He was a cross-bred hound.
He read the 'Welcome' on the mat,
So he wandered in to have a chat.
He told them he was just a stray,
And said that he would like to stay,
So Walter never went away.

I have ten fingers and ten toes.
It's just the right amount.
Apart from other useful things,
They help me when I count.

Is Archibald just a cat?
An ordinary tabby cat?
No! Archibald is more than that.

He has the habits, it is true,
Of doing things that most cats do,
But Archibald is something new . . .

Archibald belongs to me,
Which makes him special, don't you see?
I love him so, and he loves me.

I don't remember being one
Because I was so very young.
Then being two I don't recall

Because I was still very small.
The nicest year of all is three
'Cause now I can remember me.

I stand and stare. I can't believe
I'm seeing what I see.
A cow, dressed in a jumper,
Is walking straight at me.

Though odd, I agree, I'm beginning to see
The reason for it now.
The cow is wearing a jumper
Because she's a Jersey cow.

A bee, a very busy bee,
Was great on hospitality.
When she invited friends to dine
She gave them mead (a honey wine).
Her hive, it seemed, was not, alas,
Equipped throughout with British Gas.
There was no way that she could cook,
Nor did she have a cooking book.

Undaunted by this state of things,
She thought it out, then spread her wings.
She travelled far, she travelled near,
And then engaged a caterer.
It goes to show how much she cared –
She really was a bee prepared.

The moon peeped through the window.
I was lying in my bed.
It was very bright that starry night,
So I opened a book and read.

G000152912

THE STONES

A CRIME MYSTERY

By

Cate Cullington

CRANTHORPE
—MILLNER—

Copyright © Cate Cullington (2020)

The right of Cate Cullington to be identified as author of this work has been asserted by her in accordance with section 77 and 78 of the Copyright, Designs and Patents Act 1988.

All rights reserved. No part of this publication may be reproduced, stored in a retrieval system, or transmitted in any form or by any means, electronic, mechanical, photocopying, recording, or otherwise, without the prior permission of the publishers.

Any person who commits any unauthorized act in relation to this publication may be liable to criminal prosecution and civil claims for damages.

A CIP catalogue record for this title is available from the British Library.

First published (2020)

ISBN 978-1-912964-43-7 (Paperback)

www.cranthorpemillner.com

Cranthorpe Millner Publishers

A Note from the Author

Six months before I wrote this book, I could never have imagined myself as a writer - I just didn't sit still long enough! There are so many people who I need to thank for making this happen.

Firstly, my husband Steve, for his unwavering conviction that I could do this, and for his enduring patience and support. I'd especially like to thank him for the endless cups of tea - without which, there would be no book!

I'd like to thank a small but immensely important group of friends who read the first draft and who gave their advice and encouragement freely. They have pushed me all the way. Dorne and Don Werner, Allison Archer, Paula Hare, Sarah Mitchell, Jackie Crossland and Jeannette Pepper - their enthusiasm for this book has been astounding.

I'd like to thank my daughters Melissa Mitchell and Tamara Rowland for being amazing every single day. They have grown into the strongest, most capable women I know and I couldn't be more pr of them. Their friendship is my most precious possession.

I am hugely grateful to my publisher Cranthorpe Millner who I was so very fortunate to find. Thanks especially to Kirsty-Ellen Smillie for her guidance and to Victoria Roberts for her thoughtful editing.

And lastly, because this book is about a sister's love for her brother, I'd like to remember my own brothers Philip and Keith whose memory will always inspire me.

About the author

Cate Cullington is the author behind 'The Stones' - a debut novel that will appeal to readers who like their crime laced with tense family drama.

She works for the NHS in rural Lincolnshire and attended the same primary and secondary schools as Margaret Thatcher, though some years later.

When she's not at work she likes to walk, play golf and watch very old films.

Chapter 1

As the bus turned a corner into the main thoroughfare, Mark glimpsed a figure that he thought he recognised on the other side of the street. He jolted to his feet and looked back over his shoulder. Was it him? Could it really be him? He looked again; this time he managed to get a clearer view of the man. Yes, it was him, it was definitely him!

Mark grabbed his bag from the seat, pushing his way through commuters to reach the double doors at the front of the bus. He banged his fists on the glass partition.

"Please stop the bus, I need to get off."

The driver, quite unaffected by the commotion, answered in a dismissive tone, "There's a stop in about eight hundred yards, mate."

Mark, now increasingly agitated, looked directly into the driver's eyes. Flustered and embarrassed at the disturbance he was creating, his eyes beseeched the driver to submit to him in this battle of wills.

"No, no, you don't understand. I really need to get off now, it's important," he tried to explain.

The driver looked at the young man in front of him, who was red in the face with beads of sweat forming on his forehead and around his temples. He didn't know him personally, but he recognised him as someone who used this route often. He couldn't recall that the man had ever given him any trouble before, and there were plenty that had. Today he could see that his passenger was unable to hold eye contact with him for any length of time, though the young man did keep glancing at him. When they did lock eyes, the driver saw a pleading expression that was hard to ignore. His agitated passenger was unable to stand still, becoming more uncomfortable with every passing minute. Against his better judgement, and company protocol, the driver pulled over to the side of the road. While he made this manoeuvre, he gave the troubled young man in front of him some well-intended advice, "Everyone is always in such a rip-roaring hurry these days. You should slow down, mate, take it easy."

Mark nodded although he hadn't really heard the driver's words, repeatedly and frantically pushing at the button to release the doors before the bus had come to a standstill.

"Won't open until I'm in neutral, mate," the driver said, shaking his head. He knew his words were not having any effect on his passenger. "Health and safety and all that."

The bus pulled to a sharp stop. The driver released the lock on the doors and they slowly began to separate. The very second a small gap appeared, Mark pushed both of his hands through and forced the gap to widen enough for him to jump through. He was in too much of a hurry to wait for the procedure to finish.

As he sprinted back down the road he glimpsed the familiar figure again just yards in front of him. The man was just leaving a shop and about to walk off in the opposite direction. He shouted as loudly as he could up the street, "Wait, wait!"

Several bystanders turned to look, unsure of the reason for the commotion, and to Mark's relief the shout also caught the attention of the figure. The two men locked glances. From his reaction it was clear the man recognised Mark. He stopped for a moment, smiling at Mark in a curious manner, and started to put his hand up in a gesture of acknowledgement. Almost immediately his demeanour changed, and he smirked at Mark as if to goad him, running off at great pace in the opposite direction. Mark set off in pursuit.

The pair chased each other to the top of the street, deftly weaving through weary shoppers, leisurely strollers and skipping children. The two runners reached the end of the street, neither of them losing speed, and skilfully manoeuvred around the corner as they continued to run at a pace into the next road. Mark soon became breathless and knew he was losing distance on the fast-moving figure in front of him, who was much fitter and faster. Undeterred he continued, running as hard as he could.

Suddenly, the man he was chasing collided heavily into two old ladies, knocking their shopping right out of their hands and all over the pavement. The runner didn't stop to help them, and when Mark reached the confused pair seconds later he was forced to jump into the road, narrowly avoiding the spilled blockage on the pavement. As he darted past them he heard the women protesting, "Bloody idiot, took me right off my feet."

Mark looked back at the two innocent casualties of their chase. Although concerned for their predicament, he did not stop to help them, and continued pushing forward. He could only just see the diminishing figure in the distance.

"Stop," he shouted. "Stop!"

The figure paused briefly, looked back at Mark, then continued running ahead. Mark was losing ground fast, but he did not want to give up. He pushed his head tightly into his chest and drove himself onward, sweat pouring off his face. Reaching the next corner he looked up, to see if he had gained any distance on the man in front, but the figure had disappeared. Mark quickly scanned the scene around him, searching in every direction, but he could see no sign of the person he had been chasing. He was panicked and anxious, his target was nowhere to be seen, and he had no idea where to start looking. Mark stood bent over on the spot, taking big gulps of air for several minutes before he could breathe properly again. His t-shirt was drenched with sweat, he had a crippling pain in his side, and he was utterly exhausted.

"Damn," he gasped. "Damn, damn, damn!"

Teresa watched through the kitchen window as Lily skipped towards the summer house, where Mark was sitting beside an unfinished game of Ludo. The two of them had been out there playing for almost an

4

hour, with Lily periodically running on to the lawn to attempt a handstand or practice one of her ballet positions. She would occasionally return to Mark and their Ludo game to play a few moves, before running off again. Mark didn't mind. His patience with Lily was endless; he always encouraged her with great energy and involvement, applauding every complex position that she attempted, and laughing with deep mirth when she inevitably fell into a crumpled mess on the grass. They were clearly enjoying themselves and always had fun together, whether they were playing games, chasing each other, making faces or laughing at one of Mark's silly jokes that only a five year old would find funny.

Teresa was so thankful to Mark for providing Lily with a male role model in her life. Mark was Lily's only uncle; her only male relative if you didn't count her father. Lily's father had left them both when she was just a baby, and she had never known Teresa's dad, who had passed away long before Lily was born.

Teresa had married Alex, Lily's father, when she found out that she was expecting Lily, but their union hadn't lasted very long. In hindsight, it was obvious that they were far too young for such a huge undertaking. She had known Alex for just a few short months when she discovered she was pregnant, and under great pressure from his family they had taken the decision to marry. It had been a small ceremony with only twelve guests, but at twenty years old she had felt too intimidated and apprehensive to enjoy

5

herself, and couldn't wait for the ceremony to be over.

Their marriage was difficult from the start, the young couple struggling to cope financially and emotionally, especially when the baby neither of them had been prepared for arrived. Despite the pressures of parenthood, Teresa had really thought they were both trying their best to make a future for their young daughter, until she found a message on Alex's phone from one of his female colleagues. It had been clear from their conversations that they were more than just friends. Within days of Teresa confronting Alex with her suspicions he had left her and the baby to go and live with his new girlfriend, leaving Teresa heartbroken. She and Lily, who had only been eighteen months old at the time, had never seen him or any of his family since; it was like he had just disappeared. Teresa had never imagined that Alex could be so heartless.

A high-pitched squeal brought Teresa away from her thoughts and back to the scene before her. Mark had emerged from the summer house, grabbing both of Lily's ankles and lifting them high in the air, prompting Lily to start walking around the lawn on her hands, pretending to be a wheelbarrow. Their persistent and joyful laughter was infectious, and Teresa found herself smiling broadly, despite her growing concerns about Mark. Looking down at the sink she continued with the washing up. She always found herself here, washing the dishes on a Sunday afternoon. The day always followed the same routine. She and Lily would arrive at her mum's house and Teresa would cook Sunday lunch for them all, usually a traditional roast with all the trimmings. Today had been no exception; they had eaten roast lamb, infused with garlic and fresh rosemary from Mark's herb patch in the back garden, served alongside crispy roast potatoes, Yorkshire puddings, steamed vegetables and a jug of hot, thick gravy. As usual, Mark and Lily had been of little help to her in the kitchen, although they always took great care to make sure the table looked presentable. The two of them would meticulously polish the cutlery and glasses, setting all the places neatly, and always adorned the table with fresh flowers from the garden. Today they had chosen a beautiful display of delicate blue and white sweet peas, the fragrant smell of which made it feel as though summer was already here.

After every Sunday lunch, Teresa invariably found herself clearing the table and washing the dishes. She knew that if she complained Mark would offer to help, but she didn't want to spoil the fun that he and Lily had together. Lily always looked forward to going to Granny's house, and to seeing her Uncle Mark. As soon as Lily's eyes opened on a Sunday morning she would ask when it was time to go, and she would be up, washed and dressed in no time. Every week she would bounce around their small flat with such energy and enthusiasm that Teresa had no choice but to take her to Granny's earlier and earlier each week, to save disturbing the old man who lived downstairs. Even in their tiny two-bedroom flat Lily would skip from one room to another, often singing to herself as she went. She had far too much energy to walk.

Teresa smiled. She knew how lucky she was to have such an active, happy little girl. It may not have been Teresa's choice to bring a child up on her own, but watching Lily, with her boundless and infectious enthusiasm for everything, she knew it was a decision she could never regret.

"Teresa, Teresa," her mother's voice called urgently from the living room. Teresa left the sink full of soapy water, entering the living room to find her mum standing next to the armchair, dabbing at her dress with a tissue.

"I've spilt my tea, Teresa, I'm so sorry."

Teresa immediately went to help. Her mother had not spilt very much, only the last few dregs, and the tea had gone cold so there was no harm done. She had probably lost concentration, or fallen asleep again, with the tea in her hand.

"It's all right Mum, it's just a little spill. We'll soon get you cleaned up, don't worry," said Teresa, flashing her mother a reassuring smile. The old woman sat down in her chair again, sighing heavily.

"I'm sorry," she repeated.

"Don't worry," Teresa said, as she began to mop up the remaining tea from the carpet. "It's nothing, all clean now, see? Why don't you have a rest after that big meal, Mum?"

Leaving her mother in the sitting room, Teresa returned to the kitchen, adding the tea cup to the pile of dishes in the sink. 'Big meal', that was a laugh. Her mother had barely eaten at lunch, just a tiny piece of lamb and a few carrots. Teresa had only served her one small roast potato, half a parsnip and a tiny portion of mashed swede, but they had been left untouched, and she had refused to try the apple pie and custard served up for dessert. Try as she might, Teresa could not seem to improve her mother's appetite; this Sunday meal was probably the most her mother had eaten all week.

The situation had been much the same for the past ten years. Since the death of Mark and Teresa's dad, twenty years ago, the spark of life in her mother had been snuffed out. Initially, she had tried to cope with things on her own, but as the years went by her energy had gradually faded, and she had given up. These days she was permanently lethargic, and spent her days watching the television or falling asleep in her chair, before going to bed early.

Tiny and frail, her mother was a pale shadow of the vibrant, lively woman Teresa remembered. Her decreasing weight was a constant worry. Teresa did not know exactly how much she weighed, her mum had refused to step on to the doctor's scales for months, but she had been a slight seven and a half stone two years ago, and she had become considerably smaller since then. Teresa was also convinced that her mother suffered from clinical depression. It had been triggered by her father's death, and despite receiving help and support from friends and the local surgery, her mother had become increasingly distant and withdrawn. She engaged on a superficial level with Teresa, Mark and Lily, but every interaction with them was strained. Her neighbour, Mrs Philpot, would occasionally pop in to sit with her mother during the day, chattering to her about the old days and how wonderful things had been. But, despite having known Mrs Philpot since first moving in to the house, as a newly married woman, her mother just smiled vacantly during these visits, barely engaging with her neighbour.

Although her mum seemed lost in her own thoughts most of the time, a broad smile would occasionally come over her face, and in those rare moments Teresa hoped she was perhaps enjoying memories of happier times. The fact that her mother had the capacity to be happy, even if only for a fleeting moment, was a great comfort to Teresa. With Mark also laden with problems, sometimes Teresa keenly felt the burden of her family weighing down on her shoulders. They had very few relatives, as her father had no siblings and her mother had just one sister, Aunt June, who lived in Edinburgh and had no children. They hadn't seen June since Teresa's wedding, and contact was confined mainly to Christmas and birthday cards, containing short messages.

At that moment, Mark and Lily burst in through the back door, and the kitchen was filled with noise and giggles.

"Lily, you must be tired. Why don't you go and sit with Granny for a while?' Teresa asked her daughter. "She'd love the company." Lily dutifully picked up her favourite doll, from the chair in the kitchen where she had left it earlier, and skipped into the living room to see her grandmother. Mark was about to follow her, but Teresa gestured for him to sit at the table.

"Why don't you and I have a cuppa? There's something I want to talk to you about."

"Okay," Mark replied.

He was reluctant, but he knew his sister well and realised it was pointless to try and avoid this conversation. Teresa would not leave him alone until she had said what she wanted to say.

"You said at lunch that you were thinking of going away for a few days..."

"What of it?"

Teresa softened her voice and fixed her gaze on her brother.

"Are you okay?"

"Yes, of course I am."

"You know, you don't need to hide anything from me," she continued. "If you're not well, I can help. We can get you some help."

"I'm fine, really, I am."

"Why are you going away then? You said you needed a break from your life. Some time to think. What's wrong, Mark?"

"It's nothing. You know how I get. I just feel like...going away would...help. Just for a few days."

"Where would you go?" Teresa persisted, even though it was clear that Mark was becoming increasingly uncomfortable with their exchange. He avoided eye contact with her, looking down at the floor.

"I haven't thought about it. Maybe to the coast?" He smiled, trying to lighten the tone of their conversation, "I'm not going just yet. Maybe in a couple of weeks, and it'll just be for a few days so Mum will be okay. You'll hardly notice I'm gone. Try not to worry about me, I'm fine, honestly."

After their conversation, Mark had headed upstairs, giving her some excuse that he had things to do. Teresa heard him turn the key in the lock on his bedroom door, enter the room and then close and lock the door behind him. 'Try not to worry about me'. This was precisely one of the things that *did* worry her about Mark. That lock had been fitted ten years ago, at Mark's request, when he had returned from his last stay in a secure unit. As far as she knew, no one had entered that room since, except for Mark himself. When pressed on the subject, he said he needed a private space. Mark had a long, complicated history, involving his admittance to an assortment of hospitals, mental health units and safe houses, all in an attempt to help him manage his problems. He hadn't had an admission for ten years, and outwardly appeared happy and content. Although he still regularly saw a variety of healthcare professionals, on a voluntary basis, he presented himself so confidently that all of them were convinced that he was perfectly well. Teresa was not convinced. His intense need for privacy was understandable, but she couldn't figure out why he was so secretive. What was he hiding in that room? Why the need for so much solitude and isolation? It surely couldn't be good for him. She had always been very close to Mark, and was instinctively aware of his changes in mood, however subtle. She felt sure that he was hiding something from her. Teresa had never known Mark hurt anyone, other than himself. But, as much as she loved her brother, she couldn't shake the thought that something sinister was going on.

For the past two years, on the night of the Summer Solstice, a girl had gone missing from Stonehenge, and neither girl had been seen since. Mark had shown an abnormal interest in their disappearance, and Teresa was growing increasingly concerned. She lay awake at night, unable to shake the malignant thought that he might, perhaps, have been involved in some way. The night of the solstice was three weeks away, and Mark was talking about going on a trip, just as he had this time last year when the second girl went missing. At the time, he had told Teresa that he needed a break, that being in the house with mum all the time was adversely affecting him. He had just needed to get away for a little while, to take a few days to recalibrate. Today, he had said much the same thing. The events of last year that were still strong in Teresa's mind, and she remembered with great clarity the intensity of the moment when she had first heard the news about the missing girl, Claudia, the day after the celebration for the solstice…

As the sun rose at Stonehenge on the first day of summer, a young man could be seen frantically searching for his girlfriend, spiralling deeper into despair with every minute that passed, unable to resist the rising panic that pulsed through his veins. He had woken from his sleep in the field near the stones, where he and Claudia had sung and danced the previous night, partying and chanting with the gathered crowd. White cannabis trails had floated through the starlit sky, and the air had been filled with the sound of folk music: flutes and guitars, tin whistles and banjos, xylophones, shakers and drums. A man, his dreadlocked hair wrapped in a bandana, had been playing a set of kettlebells which sent tinkling sounds and booming vibrations echoing through the crowd. The sound had been intoxicating, as had the smell: incense burning, blended with a herby smell of marijuana and woodsmoke. People had been seated beside barbecues and small campfires, roasting sausages, chestnuts and marshmallows, and large pans of curry had been gently bubbling away, their aromatic scent wafting through the night air. Warm drinks had been brewing, and the aroma of strong, bitter coffee, sweet fruit infusions, and rich, sweet hot chocolate had hung heavily in the dampness of the dewy air. Others had continued to drink alcohol late into the night, Julian and Claudia among them. By three in the morning, the pair had been exhausted, and had fallen into a heavy sleep like many of the other revellers.

When he had first been roused by the murmuring of the waking crowd, Julian had not been overly concerned that Claudia was not lying next to him, assuming that she had gone to use the makeshift toilets. But after ten minutes, when she had still not returned, he had started to look for her. Picking his way across the uneven ground, he had searched the fields in the dim morning light, avoiding the many sleeping bodies lying on the floor. As he had passed through small, multi-coloured gatherings of people, he had stopped, asking if anyone had seen Claudia and showing them her picture on his mobile phone. Nobody that he had spoken to had any memory of her. Some of these revellers had also become concerned for her safety, and had helped him to look for her, while all the time the main crowd had continued to push forward, trying to get a better view of the sunrise.

The sun rose before him. Tired from his search, Julian knew that something was wrong, that something serious must have happened to Claudia. They had been planning this trip for weeks, and she had been looking forward to seeing this sunrise more than anything. Where was she? Julian suddenly caught sight of a policeman, there to control the crowds, and he knew exactly what he had to do. He ran over to him, breaking down sobbing as he told the policeman what had happened. Instantly, the policeman made a call on his radio, and within seconds the alarm was raised. Police officers started to appear from every direction, all with torches flashing, and some with sniffer dogs pulling urgently at their leads. The officers worked their way through the partygoers, taking down information and escorting people away from the area. Most were happy to go, with no resistance, and although a skirmish would break out now and again, these fights were easily contained by the officials. Above the turmoil, a helicopter flooded the field with bright light and deafening noise.

Julian slumped against a nearby rock, looking out at the chaos before him. At some point, someone put a blanket around his shoulders, but he was barely aware of their presence. He did not know what had happened, or where she was, but one thing he knew instinctively. He would never see Claudia again.

Teresa could remember watching the television coverage in her mother's living room. There had been footage from the site itself during the search, interviews with some of the crowd as they had left the scene, and, most compelling of all, a press conference. The victim's boyfriend, Julian, had appeared, still wearing his clothes from the night before and flanked by several policemen in uniform. He had looked pale, frightened and bereft, shaking as he did his best to recount the events of the previous evening. His voice had broken often; his pain palpable and raw. As absorbing as the coverage had been, Teresa could only watch her brother. Mark had watched the news item with her, and glancing at him out of the corner of her eye she had seen him grow as pale as the young man on the television. His eyes had filled with tears and his hands had been shaking, as he visibly struggled to keep his composure, gripping his hands together in an attempt to control them.

"I can't believe this has happened again, how awful," Teresa had exclaimed to Mark. "Do you think it's going to be the same as last year, do you think the same person did it?"

Suddenly Mark had bolted up from his chair, fleeing from the room and sprinting upstairs. As she had expected, Teresa had heard the familiar sequence of his bedroom door being unlocked, opened, closed and locked again. She had stared after her brother in horror, a familiar feeling of worry and fear coming over her. Mark had only returned from 'a break' earlier that day. He had only been away for a few days, but from the look of him on his return he had been sleeping rough. His clothes had been dirty and crumpled, his hair dishevelled and he had looked pale and tired. Teresa had not questioned him too much, aware of his fragile state of mind, but she had been perplexed by his reaction to this news, and had felt a growing sense of unease that Mark knew something about Claudia's disappearance.

After sitting at the kitchen table for a few more minutes, consumed by the thoughts whirling around her head, Teresa decided to go home. She knew it would be pointless to knock on Mark's door or try to contact him on his mobile. He never responded when he was in his room, he would only communicate with them when he chose to, and Teresa knew that wouldn't be today. Considering their conversation a few moments before, it was likely he would not leave his room until tomorrow evening, if then. One day last year, when he had been locked up in his room, Lily had been skipping up and down on the stairs and had suddenly misplaced her footing. She had fallen right from the top to the bottom of the staircase, twisting her ankle on the way down, and had landed in a heap, screaming in pain. Teresa's mother had heard Lily's cries and come running to help, but Mark had not reacted at all, remaining locked in his room. Teresa had been furious, and had banged her fist repeatedly on his bedroom door, shouting at him and pleading for him to come and help, but he had remained unresponsive. She had comforted Lily, wrapping a bag of frozen peas in a hand towel and holding the cold compress against her rapidly swelling ankle. The child had been shaking and sobbing in pain as Teresa had carried her to the car, but an x-ray at the local hospital had revealed that the ankle wasn't broken, and the doctor had given Teresa some painkillers for Lily, which rapidly eased the pain. During the four hours Teresa had been at the hospital with Lily, she had not heard from Mark once.

The following day, after leaving Lily with a friend, Teresa had made her way to her mother's house. She had still been angry with Mark, and on seeing him in the kitchen, calmly making himself a cup of tea, had started a blazing row with him, challenging him to explain his behaviour. When she thought back on it now, it had not been much of a row. Teresa had done all of the shouting, and Mark had not once shouted back or tried to defend his

18

actions. She remembered calling him all sorts of things, saying that he had no compassion, that he was uncaring and selfish and that she would be surprised if Lily ever forgave him. The words 'not fit to be her uncle' had really hit home though; at that point Mark had burst into tears and started repeating that he was sorry, over and over. He had become so distressed that he had curled up on the kitchen floor, holding his sides and forcefully rocking backwards and forwards at great speed. On seeing Mark's genuine remorse, Teresa's anger had subsided, her concern for her brother's mental state becoming more important than her fury. She had soothed her brother, reassuring him that Lily would be fine, that there was no serious injury, and that of course she would still love her uncle. Neither of them had ever spoken of the incident again.

Teresa often thought about what had happened that day, but this always left her increasingly perplexed and confused. She knew how much Mark loved Lily, but even though Lily had been sobbing loudly, in obvious distress, he had not left that room. What could be in there that was so important to him? Sometimes she wondered what would happen if their mother took ill when Mark was locked up in his room and Teresa was not there. Would Mark even react? Would he be so absorbed in whatever was in that room that he would fail to notice that something was wrong? This was the main reason Teresa was such a regular visitor to the house. She felt it necessary to check up on her mother and brother every day, and did not feel comfortable leaving Mark in sole charge of their mother. Teresa started to think about the room again, wondering what could possibly keep him so absorbed up there. Mark had always refused to talk about it, saying only that it was his 'safe place' and that he needed the security of the locked door to keep him calm. He had told her that if anyone else went in there he would feel violated, and that the room would not feel safe anymore.

Tired of her distressing, nagging thoughts, Teresa called Lily in from the garden. Picking up their belongings, she kissed her mother on the cheek and walked out of the door. Sometimes she did not want to be in that house and today, without warning, had turned into one of those days.

On the drive home, Teresa tried to focus on other things, like whether she has washed and ironed Lily's school uniform for tomorrow, and how lucky she was to have a steady job. Despite being a qualified physiotherapist, she was currently working at a local grocery store as a checkout operator. When Lily was born, the small, private physiotherapy practice where she used to work had been unable to accommodate the reduced hours that she needed, and she had been forced to seek alternative employment. Teresa now worked every weekday during school hours at the grocery shop, taking the weekends off to look after Lily. She appreciated how lucky she was to have a job with such flexible hours, she would not have been able to cope with being a single mother otherwise. Besides, the checkout at the shop was where she had met Dan. He was coming to see her tonight, and after the events of today, seeing him was exactly what she needed.

Chapter 2

By the time Teresa reached the flat it was six thirty
p.m., about an hour and a half before Dan was due to
arrive. This would be his first visit to her flat, and as
she looked around she felt disappointed. When Alex
had gone, she had been forced to leave their small
terraced house across the other side of town and
come here, where the rents were more affordable.
Her heart sank. It hadn't been much, but she had felt
at home in that house, and she had thought that their
future as a family was beginning to take shape. She
and Alex had chosen it together; of the many they
had looked at, it had been the only one they had both
liked. It had felt like the perfect place to start their
life together.

They had spent their weekends looking around
furniture shops and bring-and-buy sales, managing
to pick up a few pieces for the house, and had started
to decorate the rooms. With every small addition,
and the completion of each DIY project, the house
had begun to feel more and more like home. Teresa
had loved that pretty, cosy little house, her first home
away from her family, with it's small garden,
enclosed by sturdy fencing and an iron gate. She had
loved to sit on the old swing, left by the previous
owners, looking back at the house. There she had
often mused about her life; how she had been forced

22

to put thoughts of opening her own sports physiotherapy franchise to one side, because of the unexpected turn her life had taken. She hadn't planned the pregnancy, and certainly hadn't intended to be married at such a young age, but as she had gently rocked on the swing, she had counted her blessings.

At twenty years old, many had said she was far too young to have a child, but Alex had worked hard and treated her well; she and their unborn baby had been healthy. She had known she had a lot to be grateful for, and had adjusted surprisingly quickly to her change of circumstances. As she waited for the baby to arrive, she had filled her days with tasks: making curtains for their house, decorating the nursery for the little girl they were expecting and keeping the weeds in the back garden under control. Their neighbours had been friendly people, and had always smiled and waved to her when she saw them in the street. She had been happy.

Two years later, Alex had left, and the life that they had been building together suddenly crumbled around her, shattering her dreams and leaving her emotionally and financially broken. At first, she had hardly functioned, and looking back Teresa wondered how she had let herself fall so low. For days on end she had not dressed or washed herself, cooked a meal, shopped for groceries or taken care of the house. She had felt lost and empty.

Mark had got her through those first few weeks of rejection. He had visited every day, looking after

Lily and taking over the running of the house. He had shopped and cooked, and eventually encouraged Teresa to start eating again. He had brought Lily into her room regularly, leaving her there in the knowledge that Teresa could never ignore the child's cries. With Mark's support she had gradually grown stronger, eventually becoming brave enough to face the reality of her new life. Although she had found part time work, it became clear that she could not afford to pay the bills for a house that size, and she and Lily had been forced to leave. Losing the house had been upsetting, but what Teresa missed most was the back garden. At the flat they had no outdoor space, and she found being cooped up indoors all the time suffocating. She often threw open all the windows, just to let some fresh air in, but she still felt like she could hardly breathe.

She looked around the flat. There was a comfy sofa and chair that she had brought from the house, though she had given away the second chair as the flat was too small to accommodate both. The curtains were also from the old house, adjusted to fit the smaller windows in the flat. She had used the extra material to cover some old scatter cushions, which were currently piled up in a heap on the sofa as Lily had been playing with them earlier that day. There was a round, glass-topped coffee table in the centre of the room, a television on a stand in the corner and a small wooden sideboard, which a friend had given to her. The room was full, there was no space for any other furniture, and with Lily's various toys dotted around the flat seemed even smaller and more cluttered. Teresa started gathering Lily's things and rearranging the cushions, trying to make the place look more presentable before Dan arrived.

Once she had tidied the living area Teresa went to the bathroom and ran a bath for Lily. The girl was already very independent, and so once Teresa had helped to wash her hair, she left Lily playing with a few toys in the bubbles while she ran the vacuum over the living room carpet. It didn't take her long, and she was soon back in the bathroom, helping to dry Lily off and gently brush all the tangles out of her long hair. Lily's hair was so long now, reaching all the way down to the small of her back, and Teresa had to plait it to keep Lily's hair off her face while she slept.

Once Lily had her pyjamas on, the two of them went to the kitchen. It was a small room, but there was just enough space for a small table and two chairs. The smart pine table and four matching chairs from the old house had been sold, so Teresa had bought this second-hand one. She had to push it right into the corner of the kitchen, and there was only just enough room for the two chairs, but it was all they needed. Lily and Teresa had all their meals here, and now Lily was at school they also practiced her writing and drew pictures at the table. Every evening they would sit there together, and Teresa would make Lily a jam sandwich and a mug of warm milk before she went to bed. Lily loved strawberry jam, and so jam sandwiches and milk before bed had become part of their routine. When she had finished, Teresa took Lily to the bathroom to clean her teeth, glancing up at her own reflection in the bathroom mirror as she did so. She really ought to put on a bit of make-up and fix her hair before Dan arrived. Knowing that Lily would be asleep in moments after her busy day at Granny's house, she tucked her up in bed, gave her a quick goodnight kiss and then left her, sneaking back to the bathroom to tidy herself up.

At 8pm exactly there was a knock at the door. Dan was standing there with a bottle of red wine in one hand and a small bunch of flowers in the other, looking slightly uncomfortable.

"You found us then?" said Teresa, trying to break the ice.

"Yes," he replied. "I know this area quite well."

Teresa looked at the floor, her heart sinking. She was sure that he did. It was not the best area of town, and when she looked out of her window in the evening she often saw a large group of rowdy lads and girls hanging about, drinking and smoking. Police cars would often pull up and talk to them, attempting to disperse the group. Dan was a police constable, so she was not surprised to hear that he was familiar with this estate. Why on Earth had she asked him to come here? It was a terrible mistake.

Dan sensed her embarrassment immediately, and quickly stepped through the door and into the living room, chatting away in a bid to put her at ease.

"This is a nice room," he said. "It looks very, um, comfortable."

26

"Why don't you take a seat and I'll pour us a drink?" Teresa suggested, taking the wine and flowers from him.

She walked into the kitchen and sighed. This was awful. Dan was clearly feeling just as embarrassed and awkward as she was, it was never going to work between them. She had told herself not to invite him to the flat, but they had already been on three dates and it felt like they ought to move things along. Dan still lived with his parents, so he had suggested they meet at her place, and although Teresa would have preferred for him not to see where she lived, she could not come up with a valid excuse. He knew about Lily, she had told him about her on their first date, and he knew that it was difficult for her to get a babysitter. This had seemed like a good idea, until now.

She poured two large glasses of red wine, took a large gulp from one of them, and went back into the living room. Dan was holding a picture of Lily he had picked up from the sideboard. Mark had taken the photograph last summer, in the garden at their mum's house. Lily was standing barefoot on the grass, wearing a yellow sundress, with her arms and legs stretched out wide on either side of her. Her long, dark hair was blowing in the breeze and she was smiling joyfully. It was a beautiful picture, perfectly capturing Lily's energy and enthusiasm, which is why Teresa had put it in a frame. That picture *was* Lily.

"So, this is Lily? What a little beauty she is."

"Yes, and a bit of a handful sometimes."

"I bet. Is she asleep now?"

"Yes, fast asleep. She won't wake up until the morning. Lily is a really good sleeper".

Dan placed the photograph back on the sideboard, patting the sofa next to him.

"That's good. Now, why don't you bring that wine over here? I'm ready for a drink".

She passed him his glass, sitting down next to him, and he placed his hand reassuringly on her knee as he took a sip of wine. Before too long they were chatting away, the initial awkwardness and tension of the evening gone. Teresa had even put her worries about Mark to the back of her mind, determined to enjoy this evening with Dan. She had spent so many evenings here on her own, it felt really good to finally have someone to talk to. They did not leave the sofa all evening, sitting and chatting there for three hours. They talked about Dan's work; how he'd always wanted to become a police officer like his father before him, and about his ambitions to rise through the ranks of the police force to make his family proud. He told her about his family, with whom he was very close, and about his insatiable love for custard cream biscuits, which made Teresa laugh out loud. He was a local lad and wanted to stay close to his parents once he left home, which he was planning to do next year. He had a lot of friends and enjoyed playing sports with them or going to the pub in the evening. Many of his friends were now married and had started their own families, and as Dan spoke, Teresa could tell that he wanted a life like that for himself.

In turn, Teresa confided in him about her failed marriage, the unexpected pregnancy, Alex leaving and disappearing without a trace, and why she had ended up living in this flat and working at the local grocery shop. She told him about her mother's failing health, and that she regularly went to visit her. For reasons she could not fully explain, she didn't mention Mark. She was still worried about Mark and his proposed trip, and the possibility that he was somehow involved in the case of those missing girls troubled her. She felt that she could not tell Dan about Mark until she had spoken to her brother. Besides, she did not want to think about Mark and his troubles now. She wanted to enjoy this evening with Dan. The wine had worked wonders on her anxiety, and she was finally feeling relaxed and comfortable in Dan's company.

At eleven p.m. Dan decided it was time to head home. Six weeks ago, on their first date, Teresa had said to him that she had not had a relationship since Alex, and was unsure whether she was ready to start seeing someone yet. He had put no pressure on her at all, and on their following dates had given her a very quick kiss goodnight, before seeing her to her taxi at the end of their evening. This evening, as they both stood at her door, he moved in for a kiss and they embraced passionately, for longer than they had before. Teresa felt she could have stayed there all night, but he eventually pulled away and said he had to go.

"Thank you for a lovely evening, I'll call you tomorrow," he said quietly, before slowly making his way down the stairs.

She was left standing at the door of the flat, a little light-headed from the wine and barely able to contain her happiness. She had a good feeling about Dan. She hadn't been interested in anyone since Alex, and she wondered if this could be the start of a new chapter for her. Tired but content, Teresa locked the front door, put the two wine glasses in the kitchen sink and fell fully clothed on to her bed. It had been a lovely evening, and with that thought in her mind Teresa quickly drifted off to sleep.

Teresa woke with a start the next morning. Looking at the clock she gave a sigh of relief, it was only a quarter to eight. She had been so relaxed last night she had forgotten to set her alarm, and could easily have overslept. Forcing her weary body out of bed, she made her way to the shower, and by 8am she was dressed and ready for work. As she helped Lily get ready for school and prepared their breakfast, Teresa's thoughts returned to last night and Dan. She wondered if Dan would be in touch again, now that he has seen where she lived. He had not seemed too put off by his surroundings last night, and when she had gone to bed Teresa had felt positive about him. But now, in the cold light of day, her feelings of inadequacy were beginning to resurface, and she started to doubt whether Dan could really be interested in her. She was a single mother, living in a small rented flat in an undesirable part of town, with a menial job, no hobbies and few friends. Dan was a police officer, with ambition and good connections in the force. He had a supportive family and a good background, kept himself fit by going to the gym and swimming regularly, and played for the local five a side football team. On top of that, he was very good looking.

"Don't be a fool Teresa, why would he be interested in you?" she muttered to herself. "He probably stayed and talked last night just to be polite, and we had been drinking so that would explain the kiss. That's it now, you won't be seeing him again."

There was no time to dwell on her thoughts. She had to drive Lily to school and call in at her mum's house before she went to work, as she did most days. The troubled look returned to her face as she thought about the events of yesterday, and Mark's worrying behaviour. Teresa watched Lily skip into school and then drove to her mum's, letting herself in through the front door when she arrived. As she passed the living room, she noticed her mum's chair was empty. Her mum did not usually get up until she or Mark took a cup of tea up to her room and encouraged her to come downstairs. Teresa heard noises coming from the kitchen. Turning the corner, she found Mark in there, making himself a coffee and some toast. He greeted her with such a warm, friendly smile it felt as though yesterday had never happened.

"We have to talk," Teresa challenged her brother, and Mark's mood changed instantly. "I need to know what's going on with you."

"Leave it, will you?" Mark's voice was sharp, and he was clearly irritated.

"No, Mark. I can't, and I won't. I'm worried about you. You were so upset yesterday, and all this talk of going away again...I don't understand what's going on. Tell me what's wrong, please? Talk to me." Mark was refusing to look at her, staring at the floor as she continued. "Why don't Lily and I go away with you? Like we did before. We had a lovely time, remember?"

"Lily's at school now," Mark said flatly, still looking at the floor.

"That doesn't matter. I'll speak to them, I'm sure it will be fine, and Lily would love it." Mark looked up at her. His mood had become sullen and saturnine. She hated it when he was uncommunicative and gloomy like this.

"I want to be on my own," he muttered, so quietly Teresa could barely catch what he was saying, "I don't want to be with you."

Exasperated by his sour and peevish tone Teresa responded, "Okay, Mark, do as you please, you usually do. I'm going to work. Sort mum out, will you? It's time she was up."

Teresa left the house, annoyed with Mark and disappointed with her lack of progress. She knew he was hiding something from her, but she was not making any headway with him.

As she reached the garden gate, she met the postman, who was holding a parcel addressed to Mark in his hand. Mark often received small parcels, but would never say what they contained...another mystery. Teresa had always assumed he must have some sort of hobby, hidden in his room, that he ordered things for. She had never really thought too much about it, but this morning, just for a second, she thought about taking the parcel and opening it up herself. At that moment, the front door opened behind her, and Mark appeared. The postman spoke directly to Mark, walking straight past Teresa.

"Good morning, sir, another delivery for you." Mark signed for the delivery and took it from him, shooting an inquisitive glance at his sister; she wondered if he had guessed what she had been thinking. Mark went inside and shut the door, without saying a word to her, and she quickly climbed in to the car and drove away.

When she had finished her work shift, Teresa decided to pay a visit to the church on Green Lane. After parking the car nearby, she made her way through the wooden gate, past the little Saxon church, and down the narrow path to the farthest end of the churchyard. There, she walked directly to the grave of her father, laying down a bunch of flowers that she had picked up from work. She came here twice a year: on his birthday, in November, and today, the anniversary of his death. Looking down at his grave, she felt overwhelmingly sad and guilty. She did not bring Lily here anymore, although she had done when she was a baby. Her mother never came here, and as far as she knew, neither did Mark. Fortunately, the church tended to the graveyard, so at least his grave was kept tidy. As she arranged the flowers more neatly, Teresa looked at the inscription on her father's headstone:

'John George Applewhite, born February 10th 1957, died tragically May 10th 1999. Beloved husband of Maryann, and devoted father to Mark and Teresa. Gone but never forgotten'

It was a simple, but honest tribute, to the father Teresa often struggled to remember. She had been only seven years old when he had died and had very few memories of him. But the day of his death was still vivid in her mind. Mark had come to pick her up from school, which was not unusual – he often picked her up on his way home from college – but that day Mark had been strangely quiet. He had not skipped down the lane with her, or pulled her pigtails, or made funny faces at her and he had not told her any jokes. That day, he had taken her bag from her and gripped her hand tightly, as they walked home together in silence. Teresa had instinctively known that she should be quiet too. When they had reached home, the house had been full of strangers: two official looking men, one holding a clipboard, who Teresa had later learnt were from her father's work; two policemen, and a police lady. Teresa had seen a police car outside as they had walked up the street, but it had not occurred to her that they might be inside her own house. Their neighbour, Mrs Philpot, had been there too. Everyone had crowded into the living room, and she had only just been able to glimpse her mother

34

through all the adult bodies, sitting in a chair. She had looked odd. Her face had been pale, and she had looked terribly old, older than when Teresa had seen her this morning. All the people in the room had been talking to her mother at the same time, but she had sat there silently, saying nothing.

The police lady had taken Teresa by the hand, asking her if Teresa would mind showing her some of her favourite toys. The seven-year-old Teresa had not considered this an odd request, and had happily taken the police lady up to her room. After she had shown off her teddies and they had flicked through her favourite book, the police lady had sat down on the bed with Teresa, and gently told her that her father was dead. Teresa could not remember anything beyond that conversation, the rest of the day had been a blur.

Looking at his grave now, Teresa physically ached for her father. She still missed him; she felt she missed him more and more with every passing year. It certainly did not get easier, like everybody had said it would. The void that he had he had left behind when he died just seemed to be getting bigger and bigger. Sometimes, like today, it felt as though they would all be swallowed up by their grief, and there was nothing that she or anyone else could do to stop it. Tears began to roll down her cheeks. She felt completely helpless. She wished she could talk to her father, he would know how to help her, and what she should do. Teresa stood crying beside his grave for a long time, overwhelmed and consumed by her loss: the loss of her father to death; the loss of her mother, who, consumed by her own grief, was out of reach and the loss of her brother, who had once supported and encouraged her but was now so distant. She had never felt as alone as she did today.

Her thoughts turned back to Mark again. She was so worried about him, and how far his mental health had deteriorated. She remembered how strong and in control he had been when she was young, and how much she had relied on him after their father died; how he had protected her and their mum from the unwanted attention of inquisitive neighbours and the local press; how he had coped with the intrusive inquiries from solicitors, who had come asking questions about their personal lives, their routines, their relationships with each other and with those outside the family. It had often felt to Teresa like they must have done something wrong, to warrant all this attention. Mark had accompanied their mother to meetings with solicitors, going alone when she could not face it anymore. He had attended numerous court appearances regarding the charge of negligence, which they had been accused of by their father's employer; he had arranged the funeral and taken control of the family finances, as well as the day to day running of the house.

He had also taken responsibility for Teresa, not only on a practical level, getting her to school and making sure she was looked after at home, but mentally as well, speaking to her teachers and making sure they kept an eye on her moods, and arranged grief counselling for her. He had been so thoughtful and kind, making Teresa and their mum his priority, never complaining about the burden it must have been. He had been an absolute brick in those early days, and Teresa could not help but wonder whether his mental instability had come about as a result of having all that responsibility forced upon him, at such a young age. His teenage years had been stolen from him, and Mark had suffered as a result. When she was younger, her mother would tell her that Mark had gone to stay with friends for a few weeks at a time, but as she grew older and more aware of things, Teresa had realised that Mark's 'weeks away' were spent in mental health institutions. Over the years, his strength had failed, and they had gradually changed places. Teresa became the strong one, the glue that kept their family stuck together, and it was now up to her to look after Mark and her mum.

Eventually, when she heard people approaching, Teresa wiped away her tears, and with a final look at the grave she made her way back to the car. She had no choice, she had to carry on. She fixed her face in the car mirror and then drove to Lily's school, a smile fixed on her face. With Lily chattering all the way, Teresa drove to her mum's house again, pulling into the drive with a sense of déjà vu. Her mum was sitting in her usual place.

"Where's Mark?" Teresa asked.

"He must be in his room," replied her mum. "I haven't seen him all day."

Chapter 3

After dropping Lily at school the next day, Teresa raced round to the local health centre. Two elderly people were queuing at the reception desk but she barely noticed them, pushing past and speaking rapidly to the receptionist.

"Is Nell in?"

The middle-aged lady sitting behind the desk looked up slowly, glancing over the rim of her glasses at Teresa.

"There is a queue," she said curtly.

"I know, I'm sorry, but it's really important. I need to see Nell."

The receptionist rolled her eyes and fixed her gaze back on the computer screen in front of her. Without looking up at Teresa, she asked,

"Have you got an appointment?"

"Well, no," stuttered Teresa, looking around in distress.

"Would you like me to make you an appointment?"

"No. Umm…I just…I…is Nell in? It's really important."

"I'm afraid you cannot just walk in here, without an appointment, and expect to be seen," the receptionist informed her, in a sharp, unsympathetic tone. She fixed Teresa with a steely gaze, and continued, "Now, either I can make you an appointment, or you can move aside and let me see to the patients who *have* made an appointment."

The deliberate and prolonged emphasis on 'have' was not lost on Teresa. The receptionist smiled smugly, knowing that she had the upper hand in this exchange. Exasperated, Teresa left the desk, and walked back past the people in the queue, who were looking disapprovingly at her and muttering to themselves, no doubt about how rude she was.

"I'm sorry. I didn't mean to be rude. I'm very sorry."

Deflated, Teresa sat slumped in one of the waiting room chairs. She had a thousand thoughts running through her head, and it felt like they were all bouncing around, fighting for her attention. She had barely slept last night, she had a thumping headache, and was burdened with an growing sense of foreboding, dreading that something awful was about to happen. She felt tired and powerless, and even the necessary act of breathing was becoming too much for her, taking all of her concentration and effort.

"Teresa, are you okay? You look dreadful." Teresa looked up. It was Nell. She had clearly just arrived at the health centre and was still wearing her coat.

"What are you doing here? Are you ill, Teresa?" Teresa looked up at the older woman. Nell was smiling down at her, with her kind face and friendly eyes. Nell's show of kindness and concern almost drove Teresa to tears.

"I came to see you, Nell. I really need your help, but I haven't got an appointment, and they wouldn't let me see you." Teresa shot a quick glance over to the receptionist, who was busy booking in one of the elderly people Teresa had pushed past earlier. Nell saw the distress in Teresa's face, and could hear her voice breaking. Something was clearly very wrong. She looked down at her fob watch.

"I've got ten minutes before my first patient. Come through to my room."

Teresa smiled, full of gratitude, and followed Nell out of the waiting room and into one of the clinic rooms labelled 'Community Nurse'. Nell gestured for Teresa to sit down as she took off her coat. Then she smoothed down the skirt of her dark blue uniform, pulled out a thick nurse's belt from her bag, and clinched it around her ample waist. Gently, she sat down opposite Teresa, who had said nothing since they had entered the room.

"Tell me what's wrong, Teresa? Is it your mum?"

"No, Mum's fine. Well, the same."

"You look so upset. Are you ill, or is it Lily?"

"No, no. I'm fine. Really, I am…and Lily, Lily's great."

"What is it then?"

Teresa had been staring down at her hands, which were clasped so tightly in her lap that her fingers had turned white. Now she looked up at Nell, who's eyes were full of concern, and blurted out,

"It's Mark. I don't know what's wrong. He won't tell me. He's behaving so strangely. He won't talk to me. He's so distant. I just know there's something wrong. I think he must be having a relapse, but he just won't tell me anything. I don't know what to do." The relief of finally telling somebody, of not holding it tightly inside, of not having to be strong and silent, was overwhelming. Teresa burst into tears. Nell calmly passed her the box of tissues she kept permanently on her desk, putting her arm around Teresa.

"What makes you think he's having a relapse?"

Teresa recovered a little and wiped her eyes, "I don't know, really. I'm just so worried about him. He won't talk to me. Has he spoken to you? Have you seen him lately?"

"Teresa, you know I couldn't tell you if he had," Nell said in her soft, gentle voice.

"Would you go and see him? Please."

"He needs to ask me Teresa, you know that. I can't just turn up if he doesn't want to see me."

Teresa burst into tears again, "I'm so sorry Nell. I just don't know what to do."

Nell looked at Teresa. She had known this family for most of her working life, and ever since Teresa's father had died she had been regularly involved with the family, particularly Mark. She was a mental health specialist, and had supported Mark for many years, through many breakdowns, relapses

41

and mental health crises. She had a great fondness for the siblings and admired the way they had coped over the years, always pulling together to support each other. It upset and worried her to see Teresa so distressed, and although she would never say anything to Teresa, Mark's behaviour concerned her. It was very out of character for Mark to shut his sister out of the difficulties he was having, and it could be indicative that he was not coping very well.

"Tell you what, why don't I pop round to see your mum and carry out a welfare check on her? She is due one soon anyway, and if Mark is there it will give him the opportunity to talk to me, if he wants to. How does that sound?"

"Oh, would you?" Teresa dabbed at her eyes with the tissue.

"Leave it with me. But, like I said, if Mark doesn't want me to tell you, then I can't talk to you about it."

"I understand," replied Teresa, " I would be so grateful if you were to go and see him. I'm sure he would talk to you."

"Okay, I will try and arrange a health visit as soon as possible. Now, you really must go. I'm going to be late for my first patient."

"Of course, thank you so much." Teresa stood up and flung her arms around the older woman, overcome with relief and gratitude, and they hugged briefly before Nell ushered Teresa out of the room. As she sat in her car in the health centre car park, Teresa felt calmer. It had made her feel a little brighter to have told someone, and she felt that Nell was a good choice. She knew that Nell really cared about Mark, and he had always got on well with Nell…hopefully talking to her would help him with his current issues. She pulled down the sun visor to check her reflection in the mirror and was shocked at what she saw. Her black mascara and eyeliner were smeared down her face, and her eyes were bright red and puffy from crying. Her skin was pale and blotchy, and her nose was running. She was a mess. Teresa sighed, grabbed some wipes from her bag which she usually used to clean Lily's sticky fingers, and carefully removed her smudged make-up. She then pulled out a small make-up bag and tidied herself up, before driving to work, feeling more relaxed than she had felt for many weeks. Mark would talk to Nell, she was sure of it, and then everything would settle down again.

Later that day, after she had seen all her clients, Nell made her way to Mrs Applewhite's house. As she drove up the road, she took in her surroundings. It had become second nature to her now to observe everything closely while she was working. It was surprising how often her familiarity with the area, and people who lived there, helped her to connect with her patients when she needed to. Perhaps she would see something on her approach that she could talk to Mark about, to help them strike up a conversation. The area where the Applewhite's house was situated had always been considered a desirable place to live; it had been the same when she had first started working in this community. They lived in the smarter end of town, which housed mainly working families who were reasonably affluent. As she drove along, she recognised some of the people who were out and about. They were employed in everyday activities, such as walking the dog or washing the car. She had not driven up this road for a long time, but everything was as Nell remembered it. The street was lined with semi-detached houses, all built in the early 1980s, and unlike most of their modern counterparts there was a generous space between the houses. Each house had a spacious rear garden, small porch area and a decent area of land at the front; in many cases this front area had been paved, allowing a second car to park. Each house also had a garage, too small for most modern cars, but the decent driveways meant that this was not a problem.

Mrs Applewhite's house still had a grassed area at the front of the house, but although the driveway was free, Nell decided not to park there. Instead, she pulled up on the road outside, taking a long look at the property. It seemed a little tired and was in need of some attention. The garage door could do with a coat of paint, it had rust spots developing along the bottom, and the wooden surround was splitting due to age and neglect. The front door to the house was painted red, but she could see that the colour had faded badly, and the paint was now flaking and peeling off in places. Although the front lawn had been mown recently, there were large tufts of weeds coming through the paved driveway and moss growing on the path.

Suddenly, Nell noticed a shadow flickering by the front bedroom window. As she turned to look, she saw a woman with shoulder-length dark hair walk past the window. It was just a fleeting glimpse, and although Nell continued to watch the window for several more minutes, she didn't see the woman again. Reassured that somebody was at home, Nell went to the front door and knocked loudly. Mrs Philpot answered the door.

"Hello, Judith, how are you?" said Nell, with a warm smile. The two ladies knew each other.

"Oh, I'm very well thank you, Nell. I've just popped over to sit with Maryann for a while, what brings you here?" she asked, as she showed Nell through to the living room.

"I was just passing and thought I'd pop in and check on Maryann, it's been a while since I've seen her."

As she entered the living room, Nell took a good look around. The room still had the same chintz wallpaper and floral three piece suite that she had seen many times before, and the ancient patterned carpet was still in good condition. The beige curtains were heavy and fully pleated, with a huge pelmet across the top which was covered in a pink floral design to match the suite and cushions. There were also two lamps standing on either side of the bay window, with large lampshades made of the same floral fabric. The room was stuck firmly in the 1980s; Nell could remember it looking exactly the same when she had first come to the house, over twenty years ago. Everything was beginning to look shabby and a little faded now, though the room was very clean and tidy. Someone was obviously doing their best to look after the house, but the decor was exposing how long it had been since anyone had done any serious re-decorating.

Approaching Mrs Applewhite, Nell saw a frail old lady, who looked much older than her eighty-five years. She was wearing a blue dress, that Nell could see was several sizes too big, her stockings were crumpled and loose on her thin legs, and a thick, grey, woollen cardigan swamped her tiny frame. The old lady was pale, and her hair was completely white, hanging limp and straggly around her shoulders. Nell also noticed an untouched sandwich sitting on the table next to Mrs Applewhite's chair. She sighed.

"Hello, Maryann. It's Nell, you remember me? How have you been keeping? Is everything alright?"

"Hello, dear. Yes, yes, everything is fine, everything is fine," Mrs Applewhite repeated to herself, without making eye contact with Nell. She stared straight out in front of her, despite there being nothing to look at.

Nell was upset to see her looking so frail, lost and withdrawn. Maryann had deteriorated so much since she had seen her last, and Nell made a mental note to ask Dr Sissions to prescribe the old lady multivitamins when she returned to the surgery this afternoon. It wasn't much, but it might help to pep her up a bit, as the old woman was clearly missing out on some key vitamins. Not wanting to raise her concerns or make Mrs Applewhite feel uncomfortable, Nell chatted on.

"What about Teresa, how's she getting on? And Lily, how are they doing? Lily must be at school now."

Mrs Applewhite nodded, but continued to stare blankly in front of her.

"And what about Mark? How's Mark?"

There was no response from Mrs Applewhite, so Mrs Philpot replied, filling in the silence.

"Oh, you know Mark, he's just the same. Spends too much time on his own, up in that room. Needs to get out more, get a job, meet some people. He's up there now."

"He's not on his own right now, though, is he? He's got a friend with him."

"Don't be daft; he doesn't let anyone in that room. He's been up there all day, on his own, same as always. It's not healthy, if you ask me."

Nell nodded. Clearly Mark didn't want Mrs Philpot to know that he had company. She bent down toward Mrs Applewhite, taking her hand gently. It felt cold and bony.

"It's lovely to see you, Maryann. Is there anything you want to discuss with me while I'm here?"

There was no response from the old lady.

"Well, you know where I am Maryann, if ever you need anything," said Nell, patting her small frail hand.

This time, Mrs Applewhite looked at Nell and smiled, but it was empty smile. Nell sensed that the old lady barely recognised her.

"I'll see myself out."

She left the two women together in the living room and walked towards the front door, pausing at the bottom of the stairs and looking up towards the landing. She listened for a moment, and considered shouting up to Mark, but there were no sounds or signs of movement coming from upstairs. She didn't want to interrupt him if he had company. Closing the front door behind her, Nell got back into her car and drove around the corner, to the little shop where Teresa worked. Nell found her down one of the aisles, stacking biscuits. Teresa looked up in mild puzzlement, as Nell approached.

"Did you talk to him? Did you talk to Mark?" she asked, as soon as Nell reached her.

"No. I'm sorry Teresa. He didn't come out of his room. Tell me, has he got a girlfriend?"

"No, he hasn't. What makes you ask?"

"Are you sure, Teresa? I saw a woman in his room. That would explain his odd behaviour, don't you think? Maybe he doesn't want you or your mum to know?"

"He would have said. He would have told me."

"Maybe not, he's always been a bit secretive. Maybe he's not ready to introduce her to the family yet. It would be quite difficult, with your mum like she is. He might find it a bit embarrassing. To be honest with you, Teresa, I'm more concerned about your mum than Mark right now, she looks very frail. I'm going to get a prescription made up for her, when I get back to the surgery. Maybe you could pop in when you're passing and pick it up?"

"Yes, of course, I will…thank you for today."

The conversation about Mrs Applewhite's health had distracted them both from talking about Mark, and it wasn't until Nell had left the shop that Teresa really thought about what she had told her. A woman, in Mark's bedroom, could it be true? Could he really have a girlfriend? Who was she? Where did he meet her? Why would he want to keep her a secret? If it was true, then it would be the first girlfriend that Teresa had ever known Mark to have. He had never seemed interested in relationships; it was one of the things Teresa had always felt guilty about. When Mark was a young adult, he had spent his time looking after her, instead of pursuing his own life. That was why he didn't really have any friends, and probably why he had never been in a romantic relationship. Then, when she had become more independent and had not needed him so much, he had started to suffer with his mental health, and had not had the opportunity to socialise with friends or form relationships.

But Nell was right, he was a very private person, so perhaps he would find it difficult to talk to Teresa about being in a relationship. His reaction when she has first started dating Dan had not been especially positive. In fact, when she thought about it, he had been quite negative when she first met Alex

49

too. Mark hadn't liked Alex from the beginning, though he had never said as much to her. Then, when the relationship had broken down and Alex had gone, she remembered crying on Mark's shoulder, asking how Alex could just abandon them both like that? Why wouldn't he want a relationship with his daughter, even if he didn't love Teresa anymore? How could he be so heartless? Mark had said it was for the best, and that both she and Lily would be better off without him, in the long run. Teresa had really needed to believe in something, and she had come round to Mark's point of view, but even now it upset her to know that Lily had a father out there who didn't care about her at all. Alex's departure had not bothered Mark in the slightest. He had said that they did not need Alex in their lives, and promised that he would act as a father-figure to Lily; he had stood by that promise, and had always looked out for the two of them.

Now there was her developing relationship with Dan. She had shown Mark pictures of Dan when she had first met him, and Mark had initially seemed happy for her, encouraging her to keep seeing him. He had said that it was time to stop living in the past, and that she should feel confident to move on with her life. Then, as she had started to talk about Dan more, about his job in the police and his family, Mark had seemed to change his mind, saying that she could do better for herself. She had wanted to introduce the two of them, but Mark had absolutely refused to meet Dan. Whenever she questioned him about it he would become irritated, telling her that there was no point in meeting him, insisting that it would all end in tears, just like the last time. Teresa could not understand his negative reaction, but had wondered whether he might be jealous, since Mark had yet to find someone to share his life with.

Over the years, she had tried to address the subject of dating and relationships with him but he had never wanted to talk about it, and refused to entertain any of her ideas about internet dating and the like. He thought such things were a stupid waste of time. The subject had always been closed as far as Mark was concerned. So for Nell to have seen a woman in his bedroom was astonishing. Could that be the answer to his bizarre behaviour, did Mark finally have a girlfriend? Maybe he felt awkward about admitting that he had a girlfriend to Teresa, given that he had always been so horrible to her about her relationship with Dan? Maybe he was worried that Teresa would not be very welcoming towards her? It would definitely answer some of Teresa's questions about Mark's current behaviour, but still…it seemed so unlikely!

There was only one girl Teresa could remember Mark ever having some sort of relationship with. Her name was Julia. She had been studying at the same college as Mark, and it had been obvious that she really liked him, although Mark hadn't seemed to notice. She had always talked to him, and used to hang around by Teresa's school waiting for Mark to come and collect her, walking down the road with the two of them on the way home. She had been friendly and very kind, always taking an interest in Teresa. Julia would join in with the silly games that she and Mark used to play on the way home, and she had been a lot of fun, always smiling with an infectious giggle. She had been very pretty, with long dark hair, big brown eyes and freckles sprinkled across her cheeks. She and Mark had seemed to get on really well, and though Teresa had been very young at the time, she had known that Julia really liked Mark. But nothing had ever come of it. Occasionally, Julia had invited Mark out to local events, when there had been a crowd going from college, but he had always said that he had to get back to look after his mum and sister. When Mark finished college, they had drifted apart, and Julia eventually went off to University. They had not seen her since. There had been no one else…well, no one as far as Teresa knew.

Chapter 4

A troubled man, dressed casually in jeans and a t-shirt, sat alone on his bed. Around him lay various items that had spilled out of an open folder: a pile of newspapers; a bottle of nail polish; a hair clip; a bracelet; a calendar. He picked up the hair clip and held it carefully for a while, focusing on it for several minutes, before laying it very gently back down on the bed again. He did the same thing with the bracelet. He handled each item very gently, as if they were priceless valuables. Always a serious and thoughtful man, today, as he considered each of the objects spread out before him, he was deeply unsettled.

Mark was to be found sitting on his bed like this most days, deep in thought. This room, the bedroom he had grown up with and the place where he had spent most of his adult life, was where he went when he needed to think. This room had always been a sanctuary for Mark. It was silent. Clean. Uncluttered. There were no televisions; no iPods or iPads; no computers; no distractions at all. Just Mark, alone in the thunderous silence.

The room had textured wallpaper, complete with a dark blue, floral border running across the top, which had been on the wall for more than twenty years, and the soft, mid-blue carpet had several areas so badly worn that it was almost threadbare. There was also a comfortable divan bed, where Mark had slept since he was a boy. He felt safe in that bed. Sitting there, he was able to gaze out of the window, with it's faded, dark blue curtains, without anyone on the outside being able to see in. The low ceiling in his bedroom room was now off-white, and the room would have been quite gloomy if it wasn't for the size of that window, which was large enough to throw light into even the darkest corners. Mark loved to watch the clouds form and float across the sky outside, and listen to the friendly, familiar sound of the wind rustling through the leaves of the willow tree in the front garden, it's top branches swaying gracefully. He would often watch the birds coming and going, envying their endless energy. Lying on his bed, Mark could see the changing colours of the heavens above and would marvel at how the patterns in the sky constantly shifted and changed. Rainy days were his favourite, when the sky was dark and moody.

Watching the weather made Mark feel connected to the world outside of his bedroom, without him having to leave it. The bond that tied him to that room was strong, and when he was in there, Mark was calm. This room felt like his only sanctuary in the world. It was the only place where, just sometimes, the voices in his head would be silent. The endless processing of his mind would be still, and the distracting pulsating of the loud, pounding heartbeat inside his chest would be calm and quiet.

Aside from the bed, the room did not contain much furniture. There was a large, imposing wardrobe, made of rosewood, which stood directly opposite the window. It had four large doors and two drawers, with ornate handles, and fitted on to one of the doors was a full-length mirror, with tarnished edges. It was old-fashioned and worn, but Mark would often remember how happy he had been when his parents had first moved the wardrobe into his room, and how he had immediately set about sorting his clothes and organising them to fill the different spaces in the wardrobe. He had hung all his clothes neatly, employing a colour coded system that he still used today. At the very left side of the wardrobe he placed his light-coloured items, then continued through the various shades and colours until he reached the black items, which he placed at the very right-hand side. Just looking at the order and organisation of his wardrobe soothed Mark, and in times of great agitation he would open up the doors and sit staring at the pleasing gradations of colour, until he felt calmer and more placid.

The only other pieces of furniture were a small dressing table and matching stool. They were the same design as the wardrobe, and his parents had moved them in to his room so that he had somewhere to do his schoolwork when he grew older. Though he had once used the dressing table for that purpose, his school days were far behind him now. One of Mark's earliest memories was of his mother, sitting at the dressing table and brushing her hair, getting ready to go out with his father. As a small child, Mark had often sat on his parents' bed and watched his mother brush her long, dark hair in front of the dressing table mirror. She used to keep make-up, little pots of creams and various spray bottles on the table, and Mark had always watched with interest as she applied cream to her face, rouge to her cheeks, powder to her eyes and a little gloss to her lips. He had marvelled at her transformation into a beautiful and glamorous woman within the space of a few minutes. She would always finish her preparations with a spray of her favourite perfume, and even now Mark kept a bottle of that same scent on the dressing table. He would sometimes spray it in his room, the familiar smell immediately taking him back to the happier, simpler time of his childhood, when his father had still been alive and his mother had been happy.

Mark had loved his father, and still felt his loss keenly. He could remember everything about him: the way he looked; his smile; his laugh; his smell; everything. He still vividly remembered the times he had spent with his father while he was growing up, and the things they used to do together. They had spent a lot of time in the garden, and it had been his dad who had instilled and encouraged Mark's enduring love of gardening. His dad had spent many hours with him in the greenhouse: demonstrating and teaching him how to harvest and cultivate seeds; how to care for and encourage new seedlings; how to look after young plants and how to pick the best spot in the garden for them, which would allow them to thrive once they were strong enough to be planted out.

"Gardening is not about expensive visits to the garden centre, my lad. It's about hard graft, getting your hands dirty, long hours of toil and sweat, and being prepared to work hard. The rewards that you will get for your hard work are not only magnificent, they are fair. The garden is the only place you will find where life is truly fair. We are not a religious family, I hold no truck with all that, but in this garden, you really will reap what you sow."

As a boy, Mark had indeed seen this. When he neglected his plants, they failed, but the more effort he put into his garden the more successful it became. In time, Mark learned to love the simplicity of the effort and reward cycle that gardening gave him; it made sense to him, where so many other things in his life did not.

His father also had a love of sport, and he had always tried to get Mark interested in that too. His dad had watched the football every week, followed the major rugby and cricket tournaments, and had always been very knowledgeable. He had also liked playing dominoes and darts with his workmates on a Friday night, down at the local pub. But Mark had never shown any interest in sports at all, he refused to take part in sports and would not watch any either. He had always hated PE lessons and cross-country running, which they had made him do at school, and he had never joined any of the after-school sports clubs which most of the boys in his year were part of. As a result, he had struggled to make friends at school. The other boys had thought him odd, and he had found them boring, as they had only ever wanted to talk about girls or football. He had been friendly with some of the girls and had enjoyed their company, but they had often become giggly when he was around, and would gather together in groups where Mark had felt he did not belong. Unable to make friends with the boys or spend time with the girls, Mark had spent most of his time at school alone. He had also been an only child for much of his childhood, and so became accustomed to spending time alone, both at school and at home. Over time he became increasingly solitary, liable to panic if he found himself in a place with too many people or too much noise. His father had been his one companion as a child, and he had been a good dad, always helping and encouraging him. Mark missed his father terribly and wished he could talk to him now. He would know what to do, and he would not judge Mark's choices, he never had.

As ever, when Mark remembered his father, his thoughts would jump from the good times they had together to the very last day he saw him. That day had started like any other day. Mark had awoken to the sounds of his mother talking to his little sister, telling her to get herself dressed and ready for school. A few moments later, as was usual, Teresa had burst into his room and jumped on his bed.

"Mark, get up," she had said, "It's morning time now, get up."

He had known it was pointless to try and ignore her, but he would always pull the covers up over his head and pretend that he was still asleep. She would then jump up and down on the bed, shouting for him to wake up, until finally he would grab her and pull her down on to the bed, tickling her until she squealed. Their routine had been the same every morning, the two of them fooling around until one of their parents shouted for them to stop mucking about and get ready for school. That fateful morning, it had been their dad who had appeared at the bedroom door. He had already been in his work uniform, ready for a day at the factory, where he was a charge hand in the warehouse.

"Teresa, leave your brother alone," he had said with a smile. "Go and have a wash and get ready for school, your breakfast is ready, now come on. Chop, chop."

She had run off to her own bedroom, closely followed by their dad, and Mark had dressed and washed, ready for the day. Later, when they were both downstairs eating breakfast with their mum, their dad had looked in to the kitchen to say goodbye before he left for work. He had kissed both his mum and Teresa, and had given Mark a friendly slap on the shoulder.

"I'll see you tonight after work, and we'll have a go at pruning those roses while your mum gets tea ready, shall we? Teresa, behave for your mum."

With that he was gone, and their day had continued as normal. His mum had taken Teresa to school, and he had made his own way to college.

59

It had been a normal morning. Then, just before lunch, the principal had come to Mark's classroom and asked him to follow her to her office. He had thought he must be in trouble, although he could not figure out what he had done. She had asked him to take a seat, and she had sat solemnly opposite him, looking at him as though he might try to run at any moment. Then, very gently, she told him that something had happened to his father. There were no details, but she had told him that his dad had been involved in an accident that morning at work, and was now in the local hospital, St Mary's, and that Mark was to get there as soon as he could. Mark didn't remember much more about that conversation, except for telling the principal that he had double maths that afternoon. He did not recall what she had said in reply, but he could remember getting in to her car and the two of them driving to the hospital. She had led the way through the labyrinth of corridors to the emergency department, where they had met his mother, and then she had left. Mark could remember walking through the austere, white corridors of the emergency department, holding his mum's hand, following a nurse who was walking at great pace in front of them, and who kept throwing glances in their direction to make sure they were still following her. She had stopped at one of the cubicles and pulled back the curtain.

"He's in here," she had said.

Although the nurse had been smiling, Mark could remember hearing concern in her voice. He remembered straining his neck, trying to see through the mass of nurses and doctors surrounding the bed. Then, a gap had appeared, and they had been ushered to his father's bedside. His dad had been lying flat on the bed, with a green oxygen mask covering his grey face. His chest, shoulders and arms had been bare, and Mark could remember seeing his father's chest rising and falling steadily. There had been various tubes attached to his chest with stickers, and Mark had seen a larger plaster covering his wrist, with a cannula attached to it. They had put a blood line up, and Mark could recall seeing the small droplets of blood dripping through the tube and into his father's arm. There had also been a monitor at the side of the bed, displaying figures and graphs, and periodically beeping. A young doctor, dressed in blue theatre scrubs, had been watching the screen intently. Mark's mother, at his side and still holding his hand, had been so shocked at the sight that met them that she had crumbled and started to collapse. Two nurses in the cubicle had reacted quickly, catching her before she hit the floor and helping her to a chair by the bed. As this was happening, a young doctor, standing close to his father's bed, had gestured for Mark to come forward. As Mark had neared the bed the doctor had said to him,

"Please say anything you have to say to your father."

Mark had not been able to speak. He had looked at the scene in front of him, at the man lying on the bed. He had known it was his father, but he had been unable to reconcile the image in front of him with the memory of his father from that morning. Mark had looked towards the young doctor, who had nodded reassuringly. Eventually, he managed to find some words.

"Dad, it's me, Mark. I'm here, Mum's here, can you hear me?"

His father had reacted to the sound of his son's voice, moving his arm to try and remove the mask from his face. Mark had taken his father's hand.

"Don't struggle, Dad."

His father's arm had fallen heavily back on to the bed, his hand still clinging to Mark's. The doctor had pulled the oxygen mask away from his father's mouth, allowing him to speak. His voice had been quiet and Mark had moved his head closer, straining to hear what his father was saying.

"Mark," he faltered. "I can't go on. I can't do it."

"Yes, you can, Dad. Yes, you can," Mark had replied.

He had swallowed hard several times, trying to control the panic he knew could be heard in his voice.

"No, Mark," his dad had said, in a barely audible voice. "No, Mark, it's down to you, now."

At this point the doctor had put the oxygen mask back over his father's nose and mouth, allowing him to breathe more easily and compose himself. Mark had squeezed his hand, willing him to be strong, and willing him to get through. The doctor had removed the mask again, and his father had raised his head very slightly.

"You, Mark, you have to do it. Look after your Mum and Teresa. They need you. They need you to be a man. Do you understand? It's time to be a man."

The effort of speaking had exhausted his father, and his head had fallen back on to the pillow, prompting the doctor to quickly replace the oxygen mask. Mark had looked up at the doctor in panic. The doctor had held up his hand and shook his head, as if to say 'no more'. By then, his mother had returned to Mark's side, slightly recovered, and had taken his father's hand from him, standing beside the bed with tears rolling down her face. A nurse had come to stand next to his mother, and Mark had moved backwards to give them room. Those were the last words that his father said to him, the last words he ever said to anyone. Shortly afterwards, his father had suffered a massive heart attack, and died. Mark remembered those words very clearly in his mind, and he could still see that expression in his father's eyes, pleading and worried.

"I'll look after them, Dad, of course I will," Mark said now, under his breath, the same words he wished he had been able to say to his father, before he died. That would always be his greatest regret, the words he had never had the chance to say to his dying father.

Mark picked up a newspaper cutting from the bed. The headline screamed at him: 'Two years, two missing: somebody must know something'. Underneath the headline were the pictures of two girls. The first was young, and Asian, with long, glossy, straight black hair and dark, almond-shaped eyes. She had a round, flat face, with wide cheekbones and a flat nose. The picture showed her smiling and happy. Her shoulders were visible on the picture, and although out of frame, it looked like her arms were raised as if she was embracing unseen companions, who had been cropped out of the original shot. The text beneath the photograph read: 'Maisie Jones, aged nineteen. A Cambridge student reading medicine, who attended the Summer Solstice at Stonehenge in 2017, with a group of friends from university. She has not been seen since'. Further down the page was a picture of Maisie's parents, and her elder brother. The parents, first generation immigrants from China, had not spoken to the press, but her brother Samuel had given several interviews on behalf of the family. There had been a press conference in the days following Maisie's disappearance, which all three family members had attended, but her parents had once again declined to speak. Mark remembered them looking very small, old, and bewildered, seated on either side of their son at a large table and flanked by detectives from the Wiltshire police force.

The other girl, Claudia, had disappeared at the annual Stonehenge festival exactly one year later. The picture of her, used by the newspaper, had been taken on the night she disappeared. It was a selfie with her boyfriend Julian, and they were both laughing, surrounded by throngs of people. 'Claudia Merrick was twenty-three years old, blond and strikingly beautiful' the paper said, discussing the fact that she and Julian both came from London and had just moved in to their first flat together. It was almost a year now since Claudia's disappearance, and Julian had been very present and vocal in the press. He had been interviewed by all the national and local newspapers and had made appearances on both the morning news and various current affairs programmes. He had been critical of the police investigation, which he argued had centred mainly on him. In the eyes of the police, he was the main suspect, and he had told the press that he would almost certainly have been arrested and convicted by now if the police had found any link between him and Maisie. However, because of the similarities between the cases, and with no link to Maisie, the police were finding it hard to get enough evidence for the Crown Prosecution Service to support their case.

Julian had discussed how the police had trawled through his entire life, desperate to find any evidence of criminal or subservient behaviour. They had spoken to his family, friends, neighbours and work colleagues, asking about his character and inviting them to pick out anything they might consider flawed or deviant. The police had asked everyone Julian knew about his relationship with Claudia, asking them whether she seemed happy, or if she had ever hinted that something was not right with their relationship. They had also spoken to previous girlfriends, asking them if he had ever shown any aggression toward them, and they had even gone so far as to ask Julian's mother if she thought he might be capable of harming Claudia. Julian Freeman was furious, absolutely furious, and he was making no secret about it. In response to his claims of harassment, the police force had strenuously denied that they were hounding him, and regularly put out appeals for any information regarding the two young women. They refused to link the two disappearances, saying that there was currently not enough evidence to say for sure that the two cases were related, although they did acknowledge the similarities between the two events.

It was now June the fifteenth, and pictures of the girls were surfacing daily in every newspaper, along with assurances from the Wiltshire police force that the Stonehenge festival would go ahead as planned, but that they would advise those attending to stay together in groups and be careful not to get separated. They assured the public that there would be a very heavy police presence at the festival, with plain-clothed police officers, male and female, mixing in with the crowd. They were taking extra precautions, but the event would go ahead as normal.

Mark picked up two objects from his bed. The first was a shiny, blue metallic hair clip, with a butterfly on it. Maisie wore a hairclip just like it, in the photograph from the newspaper cutting. Next, he picked up a braided, yellow, blue and pink bracelet. The same bracelet as the one Claudia had been wearing, in the picture taken hours before her disappearance. Mark looked at both objects intently, then gripped them tightly in his hands. With tears rolling down his cheeks, he sat alone on his bed, slowly rocking backwards and forwards.

[faint mirrored text at top of page, partially legible]

Chapter 5

Sunday morning came around again, and as usual Lily bounded out of her bed and ran into Teresa's room. It was very early, and Teresa was sleeping soundly...until Lily jumped onto the bed. Teresa woke with a start.

"When are we going to Granny's?"

Teresa, barely awake, drew Lily close to her and gave her a cuddle. She pulled the duvet up over both of them and stroked Lily's head.

"Not yet, Lily, it's far too early. Go back to sleep for a little while."

Her words seemed to work, and Lily settled down with her mother. But, thirty seconds later, the child sat up again.

"Is it time now, Mummy?"

Teresa knew it was pointless to try and contain Lily in bed any longer.

"Okay, Lily, you win. Let's get up," she yawned.

Teresa sat up, stretching her arms out wide in front of her, as Lily jumped out of the bed. Five minutes later, when Teresa had eventually managed to drag herself sleepily into the kitchen, Lily was already sitting at the kitchen table, waiting patiently for her breakfast. Teresa had her dressing gown wrapped tightly around her and was wearing a pair of thick socks which she often wore around the flat. She poured some cereal into a bowl, splashed some milk over it, and handed it to Lily, along with a small glass of apple juice. Leaving her daughter at the table eating breakfast, Teresa went to bathroom, showered quickly and threw on some jeans and a t-shirt. She had only been gone for ten minutes, but when she returned, she found Lily practicing star-jumps in the living room. She looked sternly at her daughter.

"Lily, stop banging about. It's very early. What about poor Mr Michael downstairs? You'll wake him up."

Lily stopped jumping, immediately regretting of her actions.

"I'm sorry, Mummy. I was only doing some of the exercises they showed us at school, to keep fit. They said we should do some every day, so we don't become obese."

It was impossible to be cross with Lily for any length of time, and Teresa softened immediately when she heard the child's explanation. She smiled at her daughter.

"Well, I think that's probably enough exercise for this morning, Lily. Maybe you could do some more in Granny's garden later?"

The child skipped off happily into her bedroom, and half an hour later, the two of them arrived at her mother's house. Usually, Mark would be at the door waiting for them, as was his custom on a Sunday. But not today. The house felt eerily still and quiet. The living room curtains were still closed, and there were no signs of life anywhere.

Teresa went upstairs and looked inside her mother's bedroom.

"Mum, are you awake?"

"Yes, love, I am," came the reply.

"Good. I'll get you a cuppa."

Teresa passed Mark's room on the way back downstairs. She knew it was pointless knocking. He would have heard them arrive, and Teresa was sure he would come downstairs in his own time. She knew that he always slept more when he was going through one of his episodes, so Teresa was not overly worried that he wasn't up and about yet. She understood that he needed more rest than usual. Unconcerned, she went into the kitchen and unlocked the back door for Lily, who immediately ran outside and started to cartwheel around the lawn. Teresa took her mum the tea, then left her alone to get herself up and ready for the day.

The morning passed quickly, with Teresa kept busy tidying the house and preparing lunch. Her mother dozed in the armchair, and Lily played happily on her own in the garden. She occasionally skipped into the kitchen to check what Teresa was doing. On one of these visits she asked,

"Where's Uncle Mark?"

"He must be sleeping in, I'm sure he'll be down soon."

It was after midday, and there was still no sign of Mark, but Teresa was sure he would come down once the food was ready. They always ate together on a Sunday, and although things had been difficult between them lately, Mark did not usually sulk. He would come down soon enough, and she hoped they could have a more rational conversation than their last one. Today she was determined that they were going to have a good day. She had resolved to be more supportive and understanding towards her brother. Teresa desperately wanted to help him, not alienate him. She was even going to be brave enough to broach the subject of his girlfriend with him. She didn't want him to feel like he had to keep his new relationship a secret.

Having grown bored of waiting for Mark, Lily set the table by herself. She found the familiar tablecloth and spread it out over the large table, and polished the cutlery and glasses, as Mark had shown her how to do countless times. She set the usual four places and then went off to find some fresh flowers from the garden, returning with a pink medley of sweet peas and snapdragons, which she placed in a pleasing arrangement inside the vase which sat in the centre of the table. When lunch was finally ready, Teresa sent Lily to fetch her grandmother from the living room. Making her way to the foot of the stairs, Teresa looked towards Mark's bedroom and shouted up to him.

"Just dishing up, Mark, don't let it go cold."

There was no reply, but she didn't really expect one. She dished out the food onto four plates, the first one for her mother, containing very small portions of food, and the other three for the rest of them. As she put Lily's plate in front of her, the child immediately started to eat. Teresa smiled to herself, as she set down the last two plates and sat at the table.

"Lily, don't you think you should wait until Uncle Mark comes down?"

Lily stopped eating and looked sheepishly at her mother. Her grandmother looked at the girl and absently waved her hand.

"Carry on, child, don't wait. Mark is gone. I heard him leave early this morning."

Teresa looked at her mother in disbelief. She felt the colour drain from her face and she bolted from her chair, running up the stairs, taking them two at a time in her haste. She banged frantically on Mark's locked bedroom door, with the flat of her hand. There was no reply. She had expected that, but she was so furious that she continued to bang her hand against the door as loudly as she could. Eventually, realising the futility of what she was doing, she stopped hammering on the door and slumped to the floor, tired from her exertions. She could not control her tears as they fell freely down her cheeks, and she sat there sobbing at the foot of that door for several minutes.

After some time, Teresa recovered herself a little. Taking a deep breath, she pulled her phone out of her pocket and called Mark's number. It rang and rang. No reply. There wasn't even an option to leave a voicemail. In despair, she threw her own phone across the landing and it hit the wall opposite with a thump, falling down to the ground with a clatter and landing face up on the hall carpet, in two pieces. Deflated and fed up, she returned to the kitchen, where she picked up Mark's plate and emptied the contents into the dustbin. Returning to the table

Teresa tried to make conversation with her mother and Lily, as though everything was fine. But as she pushed food around her plate, Teresa could not stop thinking about Mark. Now she really was worried, was he about to do something stupid? Had she been right about him all along? Could he be hiding a terrible secret from her?

After lunch, she called Dan, and although she didn't say so, he could tell from the anxious tone in her voice that she was troubled.

"What's wrong, Teresa? Is it your Mum, or Lily?"

"No," replied Teresa. "It's Mark. I think...I think he may have done something terrible. Can you come over? I need to talk to you."

Dan told her that he would be there in an hour, just as soon as he had finished his shift.

Teresa's mum was dozing in her chair, and Lily was settled in front of a film, when Dan knocked on the door an hour later. Neither of them stirred as Teresa showed Dan in, and surreptitiously led him through to the kitchen. She made them both a cup of tea and sat next to him at the kitchen table.

"Tell me about this brother of yours, then," Dan said with a smile. "What's he been up to?"

Teresa burst into tears, and Dan immediately felt guilty about the way he had broached the subject. He had assumed that the young man had committed some sort of minor misdemeanour, maybe he had gotten into a fight with someone, or had failed to pay his car insurance...the usual stuff young men of

Mark's age got up to. He had thought that Teresa was probably overreacting to the situation. But her distressed response had surprised him, and he instantly changed tack.

"I'm sorry, Teresa, I didn't mean to be flippant. Is Mark okay?"

"That's just it," said Teresa, recovering herself. "I really don't know if he's okay or not."

Over the next hour she told Dan the whole story. She began by describing Mark's reaction to the news report on Claudia's disappearance last year, and his obsession with the Stonehenge story: how he kept every newspaper cutting related to the missing girls case, and turned the radio up any time it was mentioned. She also explained that he refused to discuss it if Teresa raised it with him. She outlined Mark's changes in behaviour, and told Dan that he had been growing increasingly distant from her over recent weeks. Now he had gone completely, and she had no idea where he was, but she said to Dan that she was terrified his unexpected departure had something to do with the missing girls cases. The solstice festival at Stonehenge was getting close, and she couldn't stop thinking that Mark might have been involved in Claudia's disappearance last year. She told Dan that she was worried something might happen this year too, and that Mark was going to be involved somehow.

Dan was seriously perplexed. He had not known Teresa very long at all, but he knew that she was a sensible, and level-headed person. Her

74

behaviour today was not normal. Perhaps she wasn't thinking clearly. Surely, she was not suggesting that her own brother was the person responsible for abducting Claudia?

"Tell me more about your brother," he encouraged. "What's he like?"

Teresa described Mark as a good, supportive brother, who was a kind uncle to Lily and loved her dearly. He was a dependable son, who helped Teresa to look after their mother.

"This is all good," Dan said. "I think you may be worrying over nothing."

"I haven't told you everything, yet!"

Teresa went on to explain Mark's mental health issues, his recurring bouts of depression and his admissions to various mental health units over the years. She talked honestly about his lack of friends, and his compelling and confusing need for solitude and personal space. Finally, with great reluctance, she told him about Mark's bedroom, explaining to Dan that it had been locked for ten years, and that Mark would not let anyone else in there, or even communicate with anyone while he was locked in there. The look on Teresa's face clearly showed how worried and concerned she was.

"It's just not right, is it?"

"No, Teresa, no it isn't," replied Dan in a measured tone. "It's very unusual. But it also isn't a crime. He's not doing anything wrong by wanting to spend time alone. That doesn't make him a criminal."

"What about Stonehenge? What about those girls? Why is he so interested?"

Teresa was beginning to get upset again. Dan stroked her arm to reassure her.

"It's a really big news story. A lot of people are fascinated by it, and that's not a crime either. It may sound a bit morbid to you, but I'm fascinated by it too. I've tried to get on the team a few times, but they told me I hadn't been in the job long enough. You said that he was with you when all this started, when the first girl went missing? The likelihood is that the same person is responsible for the disappearance of both girls. So, if that's the case, Mark couldn't have had anything to do with it, could he? Surely you don't really believe that he is responsible for abducting two young women, do you?"

"That's what I told myself to start with. That he was with me, so he couldn't have been involved." Teresa was calmer now. "But he's been behaving so strangely and now he's gone off again, without a word to me."

"That's not quite true, is it, Teresa? You told me yourself that he had been talking about going away. Now, I don't know your brother, but from what you've told me, he could be struggling with his mental health issues right now which isn't unusual or out of character for him. He might have gone off for a while to get his head straight. You said yourself, he's done that before, but he came back, didn't he? I'm sure he'll be back home in a day or two, you wait and see."

Dan's tone was sanguine and upbeat. He could see that Teresa had worked herself into a state over all of this, and he tried to be positive and helpful, to show her the situation from a different perspective.

"I hope you're right."

"I'm sure I am," said Dan with confidence. "Now, why don't we have another cuppa, and then you can introduce me to Lily and your mum."

"Yes, okay, why not," said Teresa. "You're right, I've probably got this all out of context. I'm sure Mark will be fine, he knows what he's doing."

Dan stayed for the rest of the afternoon. Teresa introduced him to her mum, who smiled in her distant way at him, and then to Lily, who asked him a hundred questions about being a policeman and was especially interested in whether he had caught any burglars today. Dan laughed and joked with Lily, and let her wear his policeman's hat, which dropped down onto her nose. She struggled to lift it back up and it dropped down again, which made them all laugh. Teresa felt a lot calmer after talking to Dan, and she put her worries about Mark to the back of her mind as she enjoyed the afternoon with Dan and Lily.

Later, when Dan had gone home, Teresa drove back to the flat to fetch some belongings for her and Lily. She had decided to move back into her mum's house for a short while, just until Mark came home. Lily was delighted to be moving into her grandmother's house, and packed so many toys and clothes into her suitcase that Teresa had to step in, reminding her that they were only staying for a few nights. As she was packing her own clothes, she considered the possibility of moving back into her mother's house permanently. She had thought about it once before, when she had left the old house, after Alex. Back then, she had wanted to keep as much of her new found independence as possible, and she had thought it would be unfair on her mum for her to bring a new baby into the house. Her mum would not have coped well with all of the disturbed nights and crying.

Thinking back now, she supposed that she hadn't wanted to fail her first attempt at being an adult, but that seemed irrelevant to her now. As she drove from the flat to her mum's house, Teresa was still thinking about the practicalities of moving back home for good. Right now, it seemed to make a lot of sense. She spent so much of her time there anyway. Lily loved being there, and maybe it would even be good for her mum to have Lily there more often. After all, she did seem to try harder to communicate with Lily than she did with anyone else. Teresa could also keep a much closer eye on Mark if she moved back home, but how would he feel about it? Until recently, she thought he would probably agree with her that it was a good idea, but because of how things had been between them lately, she just couldn't predict what his reaction would be. Then there was her financial situation. Of course, if she moved back, she would expect to contribute to the running of the house, but she already did most of the shopping. If she didn't have to pay for the flat, maybe she would be able to save up a deposit to buy her own house. Then, when Lily was a bit older and more independent, she could work longer hours, and maybe even get a better job. Teresa sighed. She knew she was daydreaming. She also knew that she had really enjoyed her afternoon in Dan's company, despite her worries about Mark. She hadn't felt at all awkward or uncomfortable with him, not like she had when he came to her flat. In her heart, she knew exactly why she was thinking about moving home again. She shook her head as she pulled up outside her mum's house. Maybe, just maybe, it could work.

Teresa unloaded the car and spent the next hour settling Lily into her old bedroom. Lily often played in that room, so it didn't take long to settle her down for the night. Teresa spent the evening watching television with her mum.

"It's good to have you home, Teresa, I've missed you."

Teresa smiled at her mother. She had explained to her mum several times that she was just moving back in for a few days, until Mark came home, but either her mum had forgotten, or she had chosen to ignore what Teresa had said. Over the course of the evening, Teresa continued to think seriously about moving back in permanently, and she resolved to talk to Mark about it as soon as he got home.

Dan was at the police station.

"What are you doing here? Can't keep away?" asked Jim, one of his colleagues as he walked in.

"Just remembered I needed to add something to my report about those lads we had in earlier," Dan lied. "Wanted to do it while it was still fresh in my mind."

"Very conscientious, I'm sure. Are you looking for a promotion?"

"I wish," replied Dan.

"It'll come," said Jim. "You know how it is in this job, mate. You gotta serve your time, same as the cons. Either that or crack a big one."

Dan sat down at the computer, opening the application for the National Crime Information Centre. He entered Mark's details and sat back in the chair, while the computer searched through the data. He couldn't really say if he wanted the computer to come up with something or not. Teresa was lovely, and he really liked her. He had seen himself having a serious, long-term relationship with her, but that was before the events of earlier today. She had been completely different from the girl he thought he was getting to know. Suggesting her brother could be involved with the Stonehenge girls was just crazy, he had believed that she was more sensible than that. Still, if he really did think she was crazy, what was he doing here now, running a background check on Mark? The 'finished searches' icon popped up on the computer, and Dan pressed on the 'results' button. Nothing. There was absolutely nothing on Mark Applewhite. He was completely clean, no cautions, nothing. Dan sighed with relief. Of course, it was good news. Now he just had to figure out why Teresa, a seemingly level-headed girl with no apparent malice toward her brother, had suggested such a ridiculous thing? Maybe she wasn't as level-headed as he thought.

On impulse he put Teresa's details into the search engine. He really shouldn't have. He could be asked to justify every one of these searches by his superiors, and he would find it quite difficult, not to mention hugely embarrassing, to explain why he was running a background check on his girlfriend. He changed his mind about what he was doing, but just as he was about to switch the computer off it popped up with the 'finished searching' icon again. Dan couldn't resist the urge to look, and he pressed the 'results' button. Teresa had a caution against her! In June 1998, she had been cautioned for assaulting a police officer. He scrolled through the details of the assault. Teresa Applewhite, sixteen years old, had bitten the arm of a female police officer, who had been restraining her while her brother was detained by a doctor under the Mental Health Act. She had attended a Juvenile Court and received a warning from the judge. The warning seemed to have served its purpose, as there was nothing else on the system. Dan sat back in his chair, confused about the information in front of him. Earlier, when he had been with her, Teresa had volunteered all sorts of information about her brother. But she had not mentioned this, that she had a police record. Dan would have to seriously consider this new information about Teresa. Was she really what she seemed to be? He couldn't afford to get mixed up with anyone who was unstable, he had his future to think about. He really liked Teresa, but looking at the picture in front of him of a petulant teenager, he was starting to have his doubts.

Dan turned the computer off and went up to the top floor of the building, into the Major Incident room. It was a huge room, with ten desks arranged in rows. Even though it was late on a Sunday evening, there were still several officers working. He nodded in acknowledgement as he walked past and made his way to the glass screens at the front of the incident room. Two enormous glass screens, one dedicated to pictures and information about Maisie, the other one to information about Claudia, loomed in front of him. Down the right-hand side of the screens were timelines, written in coloured pen, detailing what was known about the activities of the two girls prior to their disappearances. Dan sat at one of the desks at the front of the room, looking at the pictures of the two girls. They were both young and pretty, with so much in life left to do, and so much still to achieve. Where were they? Were they still alive? Mark may not have anything to do with this case, but somebody, somewhere did. Somebody knew.

As he sat there thinking about the girls, a young woman approached.

"Hi, Dan, haven't seen you for a while. What brings you up here?"

Megan was the same age as Dan and, like him, came from a police family. They had attended cadets together when they were younger and had joined the force at the same time. They had often been involved in the same cases, and knew each other well. Only last year, Megan had decided to sit her National Investigators Examination. She had passed with flying colours and had been immediately recruited to join the Stonehenge investigation, as a detective. It was perfect timing for her, and she had fallen on her feet. She was the youngest officer on the case, and the only female. Dan was pleased for her, but he was also a little jealous. He too had wanted to take the Investigators exam, but his father had advised him to wait until he had a bit more experience under his belt. Dan had taken that advice, but now, seeing Megan, he believed that he had made the wrong decision. He would have to wait another two years before he could apply to sit the exam. He certainly wasn't going to miss that chance when it came around again.

"Megan, how are you doing? Any progress?" he asked, nodding toward the screens.

"Very little, if I'm honest," replied Megan, shrugging her shoulders. "They just seem to have vanished into thin air. We've had very little information from the public. Most of what we have has come from crackpots. The main push at the minute is this year's festival. We've got to make sure it doesn't happen again, so well be out in force on the night: dogs, helicopters, and the lot. They're offering overtime to anyone willing to help out, it'll be an all-nighter though."

"I'll help," Dan volunteered immediately. "I'll clear it with the Sarge tomorrow."

"That would be great, it's all hands on deck. We're arranging a briefing here the night before. I'll let you know what time."

"Fantastic, thanks, Megan. I'll be there."

As Dan got up to leave Megan asked, "Dan, why did you come?"

"No reason, just curiosity, I suppose."

Megan smiled, "Okay. If you say so. See you soon."

Dan left. He realised that this would have been an ideal opportunity to tell Megan what Teresa had said about Mark Applewhite, but he hadn't taken that opportunity. He knew why he hadn't said anything. As he considered what Teresa had told him earlier that evening, he really wasn't sure if it was Mark who had something to hide, or his sister.

Chapter 6

Four days. Mark had been gone for four days and Teresa had heard nothing from him. She had been repeatedly calling his mobile, only to listen to it ring endlessly countless times, and she had sent him a tonne of messages, all unread and unanswered. She was sure that his phone was probably dead by now, but she continued to ring him, desperate for some kind of contact.

Teresa had also tried to get in touch with Dan. Now that she was staying at her mum's house, she felt a lot more comfortable about Dan coming over to visit. The problem was that he kept saying he was too busy. She hadn't seen him since last Sunday afternoon, when she'd told him about Mark and her concerns, and she'd only spoken to him on the phone once, very briefly. When she had asked him if he wanted to come to the house one evening, Teresa thought she had detected some reluctance in his voice, but she wasn't sure. He had said he was very busy this week at work, and that he would be in touch when things had settled down again, leaving things very open-ended. Teresa was excruciatingly aware that she had presented herself as a paranoid fantasist, who was a bit out of control, on Dan's last visit. She was acutely embarrassed when she remembered how she had behaved, and the last thing she wanted to do was put him under any pressure, or push him by asking why he didn't want to see her. She was sure that would just make her look even more needy. Dan had made it clear that he thought she was overreacting about Mark going away, and he had been incredulous when she voiced her concerns about Mark's possible connection to the Stonehenge girls. She did not want Dan to think she was crazy, but maybe it was already too late for that...he must deal with crazy people all the time as part of his job...what must he think of her? She had sent him a couple of light-hearted texts to maintain contact, but so far, he had not replied. Teresa now regretted confiding in Dan, but at the time he had made her feel better about things, and it had been such a relief to finally share her concerns with somebody. Although he had listened and been reassuring, looking back, it was clear that Dan felt Teresa was the one with the problem, not Mark. What if she had ruined everything between them? To top it all off, there was still no sign of Mark, and tomorrow was solstice day.

Teresa had not been sleeping well, and she was very tired at work the following day. She must have looked unwell, because her boss kept asking her if she was okay. She shook herself out of her thoughts as two customers approached the checkout. It was a mum and daughter, and as they came closer, she could hear they were talking about the solstice celebrations that night.

"I don't care what you say, Molly, I'm not changing my mind. You are not going, and that's final. Do you ever listen to the news? You know they still haven't found those two girls."

The daughter, who must have been about fifteen years old and was wearing a school uniform from the local grammar school, glared at her mother.

"Exactly! They haven't found them, Mum. Why is everybody so convinced that something bad happened to them? There's no proof. Perhaps they just wanted to disappear? I know I do!"

Molly's mum had been loading the shopping into bags, but this last sentence made her stop in her tracks.

"Molly! Don't say things like that! The problem with you is you're too used to getting your own way."

"But we always go, Mum, every year. Sally's still going."

"I know we do, love, and I'll miss it too. I'm only thinking of you and your sister. I wouldn't be able to let you out of my sight. I'd be sick with worry."

Her words didn't placate Molly at all, and the girl crossed her arms in frustration.

"It's just so unfair!"

"Well, love, life's not fair. The sooner you learn that, the better. Your dad and I have made our decision. We're giving it a miss this year, end of story."

By this time, the pair had packed their shopping into bags, and the mother was searching in her purse for her payment card.

"What do you think?" the older woman asked, looking up at Teresa as she handed over her bank card. "All this Stonehenge business, I think they should have called it off. What do you think?"

Molly jumped in before Teresa had a chance to respond.

"Mum! You always think the worst! It's the best thing that happens around here, it's not fair to stop it. People look forward to it all year."

The woman looked at Teresa and rolled her eyes, exasperated by her daughter's continued inability to see this from any perspective apart from her own.

"They just don't understand, do they? Do you have kids?"

"Yes, a little girl."

"Well then, you'll understand. It's just not worth the risk, is it?"

As the pair gathered up their shopping and left the shop, Teresa pondered what the woman had said. Teresa had never even considered Lily in all of this, and yet it was inevitable that, in a few years, Lily would want to attend the festival, just like Molly. Molly was quite right, all the local kids went. It was the biggest event on the calendar around here, and many families attended every year without fail. Most people attended in big groups, and many took time off work and invited relatives down for the event. It was a family occasion, with people of all ages coming together to celebrate. Teresa had been a couple of times herself, when she was a teenager. She had attended with her friend's family while she was still at school, and Molly was right, it was a fantastic night. At that age, just staying up all night was exciting enough, but combined with the party atmosphere, the delicious, exotic food, and the strange, ethereal music, the evening was transformed into a truly mesmerising experience.

Teresa's family had never attended, and she didn't really know why. Certainly, since her dad had died, it would have been too much to expect her mum to take the two children on her own. But, even before he died, they had never been to the festival as a family. Teresa thought about Lily. She considered her daughter too young to be taken to the festival... perhaps her dad had thought the same thing about her, too? Some people must consider that view old-fashioned, as she could remember seeing very young children sitting on their dad's shoulders, and mums breastfeeding tiny babies, in previous years, so clearly some children of Lily's age had been going to the festival all their lives.

What would Teresa do when Lily was a teenager? Naturally she would want to go, and all her friends would be going. Would she let her go? Right now, she didn't know the answer to that question, but that argument was going to happen one day and then she would have to face it. Teresa felt immensely relieved and thankful that Lily was so young and had absolutely no knowledge of what was going on. She could well imagine herself having a very similar conversation with Lily in a few years' time as the one she had just witnessed between Molly and her mum. Teresa sighed. It had been a very long day and her mind was running on overdrive. She was relieved when her shift finally ended.

Teresa left work quickly and went to pick up Lily as usual. Standing in the playground, she took off her cardigan, draping it over her arm as she felt the hot sun beating down on her as she waited for Lily to come down the steps from her classroom. All week, the weather had been warm, and the forecast was good for tonight too, with no rain, wind or clouds. It was going to be a very clear, still night, perfect for the solstice.

On the drive home, Teresa had the local radio station playing, and the regular 'hot topic' broadcast was about tonight's festival. The reporter was asking a police spokesman what his advice would be for anyone attending tonight's celebrations.

"As we've said before," said the spokesman in a particularly monotone voice, "there is no danger in attending the festival, but we are advising people to be careful. As a precaution, we ask those attending the event to arrive in a group, to stay within that group during the event, and to avoid wandering off alone. Everyone is responsible for making sure that no-one gets separated from their group. As a further precaution, there will be a heavier police presence than usual. We are not there to stop people enjoying the event, and we will endeavour to keep a low profile. However, we will be on hand if anyone requires any assistance. We also ask that if, during the event, anyone sees anything that could be considered suspicious, please report to a police officer immediately."

At this point, the interviewer tried to interrupt with another question, but the spokesman ignored her and carried on.

"All we ask of the public is that they are mindful of their own safety, and that they are vigilant. We thank everybody for their cooperation and hope that you all enjoy tonight's event."

The reporter asked whether the issuing of safety warnings and the increased police presence at the event could be considered scaremongering by the police force, but the spokesman countered that argument, insisting that the same advice was given out every year and that he could not agree that a larger police presence was anything other than pragmatic, given that the number of festival goers was increasing year on year and that this year was expected to follow the same trend. The statement had clearly been scripted, and as the discussion deviated further from the script the spokesman became increasingly uncomfortable and refused to be drawn in by the reporter. He made it very clear that it was not his place to speculate on the disappearances of Claudia and Maisie, highlighting that these were ongoing cases, and that it would therefore be inappropriate to comment further on them.

Teresa was really interested to hear more, but she noticed that Lily was listening too. Quickly, she turned the radio off, and started asking Lily questions about her day at school. She didn't want Lily to become concerned about what she had heard. As Lily babbled on about her day, Teresa thought about Dan. Perhaps he had been recruited to provide cover as part of the 'heavier police presence'? That would make sense. Maybe he really was busy with work, and not avoiding her at all? After all, he had given her no reason to think that he had gone off her. Perhaps she should just be patient and wait for all this to go back to normal. Oh, how she wished this day and night were over. She looked at the clock on the dashboard. There were still fifteen hours until sunrise.

Later that night, when Lily and her mum were in bed, Teresa sat up watching the news. She was exhausted, but she knew that she would not be able to sleep tonight. She would just have to stay awake and see this dreaded night through. She was optimistic that once this night was over, and the new day had started, she would feel much better about everything. After the news had finished, she made herself a cup of strong coffee, found an old black and white film to watch, and settled down for the night. Her phone was by her side, she hadn't had it out of her sight since Mark had left, just in case. She was also hopeful that Dan might reply to her. She snuggled down in the chair to watch the film, but twenty minutes in, it had failed to grab her attention, and she found herself flicking over to the 24 hour news station, to check for any news about Stonehenge.

Nothing. A wave of relief swept over her, and she went back to watching the film. But she just couldn't concentrate.

Eventually, she gave up on the film altogether, switching over to the news channel. The same four news items just kept going around and around in a loop, and eventually Teresa became so bored that she muted the sound and picked up her book to read. She could still see the script running along the bottom of the screen, announcing news articles as they came in. This way she could read her book and keep an eye on the news channel simultaneously. The channel also had a permanent running clock, so she had everything she needed to make it through the night.

Two-thirty in the morning: it was nearly over. Teresa told herself that once it got to six a.m. she could assume that nothing bad was going to happen and head up to bed, in the knowledge that the solstice had passed by without incident. That would give her one hour of sleep before she has to get up to take Lily to school. She wasn't working tomorrow. She had booked the day off as holiday, knowing how tired she would be.

Five-thirty in the morning: Teresa woke with a start. Oh no, she must have nodded off! Her book had dropped to the floor, and she had fallen asleep, sprawled out on the sofa. She bent down to pick up her book and glanced at the television screen, which was still silently broadcasting. In red, along the bottom of the screen, the script screamed in capital letters 'BREAKING NEWS – THIRD GIRL GOES MISSING FROM STONEHENGE EVENT'. Teresa stared at the screen as the message ran repetitively. She saw concern on the face of the newsreader. It was clear that she was talking about Stonehenge. At that moment, two pictures flashed up. One was Maisie, the other Claudia. Teresa's stomach churned and she felt the bile rise from the pit of her stomach, tasting the vile flavour in her throat. She ran from the room, and just manged to make it to the bathroom before she was violently sick in the toilet. She retched and retched, eventually slumping to the floor in exhaustion. She retched again, holding her head over the toilet bowl, waiting for the vomit. Throwing up again, she began to cry. She couldn't stop the tears. She was absolutely distraught and felt wretched. She fell onto the bathroom floor, pulled her arms around her bent knees and sobbed. Please, Mark…please…don't let it be you. Please come home…don't let it be you. That was all she could think, as the feelings of fear and horror came over her.

Teresa didn't know how long she had been lying on the bathroom floor for when she heard Lily stirring in the next room. She had to get a hold of herself. Very slowly, she stood up, blew her nose, and wiped her eyes with a tissue. She poured cold water into the basin and splashed some onto her face to wake herself up. The coldness smarted at her red, swollen eyes, and she flinched with pain. She splashed more and more cold water until her face and hands were so numb that she couldn't feel them. She dried herself on the towel and left the bathroom, just in time for Lily to race past her into the bathroom.

"You're up, Mummy! I'll be down in a minute for breakfast."

Lily, completely unaware, had not noticed that Teresa was pale and shaking.

"Okay, love." Teresa forced herself to smile. "I'll go and get it ready for you."

Teresa went to the kitchen and automatically ran through her customary morning habits, pouring out Lily's cereal and milk, and making herself a cup of tea. She knew she wasn't going to drink the tea this morning, but she still made it. Lily bounded into the kitchen, and Teresa left her eating her breakfast, walking back into the living room where the strapline on the news channel now read 'MISSING GIRL. THIRD GIRL TO GO MISSING FROM STONEHENGE EVENT IN THREE YEARS.' Teresa's heart sank even further. She had no idea what she should do now. She continued to follow their normal morning routine, completely on autopilot, thoughts swirling around her head. Lily ran past her at speed, and she followed the child upstairs to help her get dressed. She was all fingers and thumbs trying to get Lily into her uniform, and the child started to notice that something was wrong.

"Silly, Mummy, that's not the right button. Look, it goes like this."

Lily took over the buttoning of her cardigan, and even managed to get her own socks on.

"Come on, Mummy. It's time to get my shoes on, or I'll be late for school."

Teresa looked at her daughter.

"Yes, we had better get a move on," she replied half-heartedly.

Downstairs, she helped Lily with her shoes and coat, then bundled her into the car. When she returned to the house half an hour later, she really couldn't say how she had managed to get to the school and back. She had absolutely no recollection of the route she had taken, or of anybody she had seen in the playground, nothing. She sat down at the kitchen table, putting her hands around the cup of tea she had made earlier. She was looking for warmth, but of course, it was cold. It must have been over an hour since she had made it. She had no idea how long she stayed like that, sitting at the kitchen table, staring into her cold mug of tea. She just couldn't figure out what to do. She didn't want to go into the living room to watch more details unfold, she couldn't face it, and she didn't want to go and wake her mother, who would surely notice that something was wrong with her.

A loud knock at the door brought her to her senses. A smart-looking man in a suit stood in front of the house, with two uniformed police officers either side of him, one male, and one female.

"Teresa Johnson?" asked the man.

"Yes."

"I'm Detective Inspector Asrat Sabir."

He held out his identification card to show her. "These are my colleagues, Cody Bedford and Juliet

Coombes. We have a warrant to search this property. Can we come in?"

"What do you mean you have a warrant? Why? What for?"

"We are in possession of certain information suggesting that a person, or persons, residing at this address may be connected to a crime. As such, we have been issued with a warrant to search the property." With that he thrust a piece of paper into Teresa's hand.

"Do you mean Mark? He's not here. Do you know where he is? I haven't heard from him."

"Miss, I am not at liberty to discuss this any further at this time. I have a warrant to enter this property. Now, please, step aside."

Teresa opened the door a little further and the three officers pushed past her. She looked out onto the street. There were two police cars parked outside, one on their drive and the other on the street. She noticed curtains moving in the house opposite. Mrs Philpot must have seen all the activity. Teresa closed the door. The two male officers had disappeared, but Constable Juliet Coombes was standing in the hallway, waiting for her.

"Why don't we have a cup of tea?" she said to Teresa.

"Where are they? Mum's upstairs in bed. She'll be frightened."

"Come into the kitchen and sit down. I'll go check on your mum."

Constable Coombes was being kind, but Teresa did not miss the tone in the constable's voice informing her that this was not a suggestion, it was an instruction. She followed the constable into the kitchen and sat back down at the table. The police officer removed the cold cup of tea, and in no time at all had replaced it with a hot one. She hadn't once asked where to find anything, and was obviously used to finding her way around unfamiliar kitchens. The next thing Teresa was aware of was Constable Coombes walking through the kitchen door, leading her mother to the table.

"There you go, Mrs Applewhite, have a seat next to Teresa and I'll get you a cup of tea. Would you both like some toast?"

"No!" Teresa snapped at the policewoman. "I don't want toast. I want to know what you're doing here. What do you want? You didn't come here to make bloody toast!"

She felt her mother's hand on her own clenched fist and saw the bewilderment and confusion in her eyes. She knew she had to try and keep some control over her emotions. She was raging inside, absolutely raging, and felt sick to her stomach. However, as she held her mum's frail, cold and quivering hand, she said to the police officer,

"I'm sorry. Mum will have some toast please. She likes one slice with butter and a little strawberry jam on it. I'll get it for her; I know how she likes it."

"I'll get it," replied Constable Coombes with a firm tone, "and I'll get you some too. You need to keep your strength up."

Teresa didn't argue. Perhaps the officer was right. Who knew where this day was going to go?

What would happen next? When would normality return and deliver them from this chaos? She and her mother dutifully drank their tea and ate their toast. They remained there, in silence, as they listened to the noise of heavy-footed men making their way through the house. They heard doors opening and closing, floorboards squeaking, and raised voices as the men shouted between each other. After about an hour, Detective Inspector Sabir entered the kitchen.

"Can we have the key to your brother's bedroom, Miss?"

"I don't have it. He has it with him."

"There must be a spare?"

"There isn't."

"In that case, we're going to have to force the door."

"Do what you have to do."

"We'll try not to cause too much damage," he said, leaving the kitchen.

Teresa heard him shout to the other constable.

"Get on the radio. I want back-up here now, more bodies, and tell them to bring the battering ram."

Teresa resigned herself to whatever was going to happen next. She knew it was pointless to resist, and that she was powerless to stop it. Her mum was her main concern, she just had to get her through it.

Teresa's mobile phone rang. She instinctively looked at the constable, who nodded. As she picked it up from the table, she saw the call was from Dan. Dan, he chose to call now, when she had waited and waited for him to reply to her…and then she realised.

"How could you?" She spat her question down the phone as she answered the call.

"Teresa, I'm sorry, I had to."

"You had to? Why? You said I was being paranoid, that I had nothing to worry about, that of course Mark couldn't have anything to do with this."

Just then, she heard different voices, and Detective Sabir shouting.

"We're upstairs, bring the battering ram."

"They're all over the house, your colleagues. And they're about to start knocking doors down. I hope you're pleased with yourself, Dan."

She didn't give him a chance to reply, slamming her phone back down on the table.

"Can I take mum out for a walk?" she asked Constable Coombes.

"I'm afraid not," replied the constable, her voice flat and emotionless. "You both have to remain here with me until the officers have finished their search."

At that moment, Teresa heard a loud thud from upstairs, and then another one. Immediately after the third bang came a crash, and a jubilant cry from one of the officers.

"We're in!"

"The battering ram," said Constable Coombes, by way of explanation.

Thank goodness Mark wasn't there. The thought of anyone else entering his room would distress him, but this would surely have tipped him over the edge.

Chapter 7

Another policeman came into the kitchen, spoke quietly to Constable Coombes, and then left the room.

"They've finished in the living room. Perhaps we should go in there, where it's more comfortable? And they'll want to look in here, so we need to leave."

Again, this was said calmly and politely, but Teresa was left in no doubt that this was a command. She compliantly rose from her seat and assisted her mother to the living room. As they passed the bottom of the stairs, Teresa could see several uniformed officers upstairs on the landing, but there were so many of them that she couldn't see past them. As they entered the living room, Teresa's eyes quickly scanned around the room to see if anything was different. She didn't notice anything out of place, or anything missing. The television was still running silently, the strapline on the news channel now reading 'NINETEEN YEAR OLD JOANNA JADE PINKERTON MISSING. LAST SEEN AT 4:30 A.M. Constable Coombes quickly crossed the room in front of Teresa and her mother, deftly located the remote control on the coffee table, and turned the television off.

"We'd rather you didn't watch that right now."

Teresa helped her mum to get comfortable in her usual chair, then sat herself down on the sofa. Within minutes, her mum was dozing. Teresa, alone with her thoughts, wondered how she could possibly be acting so normally. This situation was anything but normal.

She could see outside now, through the living room window, and noticed three more police cars and a large police van parked up on the pavement. There was a lone uniformed officer, standing at the end of their driveway, and he nodded in acknowledgement to people passing by on the street. Teresa saw Mrs Philpot cross the street and approach the house. The police officer greeted her, and they spoke for a few minutes. Teresa could not make out what either of them were saying, but it looked like Mrs Philpot had tried to come into the house, as was usual for her at this time of day, but the officer had blocked her way, refusing entrance. She saw Mrs Philpot reluctantly return to her own house, looking back over her shoulder as she went. The whole street must be watching. Several minutes later, Detective Inspector Asrat Sabir entered the living room and spoke directly to Teresa.

"We are going to be here for some time, and we need to interview both you and your mother."

"You can interview me, but not mum. She doesn't know anything anyway, and it'll be too distressing for her."

"I'm afraid it's procedure, Miss." The inspector apologised. "She can have the constable with her though, if that will help."

Teresa resigned herself to the situation. She sighed.

"I don't suppose I have any choice, do I?"

The question remained unanswered.

"If you come back into the kitchen, we'll do your mum's interview first, and then I'll come and talk to you."

Teresa returned to the kitchen where an officer was waiting for her, leaving her mother with Inspector Sabir and Constable Coombes. She put the kettle on and made herself more tea. She had barely finished drinking it when the inspector entered.

"That was quick, is she okay?"

"She's fine, Miss. Now, I'd just like to ask you a few questions if that's okay?"

"I don't know anything, either. I don't know where Mark is. He hasn't been in touch for days now. Ask Dan, P.C. Middleton, he knows I've been worried about him."

The inspector looked at Teresa

"I'm aware of your relationship with P.C. Middleton, but that has no bearing on this case. Now, make yourself comfortable while I ask you a few questions."

An hour and a half later, the inspector snapped his notebook shut and thanked her for her cooperation. He also took Teresa's phone from her. Teresa protested.

"What if the school ring?"

The inspector had assured her that she would get the phone back that same afternoon, and that any activity on it in the meantime would be reported to her immediately.

Teresa went back to the living room. Constable Coombes was now standing guard at the living room door, and she moved aside to let Teresa in. Her mum was sleeping. Teresa slumped into a chair, going over all the questions the inspector had just put to her. He had been very thorough. It was clear from the questions that they suspected Mark of some involvement in the disappearances of the girls from Stonehenge. Inspector Sabir had said that their main priority was to find Mark as soon as possible, to find out what he knew. Sabir had asked Teresa about Mark's mental health, his background, and how he managed his condition now, including details of what medication he was on and how many days supply he had with him. He had asked about Mark's friends and romantic relationships, and about her own relationship with Mark. He had questioned her about Mark's temper, had he ever got angry with her? Raised his voice? Shown any violence or aggression toward her, or their mum, or Lily? He had asked questions about the Stonehenge girls. Did Mark know any of them? Did he have any connection to them? Had Mark ever visited Stonehenge?

The inspector had been particularly interested in their holiday together in 2017, questioning her on times, dates and details. She had struggled to recall what had happened, but he had been persistent, and had pushed her to remember. What day did they leave? What time did they leave? How long were they away? When did they get back? Where did they stay? Did she still have the address? What sort of accommodation was it? Did they share a room? What did they do on the first day, the second day? Were they together the whole time? What time did they go to bed? What time did they get up? He went on and on, asking questions.

Teresa had become exhausted, she just could not remember every detail. Why were they so interested in that holiday in 2017? Teresa thought back to that time. That was the year the first girl had gone missing, and Teresa kept repeating that to Inspector Sabir, to make sure he realised the significance of it. How could Mark have been involved if he wasn't even here? The inspector had ignored her and carried on with the same line of questioning. He clearly thought Mark was still a suspect. She was so confused by it all.

Teresa looked at the clock on the mantle. It was two-thirty p.m.

"I need to fetch Lily soon," she said to Constable Coombes. "She finishes school at three p.m."

"I'll arrange for her to be collected and brought here," replied the constable.

"Is that really necessary? I always pick her up, and she'll be frightened if the police are there. I should go. I'm not under arrest, am I?"

"No, you're not under arrest, but this is procedure. We won't send police officers to the school. Lily will be collected by two child protection officers, and they will stay with her while a specially trained police officer takes a statement from her."

Teresa was shocked at the reply. She was exhausted from the lengthily interview with Inspector Sabir, and now this.

"A statement! Don't be ridiculous! She's four years old! She can't make a statement," she shouted at Constable Coombes in frustration.

"Teresa, calm down. You will upset your mum," replied the constable, in her practiced, detached manner. "I know this is difficult. But we do need to speak to Lily. Don't worry, our officers are used to dealing with children of Lily's age. She'll be fine, I promise. And as soon as they've got her statement, they'll bring Lily here and you can make her something for tea."

"When will they be finished searching?"

"I don't know. It will take as long as it takes."

Teresa slumped back onto the sofa. Her life had been completely taken out of her control: everything she did, everywhere she went, had been taken over. She couldn't make a cup of tea. They watched her when she went to the toilet. They had her phone. They had her daughter. It had all happened so alarmingly quickly. Yesterday she had been living her life, going about her usual daily routine, as normal, without any real appreciation of her liberty, her ability to do whatever she wanted to. She recalled the warm sun on her face as she had stood in the playground the day before. Now, those simple pleasures had been stolen away from her. How quickly and dramatically lives could change, she thought. Too often, we take for granted the freedom to live our simple, parochial lives without interference or intrusion from others and, irresponsibly, we play fast and loose with those privileges. Why does something momentous have to happen for us to realise how fragile life really is? Her thoughts were interrupted by Constable Coombes' radio buzzing. She stepped out of the room to receive the call. On her return, she reported that Lily's interview had been completed, and that the child protection officers were on their way back to the house with her.

"Is she okay?"

"She's absolutely fine. I've also spoken to Detective Inspector Sabir, and he's happy for you all to remain here, on the condition that you contain your activities to the downstairs area for now. We have concluded our searches downstairs, and we are now limiting the search activity to one room upstairs. So, Teresa, if you could carry on as normally as possible when Lily gets here? But please don't allow her to go upstairs. You can now use the back garden as well, if that helps?"

"Are we allowed to have the TV on, too?"

"Yes, of course."

Teresa immediately put the news channel on again. There was a picture of Stonehenge and the third missing girl, Joanna. Teresa stared at the photograph. Joanna looked so young, and she was strikingly pretty. She had pale blue eyes, alabaster skin, and a heavy sprinkling of freckles across her nose and the top of her cheeks. Her long, straight hair was glowing in the sunshine, and she had a broad, engaging smile. How could anyone want to harm her? The report said there was no further news on Joanna's disappearance, but that the police did have a suspect and would be releasing a statement soon.

"A suspect. Is that Mark?"

"I'm not at liberty to discuss that with you," replied the constable.

Teresa became annoyed again.

"Really? They are going to release a statement shortly. Is that how you're going to inform me that my brother is suspected to be involved in the disappearances of three young women?"

Constable Coombes considered this for a moment.

"I'll get the D.C. to come and have a word with you."

She left the room.

Teresa continued to watch the news item. The news reporter was talking to several people who had attended the solstice event, asking them if they had thought the police presence was strong enough.

From the other side of the room, her mum had woken up, and was reading the news headline.

"Teresa, Mark didn't do this. I know what they think, but they're wrong. He didn't do it."

"I do hope you're right, Mum. But it isn't looking good, is it? Where the hell is he right now?

If he's got nothing to hide, why hasn't he come home?"

Inspector Sabir entered the room.

"I've come to give you an update." He sat down and looked at the two women, his face grave and serious. "Our search has produced some items that we believe may be connected to the missing girls."

Teresa looked at him in disbelief.

"This can't be happening. You must have got it wrong. What items?"

"I can't say. We need to do further analysis before we can confirm our findings, but I must tell you both that Mark is now officially a person of interest, regarding the disappearance of all three girls. As such, we have issued a warrant for his arrest. All available officers are looking for him right now. We will shortly be putting out a press release, and Mark will be named in that statement as a suspect. One more thing, we will need a recent photograph of him."

Teresa was shocked. She could barely get her words out.

"No, you can't."

"We have to," replied the inspector. "We need the public's help with this. We need to find your brother, and quickly."

Teresa went over to her mother, who was sobbing.

"He couldn't hurt those girls, Teresa, he just couldn't. He's always been a good boy."

"I know, Mum, I know," Teresa replied in a soothing voice, taking hold of her mother's hand. She looked at the detective.

"What happens now?"

"Well, you and your mother are not considered suspects. You are not under arrest, and you are free to go about your business as usual. However, we will remain here and continue searching Mark's bedroom, so there will be a police presence here throughout the night. The choice is yours, you can stay here, or you can go and stay with relatives or friends until this all dies down."

"We have no relatives. I've got the flat, but Mum wouldn't cope there. She wouldn't be able to manage the stairs. I can't move her out of here."

"That's fine with me," replied Sabir. "As I said, you are not considered suspects. I will provide a family liaison officer to stay with you, and to keep you informed with events as they unfold. There will be a continuous police presence at the front of the house, to keep unwanted callers and the press at bay. There will also be a police officer stationed at the entrance to Mark's bedroom, which none of you must attempt to enter. We must preserve that room exactly as it is. These officers will remain in place until we have concluded our investigations. If you are happy with these conditions, I see no reason why you cannot remain in the property."

Teresa nodded. Although she had heard everything the inspector had said, she couldn't believe that any of it was real.

"In addition to these conditions, I recommend that you do not go to work, that Lily stays at home, and that you remain in the house. You are not obliged to follow these instructions, but I advise that you do so for your own safety. There are several members of the press out on the street, but we are maintaining a cordon, so they are unable to get too close to the house. Also, there has been press activity on your mobile phone, but we are managing these calls at present. We will continue to keep hold of your mobile for the time being, in case your brother tries to contact you. The family liaison officer that I assign will be able to run any errands for you. I suggest that you comply with this advice until we locate Mark.

"Okay."

That was all that Teresa could manage. She had amazed herself at how compliantly she had accepted the conditions. This fight was far too big for her. She had to think about her mum, and Lily. She could do no more for Mark, now. He was out there somewhere, with an entire police force looking for him, and once the police statement was issued, in a few minutes time, he was going to find it very difficult to remain in hiding.

A car drew up outside, and Sabir glanced out of the window.

"Lily's here, I'll leave you to it. Try to keep things as normal as you can, for Lily's sake. Stick to her usual routines and try not to show her that you are worried. Oh, and turn off the news. She's a bright kid, it won't take her long to work it out."

Teresa did as she was told, turning off the news channel and going out to greet her daughter. As soon as Lily saw Teresa at the front door, she let go of the woman's hand she was holding and ran to her.

"Mummy, mummy, where were you? Why didn't you pick me up from school? Sarah said that they can't find Uncle Mark, is he lost?"

Teresa threw her arms around the child and hugged her tightly.

"Who is Sarah?"

"This is, Mummy. This is Sarah. She brought me home from school, and she's got a yellow car."

The lady that had been holding Lily's hand introduced herself.

"Good afternoon, Mrs Johnson. My name is Sarah Montague. I'm from the Child Protection Unit. I visited Lily's school earlier today, alongside a police colleague of mine, to ask her some questions."

"Don't you need my permission to do that?"

"No, we don't. We can question any child who may have witnessed, or been part of, a crime. I can assure you that Lily was very cooperative, and everything is above board."

"She doesn't know anything. She's four years old."

Lily interrupted the conversation between the two women.

"Mummy, where's Mark gone? If he's lost, we should go and look for him."

Teresa turned her attention to Lily.

"There are lots of people looking for Uncle Mark, sweetheart, and I'm sure they will find him soon. Now, let's go and get you something to eat."

The child ran past her into the house, and Sarah handed Teresa a calling card.

"These are my details. If you have any more questions, please give me a call."

Teresa took the card without replying, closed the door, and went to find Lily in the kitchen. She really wanted to ask Lily about what the police and Sarah had said to her, but Constable Coombes was in the kitchen so she didn't.

"Do you want hot dogs for tea?"

"Yes, please, Mummy."

Lily sat at the table with her book. She called it her reading book, but it didn't contain any words, just pictures. Lily would make up a story up from the pictures, and each time she told the story, it would be a little different. Some small details always changed. How could the police possibly use anything Lily had said to them? Her imagination was so active.

Teresa was also concerned about what the police might have told her. But, looking at her now, Lily seem untroubled by all the chaos, and was showing the book to Constable Coombes as if it was perfectly normal to have a police officer in the kitchen! Teresa got on with making dinner, preparing two hot dogs for Lily, her favourite, and warming up a frozen meal for her mother, taking it to her on a tray. Teresa wasn't hungry, so she made herself another cup of tea.

After a while, a young woman came into the kitchen, introducing herself as Samantha Blight, the family liaison officer assigned to her case. Samantha was very young, in her early twenties perhaps, and seemed very friendly. Teresa instantly felt comfortable in her presence. Apparently, Samantha was not short on confidence either, as was evident when the young woman addressed Constable Coombes.

"I think you can go now. There is no need to maintain a police presence here. Could you please ask Inspector Sabir to confine his staff to the upstairs area, or to the outside of the property, so that the family can regain some normality? I understand they are not considered suspects in the case? Thank you."

With that Constable Coombes was gone, and Samantha turned her attention to the little girl.

"Now, Lily, let's go into the living room and find a good film to watch. One that your Gran might like too, what do you think?"

"Can I, Mummy?"

"Of course."

"Yay! I'll go and find one."

"I'll be there in just a minute," Samantha said to the child, as Lily disappeared into the living room.

"Teresa, I am here to help you. I don't work for the police, I work with them. I will be the link between your family and the investigation. They will keep me updated with any developments, and if it's appropriate, I will share that information with you. I am here to help you practically and emotionally, as well. If you need anything, or have any questions, just ask me and I'll see what I can do."

"Thank you. I really don't know what I need, or what I want. This is all just completely crazy."

"It must be very difficult for you to take in, and I'm sure you've had an awful day. Why don't you take some time to yourself? I'll keep Lily occupied until bedtime."

"Thank you, Samantha, you are so kind."

A few minutes later, when Teresa popped her head around the living room door, she saw her mum dozing in the chair and Lily and Samantha sitting on the sofa, engrossed in one of Lily's DVDs. Lily looked up briefly at her mum, and then turned her attention back to the screen. She was obviously just fine. In fact, you wouldn't know anything was wrong, looking at the cosy scene in front of her. It all felt so wrong!

Teresa poured herself a glass of water and went into the back garden, sitting herself down on the swinging seat. It was a relief to be on her own, a relief to feel some fresh air on her face. She hadn't been outside since taking Lily to school this morning. As she sat there, gently rocking on the swing and looking across the garden, alive and beautiful with the fruits of Mark's labours, she felt a single tear on her cheek. How it had all changed. She had been sitting here, just a fortnight ago, chatting away to Mark as he had weeded the flower beds. It had all been so perfectly normal, and it seemed so far removed from today's events that she couldn't believe it was just two weeks ago. Was her brother as dangerous as they were saying?

Inspector Sabir came into the garden, looking for her.

"We're going to call it a day upstairs. Forensics will be back in the morning, and as I mentioned earlier, there will be police officers here overnight. Miss Blight will also remain here overnight, and we will re-assess the situation tomorrow."

Teresa fixed the inspector with a searching look.

"Do you really think this is down to Mark?"

"We need to find him and ask him some questions first, but we do have reason to believe that he is involved, yes."

"But I told you, he was with me when this whole thing started, in 2017."

Sabir sighed.

"I know. We know he wasn't here in 2017, but sometimes, when people get fixated with a crime, they become so obsessed with it that they try to emulate it, or imitate it in some way."

"Like a copycat?"

"Exactly like a copycat. So even if Mark was not involved with the first disappearance, and we haven't established that yet, it doesn't mean that he is not responsible for the other two. It's something we've got to consider. We're leaving now. If you need anything, talk to Miss Blight, she knows how to contact us. We will be back first thing in the morning."

He left her there with her thoughts. Mark, a copycat kidnapper! None of this was real, it just couldn't be!

Samantha appeared at the back door and called to her.

"Teresa, Lily says it's her bedtime. She's had a wash and cleaned her teeth, but I thought you might like to take her up?"

"Yes, of course. I'll come now."

Teresa led Lily, already in her pyjamas, upstairs and past the policeman standing guard outside Mark's bedroom door. The child looked quizzically at the officer and asked,

"Are you waiting for Uncle Mark to come home?"

The office smiled at the child.

"Yes, Miss, that's right."

"Come on, Lily. Let's get you to bed, it's been a long day."

The child ran ahead. She was already in bed and had her arms wrapped around her teddy when Teresa reached the room.

"Mummy, why did they ask me if Uncle Mark had ever been odd with me?"

"What do you mean?"

"They said, has he ever been unkind, or odd with you? They asked me if he had ever touched me."

Teresa's heart sank. Could this get any worse? She looked at her daughter and stroked her face gently.

"What did you say?"

"I said he touched me all the time. He's always tickling me, isn't he, Mummy? And he throws me in the air sometimes too. Do you think he'll come home tomorrow?"

"I do hope so. What else did they ask you Lily?"

"They gave me a doll and told me to show them where Uncle Mark tickled me. They asked me if he ever tickled me in my knickers. That's a silly question, isn't it?"

Teresa physically slumped at the words that came from Lily's mouth. It felt like someone had punched her hard in the stomach. The small amount of strength she did have left her immediately. Her knees buckled, and she struggled to remain on her feet. At once, she felt intensely angry, hugely disappointed, and wholly crushed. They had questioned her four-year-old daughter to see if she had been abused by her brother! Although her spirit was completely crushed, she managed to pull herself together enough to reassure the girl.

"Policemen always ask silly questions, that's their job, asking silly questions. You get some sleep, sweetheart. I'll see you in the morning."

Teresa walked in an unsteady daze back downstairs, trying to take in what her daughter had just said to her. There was a soft knock at the front door. She opened the door and there stood Dan. Teresa was furious, and almost shut the door in his face.

"Are you kidding me? What the hell are you doing here?"

"I'm really not supposed to be, but I had a word..." he nodded towards the constable standing at the end of the drive. "He owes me a favour."

Teresa spat her words out at him.

"Is this just a joke to you, Dan? Have you got any idea what you've done?"

"I had to, Teresa. You told me yourself, you were worried. I had to call it in. It's my job."

"Your job? Your fucking job? This is my family! My brother is missing. He's out there somewhere on his own, being hounded by your mates. And my daughter is upstairs, after being questioned by police, who asked her if her Uncle Mark had ever touched her! Don't tell me you were just doing your job. You have ruined my life, and I will never forgive you for this!"

"I'm sorry, Teresa, really. What was I supposed to do? Maybe I can help?"

"Get lost, Dan. I don't want your help. You've done enough. I don't want you round here. Get lost!"

She slammed the door shut. She slumped to the floor, screaming silently, her eyes filled with tears of desperation and hopelessness.

Chapter 8

"Police emergency. How can we help?"

"I think I've seen him, that bloke you're looking for. The perv. The one who took those girls from Stone'enge."

"Thank you, can I take your name, caller?"

"I don't wanna give my name, do I?"

"Alright, that's fine. Would you like to give us some information?"

"Yeah, that bloke, the one on the tele, Mark somethin' or uvver. I just seen him, aint I?"

"Where did you see him?"

"He's holed up under the stairs, at Morton's Cross, the multi-story. I fink it's him."

"Police emergency, can I help you?"

"Hello, good evening. My wife and I have just left the theatre. There was a vagrant under the stairwell of Morton's Cross multi-story car park, the East Street entrance. We didn't take much notice at first, there are often unsavoury types hanging around there at night. We just thought he was drunk. There was a half-empty bottle of whiskey next to him."

"What time was this, sir?"

"Well, it was around seven p.m. when we first saw him. The thing is, when we left the theatre, about eleven p.m., he was still there, in the exact same position. I think he might be dead. I'm not sure, and I didn't like to touch him, just in case."

"Okay, we'll go take a look."

"Sierra twelve? Can you get yourselves over to Morton's Cross multi-story car park, East Street? We've had a couple of reports in. Could be suspect Mark Applewhite. Could be deceased. Approach with extreme caution. Call for back-up if needed. Copy that Sierra twelve. Over and out."

"Sierra twelve receiving and on our way. Over and out."

The police car pulled up outside the East Street entrance to the car park, ten minutes later. The two police officers quickly located the man under the stairwell of the second floor, as reported. He was lying under an old coat and had a dirty piece of cardboard draped over him. The whiskey bottle was still lying next to him. As the two officers drew nearer, they noticed some pills, spilled out on the ground around the prostrate man.

"Don't look good, this one, Jim. Get on the blower for an ambulance, quick as you like."

"Okay, mate, will do."

Jim put the call through for an ambulance, while the other officer pulled on a pair of disposable gloves and checked the man's wrist for a pulse.

"He's alive, Jim, just. Tell them to get a move on."

Twenty minutes later, the ambulance crew arrived at the scene. The man was still lying in the same position.

"We can't get a response from him, mate. Not sure who he is. No identification on him. There's a phone in his pocket, but it's dead. We think he might be our missing suspect, Mark Applewhite, so I'd better come with you to the hospital."

The paramedic looked at the dying man.

"We need to get him on some oxygen first, looks like he's in a pretty bad way."

The two paramedics and the two police officers manhandled the lifeless man onto a stretcher, loading him into the ambulance. Once inside, they immediately attached him to an oxygen cylinder and turned on the valves, covering him in two blankets to keep him warm, and strapped him tightly to the stretcher, locking it in place. Constable Carver picked up the whiskey and the pills, climbed into the back of the ambulance, and accompanied them to the hospital. Jim Waring followed behind in the patrol car, both vehicles driving through the town with their blue lights flashing and their sirens cutting through the silence of the night. In the back of the ambulance, a pulse oximeter was attached to the end of the casualty's finger.

"How's he doing?" the constable asked the paramedic.

"It's not looking good. His oxygen levels are very low, pulse is high and there are signs of cyanosis. Could be looking at pneumonia. Is it your man?"

"Think so, he matches the description."

"Well, he's not going to be going to be in a fit state to go anywhere for a while."

The ambulance pulled up outside Accident and Emergency department, and the young man was carried into a cubicle. He was immediately examined by medics, while the ambulance crew gave their report on the situation.

"Male, approximately late thirties, currently unidentified. Found sleeping rough under partial shelter. How long he has been sleeping there remains unknown. No medical history currently available. Primary assessment revealed no visible injuries. Unconscious at the scene, accompanied to hospital by police officers. Blood pressure is ninety over sixty, temperature of 38.5 degrees C, pulse one hundred and twenty beats per minute and oxygen saturation down to ninety percent at last reading, approximately fifteen minutes ago. As you can see, cyanosis of lips, fingers and toes, indicating a reduced blood supply. We've got another call waiting, so we'll leave him in your capable hands. Good luck, fella."

The doctor listened to the man's chest.

"I want a chest x-ray as soon as possible," he instructed. "And get some intravenous antibiotics up, while we're waiting for the results."

Constable Carver's phone buzzed.

"Carver, it's Detective Inspector Sabir. Is it our man, is it Mark Applewhite?"

"Looks like it. But we can't get a positive identification yet, he's got nothing on him except a dead mobile phone."

"What state is he in?"

123

"Not good. They're taking him for an x-ray. He's still unconscious."

"Okay. Stay with him and don't let him out of your sight. Tell Waring to take the mobile back to the station, so C.I.D. can get some juice in it and see what we've got."

"Yes, sir."

"Oh, and a complete press black-out until I say otherwise, at least until we know if we've got the right man. If they find out, they'll be crawling all over the hospital"

"Right you are, sir."

At eight a.m. the next morning, Sabir arrived at the house. Teresa was just getting up. She had taken herself to bed after Dan had called last night and had been deeply asleep, until ten minutes ago. She couldn't believe it when she saw the time, she really must have been exhausted. They walked into the kitchen together, where Samantha was making tea.

"Have you found him?" Teresa asked Sabir.

"Yes, Miss, we have, but it's not good news I'm afraid."

Teresa looked aghast.

"Oh my God, he's dead, isn't he?"

"No, he's not dead, but he's very ill indeed. He's in hospital being treated for pneumonia. He's extremely poorly."

"Where has he been?"

"We don't know the answer to that, Miss. He was found sleeping rough last night, and we have been unable to speak to him."

"Can I see him?"

"We need to interview him first. We'll let you know as soon as he regains consciousness and we've been able to speak to him."

After Sabir had gone, Teresa sat at the kitchen table and Samantha handed her a cup of tea. She was so relieved that they'd found him. But now what? Surely when Mark woke up and they spoke to him, they'd see they'd got the wrong man, wouldn't they?

Lily entered the kitchen and climbed onto Teresa's knee.

"Mummy, I've just seen a lady in a white suit, with blue plastic bags on her feet. She looks like she's going to the moon in a space rocket. She's going upstairs."

"That'll be forensics," Samantha said. "They're part of the Crime Scene Investigation Service. They'll be collecting evidence and taking it away for analysis."

"I have no idea what's in that room. I haven't been in it for ten years." Teresa said.

"Shall I get ready for school, Mummy?" Lily asked.

"I know," Samantha said to the child. "Why don't you have a day off today? We can do that big jigsaw together, if you like? The one you showed me yesterday, how does that sound?"

Lily was disappointed.

"But I like school."

"I know you do, sweetheart, but you can have one day off. And Samantha can stay all day and play with you, that'll be nice, won't it?" Teresa reassured her daughter. Apparently, the concept of spending all day playing with Samantha was enough to pacify Lily.

"Okay, can I have breakfast now?"

"Of course. Go upstairs and clean your teeth, and I'll get it ready for you."

Lily slipped off Teresa's lap and skipped upstairs.

"I'm going to see him," Teresa said to Samantha.

"That's not a good idea, Teresa. Besides, they won't let you."

"They have to let me, I'm his sister."

"They don't have to, he's a suspect."

"Yes, but they haven't arrested him yet."

"The only reason they haven't arrested him is because he's not well enough. As soon as he regains consciousness, they will arrest him. You know that. You heard Sabir."

"I need to go. Will you watch Lily?"

"Of course, I will. But I'm advising you not to go. The press are camped outside, and they'll follow you. Then they will know where Mark is too. It's not a good idea."

"I'm going. I can get out the back way without them seeing. And I'll wear a hat. No-one will recognise me."

Samantha sighed. She could see how determined Teresa was.

"Fine, if you must. I can see I'm not going to be able to stop you. If you really must go, then go. I won't lie to Sabir, though. When he asks me, I'll have to tell him where you've gone.

Teresa got herself ready. She decided against the beanie hat that she'd first selected. It was the middle of summer, and she'd look out of place. Instead, she pulled her hair on top of her head and tied it in a loose topknot. She never wore it like that. Then she put on a pair of enormous sunglasses and wrapped a floaty scarf of her mum's around her neck. As she looked at her reflection in the mirror, she hardly recognised herself, so she wasn't worried about being noticed. Now all she had to do was get out of the house, and away from the street, and she'd be fine.

"I won't be long, Samantha. I just need to see if he's alright."

Samantha contemplated trying to talk her out of it again but decided against it. Teresa was clearly determined to see her brother.

"Don't worry about Lily, or your mum. I'll look after things here."

Teresa left the house by the back door and went through the back gate. There was a narrow path that ran between the houses on her side of the road and the houses on the adjacent street. About three hundred yards up, there was a gap between two houses, and Teresa took this route to come out on to the next street. She then walked to the end of the road and waited for a bus into town. She had no idea about the timetable, but there were two elderly ladies waiting at the bus stop, so she assumed a bus would be along soon.

She could hear the two old ladies gossiping as she approached the bus shelter.

"They reckon they've got him," whispered one.

"Thank goodness for that," replied the other.

Teresa knew immediately they were talking about Mark. They must have put an update out on this morning's news. Teresa hadn't seen or heard the news since yesterday, and of course she didn't have her phone. She pulled the scarf up around her mouth and chin and looked down. The scarf smelled of her mum, and she was briefly distracted, thinking maybe she should be with her mum. She felt awkward and guilty, like she shouldn't be doing this.

"Three pretty young girls like that. It doesn't bear thinking about, does it, Jean?"

"No, he can't be right in the head, can he? I'm glad they've got him. Put the wind up me it did, him living so close."

"I know what you mean. I've been scared to death. I haven't let the cat out since they said where he lived."

The two women carried on with their conversation, oblivious to Teresa, who was listening to every word, consumed with shame and embarrassment. Her heart sank to the floor. She imagined there would be lots more conversations just like this one going on all over the town. She thought about all the people that knew them: people at work;

people at school; people in her block of flats. How was she ever going to live normally again?

The bus arrived and the three women got on. The two old ladies sat down together at the front of the bus and Teresa deliberately sat right at the very back, well out of earshot. She didn't want to hear any more of their conversation. There were three more stops before the bus stopped at the hospital, and although several more people got on, nobody took any notice of her, and thankfully, nobody was talking about Mark.

"I've come to see Mark Applewhite. Could you tell me which ward he is on, please?" Teresa asked the receptionist. If the receptionist was aware who Mark was, she didn't show it. She looked at her screen, tapping a few keys on her keyboard.

"Certainly, he's in our I.C.U. ward, Intensive Care. If you follow this corridor to the very end, turn right, then take the lift to the second floor. It's all signposted. Press the buzzer when you get there, and the ward clerk will let you in."

"Thank you for your help."

Teresa walked down the corridor. She felt very conspicuous, and she was dreading seeing anybody that she knew. What on Earth would she say to them? This wasn't the time for small talk. Although she hadn't seen any news this morning, Teresa was aware that the photograph she had given to Sabir had been broadcast on last night's news, and that Mark had been named as the main suspect in all three disappearances. The public had been asked to call 999 if they had any information concerning Mark, and they had also been warned not to approach him as he could be dangerous. Dangerous! Mark had never been a danger to anyone except himself. Had she really got all this so terribly wrong? After all these years of being so close to her brother, did she really know him at all? She had been concerned about his recent behaviour, but she could never have imagined that something like this was behind it. She just could not contemplate Mark going around, kidnapping and possibly harming young women. It was utterly impossible.

She walked with her head down, looking at the floor to avoid making eye contact with anybody. As she did so, she followed the patterns of blue wavy lines on the greenish-blue floor. It made her think of the sea. What she wouldn't give to be sailing off somewhere right now, anywhere. She was so engrossed in the pattern that she nearly missed her turning. She felt so incredibly guilty, like she had done something wrong. Perhaps she had? After all, she hadn't noticed anything. Well, she had noticed something, but she hadn't done anything about it. Well, she had told Dan, and look how that had turned out!

Dan, she couldn't think about Dan right now. She felt so betrayed by him. She was angry and hurt by what he had done, but she also knew, deep down, that she felt guilty about Dan, too. She was the one who had decided to confide in him. She knew he was a police officer. If, God forbid, it turned out that Mark was guilty, then Dan would be proved right in the actions he had taken, wouldn't he? That was Teresa's problem. If she accepted that Dan had behaved reasonably, given the information he had, then she would also have to accept that her suspicions had been more than correct; that she had been right to be concerned about Mark's behaviour, and that, considering all that had happened, Mark looked guilty, very guilty. But despite the wake-up call of the last two days, she just couldn't believe that Mark was to blame.

She reached the Intensive Care Unit and pressed the ward buzzer. No voice came through the intercom, but she heard the door lock click and she walked in, heading towards the nurses' station in front of her. She could see two nurses deep in conversation with a doctor, and the ward clerk sitting at the desk with a telephone to her ear. The ward clerk covered the telephone mouthpiece with her hand.

"I won't be a minute."

"No problem."

Teresa used the pause to pluck up some courage and plan how she was going to tell them why she was here. When the ward clerk had finished on the phone she smiled at Teresa and apologised.

"Sorry about that, it's a bit crazy in here today. Now, what can I do to help you?"

"I'm here to see Mark Applewhite. I'm his sister."

The ward clerk reddened and became flustered.

"Well…umm…yes…umm. I'm not actually sure if he's permitted to have visitors right now."

One of the nurses behind the desk had heard Teresa introduce herself and approached the pair.

"You're Mark's sister?" she enquired with a smile.

"Yes."

"Come this way. He's in a side ward."

As they walked together through the ward, the nurse asked Teresa a question.

"You do know he has a police officer with him, don't you?"

"I thought he would have, yes."

"That's okay, then. I just didn't want it to be a shock for you."

They turned a corner and Teresa could see a police officer standing guard outside the door. The nurse spoke to the police officer.

"This lady is Mr Applewhite's sister.

"I'm afraid I can't let anyone in except medical staff right now," said the officer. "I'm under orders."

"Surely his sister is allowed to see him for a moment?"

"No, Miss, I'm sorry. No-one is allowed in until we have questioned him."

The nurse turned to Teresa.

"I'm really sorry. I thought they would let you see him."

"That's okay. Can you tell me how he is?"

"Of course. I'll get one of the doctors to come and talk to you, and I can open the blind in his room so you can see him through the window. You're not going to object to that officer, are you?"

The officer winked at the nurse.

"I have no orders about people looking through windows."

She guided Teresa past the officer and around the corner, to a window that had blinds pulled down.

"You wait here, and I'll lift the blinds so you can see him. But first, I'll go and find that doctor. Mark is still unconscious, and we have a lot of wires and monitors on him. Don't be alarmed. It's all perfectly normal."

Teresa nodded and the nurse disappeared. Normal! There was absolutely nothing normal about any of this. Teresa wasn't sure if she would ever know normal again. A young male doctor approached and addressed her.

"Mark Applewhite's sister?"

"Yes."

"I'm Doctor Madhavan, one of the Critical Care doctors. I've been looking after Mark."

"Thank you for taking care of him. How is he doing?"

"Mark came to us from Accident and Emergency in the early hours of this morning. He has taken an overdose, and appears to be suffering from pneumonia. It looks like he's been sleeping rough, and we think that he had been drinking, causing him to vomit. This may have resulted in him picking up a dormant infection from his stomach, which is now attacking his lungs."

"Oh my God, an overdose! He doesn't usually drink. Do you think he was trying to kill himself?"

"If he's not used to drinking, that could explain the vomiting," reasoned the doctor. "I can't say whether he was trying to take his own life or not, but I do know that he is very poorly right now. We are waiting for blood tests to come back to confirm the exact type of infection he has, but we are currently treating him for pneumonia."

At that moment the nurse drew the blind up, and Teresa saw her brother for the first time in a week. She gasped audibly, and her hand flew involuntarily to her mouth. He looked so different, she could only really recognise him by his hair. There was a huge tube in his mouth, and straps across his face to keep it in place. The machine attached to the tube was flashing with several sets of readings. There was another tube coming from his arm, attached to two drip feeds, one containing blood and the other filled with a clear liquid, which was dripping down the tube. There was a cannula stuck to the back of his hand, and as she watched, the nurse drew up some medication in a syringe and administered it through the cannula.

"Antibiotics," explained the doctor. "We're hoping they'll start to work soon, and then we should see some improvement."

"Why is he that colour? He's blue!"

"That's the lack of oxygen. We're struggling to get his levels back to normal. The pads on his chest are to monitor his heart, because while his levels remain this low, he is at increased risk of a heart attack."

"He's only thirty-seven!"

"I'm afraid it's got nothing to do with age. His lungs aren't functioning properly, so there isn't enough oxygen getting to his heart, which could trigger a heart attack. We are doing everything we can, but he is in a very critical condition."

"What about the police?"

"The police are nothing to do with me. Mark is my patient and I will treat him accordingly, as I do with all my patients. Now, I really must get on. There are a lot of very sick people on this ward. Do you have any more questions before I go?"

"No, thank you for your time. You've been very helpful. And thank you for everything you're doing."

"You're welcome."

With that, the young doctor disappeared back around the corner, to carry on with his day.

Teresa's day had halted abruptly in its tracks. All she could do now was stand at that window and watch, as her desperately ill brother fought for his life. Was he even fighting, though? Did he want to survive? Had he given up? Was this his choice? He must have taken those pills and the drink because he wanted to die. Perhaps he had chosen not to wake up and face the nightmare that was now their lives?

She must have stayed watching at that window for nearly two hours. She watched the rise and fall of his chest, and watched his eyes to see if he might be rousing from his comatose condition. She watched the orange numbers on the monitoring screen flashing, the regular drip of the liquid in the tube, the concern on the faces of the doctors and nursing staff as they took his temperature, gave him medication, adjusted his bedclothes, wrote their observations on their charts and discussed his condition between themselves. Most of all, she watched his hands. She watched for the faintest movement, the smallest sign of life, the slightest suggestion that his condition was improving. She saw nothing, not even an involuntary flinch when the nurses touched him. Nothing. He just lay there, lifeless and passive. Teresa had come here for answers, but she knew she wasn't going to get any from Mark today.

Chapter 9

Sabir arrived at the hospital ward, looking angry and annoyed.

"Teresa, what are you doing here? I asked you to stay at the house. How the hell did you get here?"

Teresa looked up at the inspector, and he immediately felt a pang of pity for her. Her voice was weak and unstable, and he heard an unmistakable note of hopelessness in it.

"I know you did, but I just needed to see him. I caught the bus."

She looked pale and she was shaking. Her eyes had dark patches under them, and he could see that she had been crying. This was the first time he had stopped focussing on cracking the case and had seen things from her perspective. He softened his voice and spoke to her with sympathy.

"How is he doing? Have they told you anything?"

Teresa glared at him.

"Don't pretend to be interested in his welfare. You don't really care, do you? If he never wakes up, he won't be able to tell you that he's innocent, that he didn't do it, and that would be just perfect for you, wouldn't it? Job done. Well done, Detective Inspector Sabir, big slap on the back for you, you'll probably get a promotion."

The older man looked at her with no hint of irritation or annoyance.

"That's not true, Teresa. I'm a policeman. I became a policeman because I care about justice, and I care about the truth. I want the truth, here. We all want the truth. So far, all roads lead to Mark, and I know that's very hard for you to hear, but that is the truth. I promise you."

Teresa didn't soften, her expression rebellious and recalcitrant.

"If you say so."

"I'm afraid I've got more bad news for you. Mark's mobile is now charged up, so we've been able to track his recent locations. We know that he was at Stonehenge at the time of Joanna's disappearance. I'm sorry, I know it's not what you wanted to hear. But that is the evidence. We're trawling through hours of local CCTV right now, to see if we can find footage of him before and after the event."

"I don't even know if I want him to wake up anymore," Teresa said, resigned and upset. "Maybe it is better to be innocent and dead, rather than guilty and alive, what do you think?"

"That's not a question for me to answer," said the inspector, looking at her with genuine concern. "Would you like a lift home, Teresa?"

"No, thanks. I want to stay here. He might wake up."

"You're not doing any good here. Even if he does wake up, I'm afraid we're not going to let you speak to him. He's in the best place. He's getting the best care. There is nothing you can do, Teresa. I promise you, we will let you know as soon as he wakes up. Come on, let's get you home. Lily will be missing you."

Teresa had lost her internal fight. She didn't have the energy to argue any more. She allowed Sabir to lead her away from the window, through the ward, and back towards the main entrance of the hospital. This time, she could hardly see where she was going, not because she was looking at the floor out of shame and guilt, but because her eyes were full of tears. She was consumed with a deep, deep sadness; her heart physically ached with pain and sorrow. She didn't know if the tears were for herself, for those beautiful, lost young women, or for her brother. Her brother, her only brother. She felt guilty to be related to him, but she also loved him. He was lying there, lifeless, barely able to breathe, desperately poorly, and unable to give his side of the story. She should be defending him, standing up for him, protesting his innocence while he was unable to himself. She thought back to all the times in her childhood when Mark had stuck up for her. He had been there for her through thick and thin. She remembered when she was six years old, and had knocked the biscuit jar off the shelf in the kitchen. It had clattered noisily to the floor and smashed into a million pieces on the floor. Their father had told her so many times not to reach up and pull it down; to always ask for help. But she had ignored his advice. Mark had been on the scene first, and had known immediately what had happened, as he had looked at the mess on the floor and seen his sister's guilty face.

"Dad's going to be so cross with me," she had burst out. "He told me not to pull it down."

Mark had swung into action instantly. He had wiped Teresa's tears, and reassured her that it would all be alright. Then he had set about clearing up the mess she had made. When their father had come in from the garden a little later, Mark had taken full responsibility before she could even say a word.

"Sorry, Dad, I've knocked the biscuit jar off the shelf. It's a goner, I'm afraid."

Their father had chided him.

"You are so clumsy sometimes, Mark."

Mark had shrugged his shoulders and winked slyly at his little sister.

That was just one instance where Mark had sailed in and rescued her. There must have been dozens over the years. When she was a teenager, she had regularly fallen out with her girlfriends over ridiculously trivial things, and Mark had always taken her side. He had never laughed at her or told her to grow up. He had just been there, all the time, putting her first, making her his priority, just like when Alex had left her. Mark had got her through the toughest time of her life, and she knew it. She didn't know where she would be without him. Surely it was her turn, now? Her turn to take the blame for him; her turn to defend and support him, no matter what he had done.

As she left the hospital with Sabir, she heard her name being shouted from outside.

"Teresa, Teresa."

She looked up. A tall man had a camera trained on her face, and as she looked at him, she was startled by bright flashlights. She held her hands over her face to protect her eyes. There were photographers, cameramen, and reporters everywhere. Beyond them, she could see a small cluster of people thronged together, watching the developing situation. The crowd in front of her were being held at bay by three police officers. One of them shouted at the crowd as the pair edged forward.

"Stand back, please. Let them through. Come on, make some room."

Teresa was utterly bewildered. She had no idea that the press were here, they hadn't been there when she had arrived earlier. There were so many of them, and as Sabir led her through, she could hear questions being shouted at her from all sides.

"Is Mark alive?"

"Where are the girls?"

"Do you know what he has been doing?"

"What's he done with them?"

"Are they dead?"

"Has he told you anything?"

"What have they found at your house?"

Sabir intervened. He stood in front of Teresa, protecting her from the flashlights.

"That's enough! Mrs Johnson is not a suspect. She will not be answering any of your questions.

Now, stand back, and let us through, before I have you all arrested."

The group stopped pushing forward immediately, and the two managed to walk a little further on, eventually reaching the waiting police car.

"One more thing," shouted the inspector. "If any one of you attempts to access Mr Applewhite while he is receiving medical care, I will make it my personal responsibility to find that person and charge them under Section 51 of the Criminal Justice and Public Order Act of 1994, for interfering with a witness. If you fancy five years in jail, go right ahead. I will prosecute."

Sabir opened the car door, and Teresa was relieved to escape into the sanctuary of the back seat. As he closed the door, the noise of the press died down, but she could still hear abuse coming from the crowd.

"Hang the bastard."

"Filthy pervert!"

"Scum, I hope he rots in hell!"

"Oh my God," gasped Teresa, as Sabir climbed in next to her from the other side. "How did they know he was here? Was it me? Did they follow me?"

Sabir pulled his seatbelt across and fastened it.

"I doubt it. We didn't even know you had gone. Anybody could have leaked the information, someone from the hospital maybe? Who knows how they get their information, but once one person finds out, this is what happens. Now do you see why I wanted you to stay at the house?"

"Yes, I do. It's horrible, and really frightening."

"Take us back to the house," Sabir instructed the driver. As the car made its way out of the hospital car park, Teresa caught the eye of a large, imposing man in the crowd. He was holding his hand in the air and had his head cocked to one side, miming the act of being hanged. Teresa was horrified.

"They're so angry. Is Mark safe?"

"They won't get onto the ward. I've doubled the security. I can't stop anyone going into the hospital. That would just play into their hands and make them even angrier."

"Can we move Mark? Somewhere safer?"

"Under normal circumstances, yes, we could. But he is so ill that the doctors have advised against it. I can't go against medical advice We're just going to have to manage the situation here as best we can."

Teresa was silent for the rest of the journey, lost in her thoughts. It had been such a shock to her: the press, the angry crowd…she had never experienced anything like that before. But then, what did she expect? Three young, innocent girls were missing, and it looked like Mark was responsible. People were angry, and they had every right to be. She should be angry too. How could she be concerned about Mark's welfare, while the whereabouts of the girls remained a mystery? She didn't know anything anymore.

The car pulled into her street. Another set of reporters were waiting. This group were being held at the end of the street by parked police cars, and a taped barrier which read 'POLICE LINE – DO NOT CROSS'. As they approached, an officer raised the tape to allow them access, and they drove up towards the house. The street itself was eerily quiet, there was nobody to be seen at all, for which Teresa was extremely thankful. They got out of the car, passing the policeman on guard outside.

"Any problems, John?"

"No, sir. The cordon is holding at the minute. It's all under control."

"Well done. Keep up the good work," Sabir encouraged.

Once inside, Lily ran to her mother.

"Where have you been? Have you been looking for Uncle Mark? Have you found him yet? Look at the jigsaw! Samantha is helping me with it. She's really good at jigsaw puzzles."

Teresa was overwhelmed by the child's questions, and Samantha distracted Lily again while Teresa went into the kitchen with Sabir.

"You need to eat something, Teresa. You look awful. I know this is hard for you all, but it's not going to help the situation if you get ill as well, is it?"

Teresa collapsed onto a nearby chair. She knew Sabir was right. She felt weak and disoriented, and she had a blinding headache.

"I know, you're right" she conceded. "I just don't know what I'm supposed to do. How can I

144

carry on like everything is okay when Mark is lying in the hospital, there are three young girls missing, the press are hounding us, and the public are baying for blood? I'm totally out of my depth here, really I am."

"Teresa, anyone in your position would be feeling the same," reasoned Sabir. "Leave the press and the public, and Mark, to me. That's my job. It's what I do. You just focus on Lily and your mum, and yourself. You must look after yourself."

Samantha entered the kitchen.

"Just in time for lunch. I'm making jam sandwiches for Lily, because I know how much she likes them. We've got some cheese and tomatoes in the fridge. Shall I make you a sandwich, with a cuppa? You look done in."

Teresa nodded. Samantha busied herself making lunch for everyone, while Lily babbled on about the jigsaw and how Samantha had done her hair in a fishtail plait, just like the mermaid's in her book. Teresa consciously applied herself to the conversation with Lily and Samantha, she had to try and act as normally as possible.

Sabir soon appeared again in the doorway.

"Can I have a quick word with you, Teresa?"

She followed him into the passageway.

"We've found some items in your brother's bedroom that we would like to ask you about."

"Okay," replied Teresa. The officer held up a pale pink dress.

"Does this belong to you?"

"No. I've never seen it before."

"What about your mum?"

"No. It isn't hers either."

"Are you sure?"

"Completely sure. That was in Mark's room?"

"Yes. You're sure you don't recognise it? It couldn't be an old one that you threw away or something?"

"No. Definitely not. In any case, it's far too big for me or my mum."

Sabir held the dress up and looked at it again.

"I suppose so," he agreed. "I'm a bit hopeless with women's clothing."

Out of politeness more than anything, Teresa took a good look at the garment. It was made from a light, floaty material, probably chiffon, and had a round, gathered neckline. It was a mid-length dress, with a tie waist detail, not the sort of thing she would wear at all. It was far too fancy.

"It must be at least a size eighteen," Teresa said. "I'm a ten, and mum is even smaller, probably a size six."

Sabir was a little embarrassed by the conversation.

"Right. What about these?"

He produced a pair of baby pink shoes. They were a low court shoe, with a small kitten heel, and a small ornamental knot detail at the front. Again, Teresa had never seen them before.

"No, they're not mine either, and again, they're far too big for me. Not that I ever wear shoes like that anyway."

146

Sabir turned one of the shoes over.

"Size forty-one to forty-two."

"That's a European size, probably about a size nine."

"I'm a size nine," said Sabir. "That's quite big for a woman, isn't it?"

"I suppose so, my mum and I are both a five, so they're definitely not ours. They look quite wide too. I have no idea who they belong to."

Suddenly, Teresa remembered her conversation with Nell, the practice nurse, a couple of weeks ago. Sabir noticed the change in her.

"What is it, Teresa? Have you thought of something?"

"I'm not sure. It's just that, a couple of weeks ago, Nell, who works at our GP practice, asked me if Mark had a girlfriend. She came here to check on Mum, and she told me she had seen a woman through the window, in Mark's room. I suppose they could belong to her?"

"And you don't know who this girlfriend is?"

"No. Mark has never mentioned her to me. But that would make sense wouldn't it?"

"What is this Nell's last name? Where can I find her?"

"Nell Hewerdine. She works at the Gatley Street Practice. She's known Mark for years."

"Okay. Thank you. I'll send someone down there to have a word with her. You've been very helpful."

147

Later that afternoon, Lily and Samantha were sitting watching the television, her mum was settled in her chair, and Teresa was busying herself in the kitchen, washing the endless pile of dirty mugs. The police had asked her if it was okay to use the kitchen, and she had not objected, but that was before she had discovered that police officers were not very good at washing up. She felt a little better now that she had eaten something, and taken painkillers for her headache, so she had decided to get on with some chores.

As she worked, she tried to recollect exactly what Nell had said to her, that day she had called in at the shop. She had told her that there had been a woman in Mark's bedroom window, but she had not described her at all. Why hadn't Teresa asked her for more details? She hadn't even asked her what the woman looked like. She was obviously a larger lady, judging by the clothes Sabir had shown her. That had been odd too...they weren't really everyday clothes, more the sort of thing you might wear to a party, or a wedding maybe? The style was quite classy and mature too. Was Mark's girlfriend older than him, perhaps? Is that why he had kept her a secret? She wondered why the clothes had been in Mark's bedroom. Perhaps she had got changed after they had been out somewhere together? Could Mark really have a mysterious girlfriend who had been coming and going from the house without her knowing? Surely her mum, or Mrs Philpot, would have said something? Mrs Philpot would certainly have said something, if she knew. She wasn't the type to keep

148

secrets. Teresa was sure that the police would have questioned Mrs Philpot by now, so she couldn't possibly have known. In which case, Mark must have been sneaking this mysterious woman in and out without anyone knowing. Well, she had just managed to sneak out of the house and avoid half of the county's press, so it wasn't beyond the bounds of possibility, was it?

Sabir interrupted her thinking as he entered the kitchen.

"I am sorry to bother you again, but I need to ask you some more questions."

"More questions? I've already told you. I don't know anything about his girlfriend."

"Teresa, we are not even sure he has a girlfriend."

"What? Did you speak to Nell?"

"Yes, we did. She gave us a description of the woman she saw through Mark's window, but she only caught a glimpse, so it wasn't much help. She did, however, give us some information about Mark's psychiatric condition."

"It's no secret that he suffers with mental health problems."

"Yes, I'm aware of that. But Ms Hewerdine indicated that his diagnosis has changed recently, and that she believes his mental instability may have progressed into something more serious. She mentioned a split personality disorder as a possibility, where at least two personalities exist within the same person."

Teresa looked at him with confusion.

"What made her come to that conclusion? Is that how you explain Mark being responsible for all this stuff? It wasn't really him, it was someone else in Mark's body? Is that what you're suggesting?"

"Well, to be honest with you, I don't really know what I'm suggesting," Sabir admitted. "But after talking to Ms Hewredine, and taking account of the things we found, I think we have to consider it as a possibility."

"What things? The dress and the shoes, you mean?"

"We have found more items since then. All sorts. Clothes, shoes, wigs, make-up, the lot. And we have been looking through the photographs on Mark's mobile. We were originally looking for photographs of his girlfriend, to see if we could identify who she was. Instead, we found pictures on there of Mark wearing these items."

Teresa stopped what she was doing. She couldn't take in what Sabir was telling her.

"Are you telling me Mark is a transvestite?"

"He could be, yes. Have you ever seen him wearing women's clothes?

"No! Never." Teresa was absolutely confounded at this new information.

"When I spoke to Ms Hewerdine, she told me that a multiple personality disorder can develop from a major depressive disorder, which Mark is known to have suffered from for a long time. It's a complex psychological condition, and I'm no expert, that's for sure. We have requested access to his medical records, and as soon as we get them, we will be getting expert advice on this. It's a bit out of my league."

"Could this explain why he has been so distant with me, lately?

"I suppose it could. If it's okay with you, I'm going to ask one of our mental health experts to pop in later and talk things over with you. You might find it useful."

"If you think it would help, that would be great, thanks."

Sabir left Teresa with her thoughts once more. Mark, a transvestite, with a split personality! It was unbelievable! And yet...was it more unbelievable that he was responsible for these crimes himself, or that some other personality within himself was responsible for these evil things he had been accused of? Certainly, the Mark she knew was not capable of doing such things...so perhaps there was some justification to the theory? Sabir didn't seem to think there was any doubt about the clothes. He had seen pictures of Mark wearing them, so she had to believe him. Could this be what Mark had been doing up in that bedroom, for all these years? Teresa wasn't sure she even wanted to know. Mark had been at Stonehenge for the solstice, the police could prove that. Now, they were finding out all sorts of things that she had never known about. He dressed in women's clothes? He might have a split personality? What next?

Later that night, as Teresa lay in bed, she thought about her childhood. She remembered that Mark, although a lot older than her, had always played games with her when she was a little girl. She hadn't realised, until she was much older, just how unusual that was. Her school friends had always complained about their brothers. About how they would always ruin their belongings and pull the heads off their dolls. Even then, she had just thought they must have horrible brothers. As she grew older, and she heard more and more of these stories, she had realised that it was her brother that was unusual, not theirs. But she didn't consider it a problem, or anything to worry about. She just thought she was very lucky to have a nice brother.

Looking back, she remembered Mark letting her paint his nails and put bobbles in his hair; he still let Lily do that now. He used to go shopping with her in town, on a Saturday, and help her choose outfits. He had always been constructive and had a knack for picking things out that really suited her. He had never seemed to get bored with it either, the endless trailing around women's clothes shops. He had never cared about his own clothes, and had refused to look around the men's section, always saying he couldn't be bothered, or that he would look some other time.

Yes…looking back, there were clues. She just hadn't seen them, and now she wondered how she had ever missed them! Had his whole life been a lie? Had he wanted to be a girl? That would explain his closeness to Teresa, he had always been more like a sister to her than a brother. Why had he carried this secret around all his life? Why hadn't he confided in her? She felt awful, like the worst sister in the world. How had she not noticed? The signs were all there, and always had been, if only she had looked! He had denied himself the life he really wanted, because he hadn't been able to tell her. He had hidden himself in that bedroom for years, transforming himself into himself up and wearing make-up. He had hidden away for so long. Perhaps he had been too embarrassed or ashamed? She could understand that when they were younger, when the world had been more old-fashioned, and less forgiving. But surely, now that society was more accepting and progressive, he could have spoken up about it? She wondered if he had ever told anyone about any of this…Nell perhaps? Or their parents?

Sabir had driven back to the station, to think the case over. In his office, he picked up a document that had been put together for him three years ago, when the first girl had gone missing. It was an academic piece, assembled by one of the history professors at the local university. Sabir started thumbing through the document, despite knowing most of the contents by heart, having periodically leafed through the pages to stimulate his thoughts over the last three years. He had tried to understand as much as he could about the history of Stonehenge, in case the monument itself held any clues regarding Maisie's disappearance. The feeling that the stones must somehow hold the key to unlocking this mystery grew within Sabir each year. Why had these girls going missing from there?

What was the significance? The stones themselves were still a mystery, a five-thousand-year-old mystery that had yet to be solved, and here he was, faced with a mystery which he too was struggling to solve.

Nobody knew why Stonehenge was there, or what its purpose was, although there was much theoretical speculation on the topic. Because of its alignment to the sun, many believed it was built as a temple to the sun, and it attracted druids and pagan worshippers throughout the year, especially during the summer and winter solstices. The first signs of development at Stonehenge could be traced back to the Neolithic period, which marked the end of the Stone Age and the beginning of a progression towards farming, agriculture and the establishment of small, sedentary settlements and community living. Much of the local area would have been forested at that time, and so the impressively large, open clearing at Salisbury Plain would have been a major attraction for ancient peoples.

But that still didn't explain the erection of the stones. There were many stone circles in the local area, and nearby Avebury boasted the largest stone circle, even larger than Stonehenge. But none of these sites were as famous or iconic as Stonehenge. The burial plots found at Stonehenge suggested a link between the monument and death, which had always troubled Sabir. Those buried at Stonehenge had been travellers from as far afield as Wales, one hundred and forty miles away, which would have been a long journey at the time. Interestingly, some of the stones, the distinctive blue stones, had been mined from that same part of Wales where the travellers were thought to have come from. The larger, Sarson stones had been sourced more locally, but they had still been transported from at least twenty miles away. Each stone was estimated to weigh between twenty and thirty tonnes, so moving the stones such a long distance would have been a huge feat of engineering, even by today's standards, especially considering the fact that the circle was created before the invention of wheeled transport. The whole structure was mind-blowing, truly phenomenal when you thought about it. It seemed to Sabir that the more they discovered about Stonehenge, the further the mystery deepened. He hoped that the more he discovered about Mark Applewhite, the clearer this case would become. Teresa's brother was their strongest lead in three years, and Sabir was determined to find out as much as he could.

Sabir also contemplated his own knowledge of the monument. He had been involved in the management of both the summer and winter solstice events throughout his policing career, initially as a uniformed officer, and now as a detective inspector, leading an investigation. Until Maisie's disappearance, most of the crimes associated with these events had been related to drug possession. Every year the police would take the sniffer dogs out, and every year they would make more arrests for cannabis possession in those two nights than they did across the rest of the year. Often the police cells would be filled with repeat offenders, with many protesting that it was part of their religion. Most were let off with a caution, and as a young officer, he had been encouraged to keep the policing at these events as light as possible, and even to facilitate the party atmosphere as long as people were being sensible and keeping within the law.

Those comparatively innocent days now seemed like a lifetime ago to Sabir. Since he had become bogged down in these awful crimes, he hadn't been able to look at the stones in the same way. Instead of mystery and awe and wonder, they conjured within him the notion of a place of horror, pain and distress. He knew they should represent hope and light, reverence and dignity, but Sabir could only now focus on the darkness and secrecy surrounding the stones. He could only think about the suffering those girls must have endured; the desperation and hopelessness of their tortured families, and the heavy burden he carried as the one in charge of bringing this nightmare to an end. What could possibly connect the stones to the disappearance of these three girls, and then to Mark Applewhite? It seemed to Sabir, like the story of the stones themselves, that the more information he gathered together, the more confusing the picture in front of him became.

Chapter 10

Teresa slowly raised her head, lifting her heavy eyelids to look out across the dim bedroom. She tried to get her eyes to focus, by fixing her gaze on the objects on the dressing table, but her head felt fuzzy, and she could have easily let her head sink back into the comfort of the soft pillow beneath her. She could hear people talking, that must be what had stirred her. The voices, barely audible at first, were coming from outside, just underneath her bedroom window. Within minutes, more voices joined in, and soon there was a small commotion.

Too curious to surrender to her tiredness, Teresa softly made her way across the room to the window. The voices were louder now, but she couldn't quite make out what they were saying. What could be causing all this activity, so early in the morning? Taking great care not to draw attention to her actions, she pulled the curtains open a little and looked down onto the driveway below. She could see a group of four people, three men and a woman, all wearing white disposable forensic suits, 'the spacemen' as Lily called them. They were huddled together on the drive, and as Teresa peered out, two of the men high-fived each other. Her interest was piqued, and she gently and silently opened the window, so she could hear their conversation. She could hear excitement in their voices.

"We've got him!" one of them exclaimed.

"Yes, a job well done," said another. "Our perseverance has paid off."

Teresa felt sick to her stomach. They were pleased with themselves, victorious even. She was at rock bottom. She felt, deep in her heart, that the time had finally come. She had to stop telling herself that Mark was innocent. She had to stop convincing herself that the police were clutching at straws, or fabricating evidence, or inventing a case against him. She had to stop believing that they were only accusing him because they were under pressure to convict somebody for these crimes, and they could fit Mark into their narrative. It was time to trust what they were telling her; to accept what they had said from the very beginning. Mark was guilty. Mark was responsible for these awful things. She had to understand that the brother she knew, or thought she knew, had gone.

Teresa was suddenly consumed by an overwhelming sense of heartbreak and loss. She grieved for the brother she had known and loved the whole of her life, now lost to her. She recognised this feeling of desolation and deep, deep sadness, from when her father had died all those years ago. But this felt even more painful, because Mark was still there, he was still alive.

Teresa's thoughts turned to Lily. She was going to have to talk to her daughter, and soon. She knew she had been avoiding it. The problem was, she hadn't got any idea how she was going to start that conversation. How was she going to explain to Lily that the uncle she adored had done some horrible things; that he would most likely be sent to prison for the rest of his life, and that she would never see him again? That is…if Mark actually made it to the court case…she knew his life hung in the balance. Even if he did die, she was going to have to talk to Lily. She couldn't bear the thought of Lily mourning and missing Mark, believing him to be a loving uncle, only to find out, when she was older, what a monster he had been. No, she couldn't keep it from her, that wouldn't be fair. It would be impossible anyway…unless they moved away, out of the area, or maybe even to a different country? Could she just move away from this place, so that Lily could enjoy a relatively normal childhood?

She dismissed the thought instantly. What about her mum? She would never be able to convince her mum to move away from everything she knew; from the house where she had lived happily for so many years. Her mum was terribly frail, and already existing on the periphery of life. The move would undoubtedly kill her. No, moving was not the answer. They were going to have to find some way of existing around here, as the family of a kidnapper, maybe even a murderer. What if Mark didn't wake up, and they never found out what he had done with those girls? She couldn't bear the thought of their parents' pain. She, the sister of a monster, would have her daughter, safe by her side, but they would never know what had happen to theirs.

A dreadful thought hit her like a thunderbolt. What if somebody took Lily? What if someone decided that they deserved to be punished for being in Mark's family, that taking Lily would serve as some kind of justice, or as retribution, redressing the balance? Or perhaps they would see it as an act of vengeance, punishment for the pain and suffering that Mark had inflicted on others? Oh God! She hadn't considered that Lily could be in any danger, but now…it seemed like a natural conclusion. After all, if Lily had been taken from her, wouldn't she want to punish the person who had taken her, harmed her? Yes, she would.

Teresa considered whether she should ask for police protection. She knew she couldn't stay in this house, with officers guarding the door and protecting them, forever. But when they were gone, how would she protect Lily? She didn't know much about police protection, but she knew they would have to move away; be given new names; new identities. They would have to forge a new life for themselves. She thought about Alex. Would Lily's dad be informed of their change in identity? Of where they had moved to? Perhaps Lily could go and stay with Alex, the man who had walked out when she was just a baby, to protect her from the media? Would he want her now? Teresa sighed. She would have to overcome her bitterness towards Alex, and forgive the hurt he had caused them both, to give Lily the opportunity to lead a normal life.

A car pulled up outside and Detective Inspector Sabir got out, addressing the small group of forensics who were huddled on the driveway.

"Bit early for a tea break, isn't it?"

"We've just had a phone call, sir. I think they've been trying to get a hold of you. We've got him!"

"Really?" queried the inspector.

"Well, all the items we recovered from the suspect's bedroom, that we believed belonged to the missing girls, have been tested. It looks like we've come up trumps in all areas: the hair clip that we suspected belonged to Maisie Jones has her DNA all over it, and the friendship bracelet that we suspected belonged to Claudia Merrick has her DNA on it. So, we've done it! We've got a link between the evidence and the suspect; got him bang to rights on the first two girls."

Sabir smiled broadly and shook hands with each member of the group.

"That's brilliant news, well done team. I know how hard you've worked, and the hours you've put in to make this happen. Frankly, all the other evidence we've got at the minute is circumstantial, so this is a huge breakthrough. Should be enough to convince any jury, and make it impossible for anyone to find him innocent. Fantastic work."

"Thank you, sir. I'll get the lab to send you the detailed report as soon as it's ready."

"Are you finished here now?"

"Yes, just a bit of clearing up to do and then you guys can go in and bag whatever else you want for evidence. We've got everything we need."

Teresa sat back on her bed, trying to take in the news she had just heard. She pulled her knees up towards her chest, wrapping her arms tightly around them, and sat rocking back and forth on her bed as the tears fell down her cheeks. This really was the end of her life, and Lily's. Outside, Sabir was still talking to the forensic team, completely unaware of her distress. They paused in their discussions as one of his officers approached.

"Sir, I've collected the post for the house. All the usual stuff, circulars and bills mostly, but you may want to look at this."

"Okay, Jim, what have you got?"

"It's a small parcel, addressed to Mark Applewhite."

"That's not unexpected. Apparently, he was always getting parcels. Turns out it was mostly stuff he'd ordered off the internet. It's probably a piece of jewellery, or some make-up that took his eye. Pass it over, I'll take a look."

Jim handed the small parcel over to Sabir.

"Doesn't look like mail order to me, sir," the officer said.

Sabir examined the parcel. Jim was right. There was no branding of any description, and no barcodes either. The parcel was wrapped in plain, brown ribbed paper, held together with parcel tape, and the address label was a piece of white card with

Mark's name and address handwritten in blue biro. Maybe Mark had ordered something from a private seller? He thought about opening it but changed his mind, handing it to one of the forensics.

"Since you're finished here, would you have a look at this for me?"

"Of course, sir, no problem at all. Drop it in here."

Sabir dropped the parcel into the open evidence bag.

"It's probably nothing, but we don't want any loose ends at this stage, do we?"

"No problem, sir" repeated the forensic officer. "We should have the first findings back for you later on today, now that we've wound everything else up."

"Great, we'll talk later."

Sabir left the group and entered the house, while the forensic investigator sealed the evidence bag, wrote on the front of it and placed it in the van, ready to take back to the lab for analysis.

Samantha and Lily were both in the kitchen when Sabir entered.

"Where's Teresa?"

"She's not down yet. I'm just going to take her a cup of tea, as soon as I've made Lily some breakfast.

"How are you this morning, young lady?" Sabir asked Lily.

"I'm fine, thank you," the little girl replied. "But I am very worried about Uncle Mark. He's been gone for a long time now, even longer than when teddy was lost in the garden. And teddy had fallen into a plant pot! Uncle Mark is too big to fall into a plant pot, isn't he?"

"Yes, Lily, he is."

Sabir looked at the little girl with concern. He had a granddaughter of a similar age, and although they looked nothing like each other, Lily reminded Sabir of her. It was probably the incessant chattering and constant questioning that felt familiar. His own family always joked that his granddaughter would be a detective one day too, because of her endless questioning. Sabir could tell that Lily was equally bright and inquisitive. He needed to talk to Teresa about her. The child should be told the truth. She needed to know that Mark had been found and was in the hospital. Just how much more she should be told would be up to Teresa.

"I'll take that tea up to her, Samantha. You stay here and have some breakfast with Lily."

Samantha poured the tea and handed it to Sabir.

"Thank you."

Upstairs, Sabir knocked on Teresa's bedroom door.

"Teresa, are you awake?"

"Yes."

"Are you decent?"

"Yes."

"Can I come in?"

"I suppose so," Teresa answered wearily.

164

Sabir opened the door and saw Teresa sitting curled up on her bed. It was obvious that she had been crying. He handed her the tea.

"Drink this, it'll make you feel better."

She took the tea from him, and Sabir sat on the end of the bed and looked at her.

"Bad night?"

"Nothing is going to make this better, is it?" Teresa sighed. "Nothing will ever feel better again."

"Teresa. We need to have a long chat later today. I want to update you on the case. But first of all, I want you to see a doctor. I know how hard this has been for you and I want you checked over, to make sure we are doing everything we can to help you."

Teresa was despondent.

"I don't think a doctor will be able to fix this."

Sabir looked at her with concern in his eyes.

"Maybe not, but there's no harm in seeing one, is there?" And I think you should speak to Lily today, too. She still thinks Mark is missing, Teresa. I think she needs to be told the truth."

"I can't tell her the truth."

"Maybe not all of it. Maybe not right now. But she's worried about him, Teresa. She still thinks he's out there somewhere on his own. It's not fair on the child. At least tell her that he's been found and he's in the hospital, being looked after."

"I know you're right," Teresa conceded. "I will, I'll talk to her later."

"Samantha will help. Lily adores her."

"Yes, I know."

165

Sabir got up and made his way to the door. He looked back at the young woman.

"Have a long shower, Teresa, and get yourself ready. It's going to be a tough day." Then he left her sitting on the bed, sipping her tea.

On her way downstairs, Teresa met Samantha, who was just about to take a cup of tea to Teresa's mother.

"I'll take that," said Teresa.

"No, it's fine," Samantha replied. "You go and see Lily. She's been asking after you."

"I'll talk to Lily soon, I promise. But first, I need to speak to mum."

Teresa took the cup from Samantha and headed back up the stairs to her mother's bedroom.

"Mum, it's time to get up."

Usually, she would put the tea down on the bedside cabinet, leaving her mum to get up in her own time. But this morning, Teresa sat on the small chair next to the bed and waited for her mum to rouse. Seconds later, her mum sat up and yawned.

"Thanks for the tea, love."

"Mum, I need to talk to you about Mark," Teresa began.

The old woman avoided eye contact with her daughter and looked down at the bedclothes.

"I can't."

"You have to, Mum. There are so many questions, and there is no-one else to ask."

"I don't know anything. I don't know what he's been up to. How could I? You know yourself, what he's been like. I don't know what he's been doing in that room, for all these years."

"You didn't suspect anything?"

"I can't talk about it, Teresa, those poor girls...I know what they're saying about Mark, but I can't believe it."

Teresa felt her eyes brim with tears as she heard the helplessness in her mother's voice.

"I know, Mum. It's just awful."

"It's no good you and me talking about it, Teresa. It's not going to change anything, is it?"

"Did the police tell you about the clothes, Mum? Mark has been dressing up in women's clothes and wearing make-up."

"Yes."

"Did you know about it before?"

"No."

"Did you have any idea? What about when he was a child? Didn't you notice anything odd about him?"

The old woman began to cry, the tears falling on her grey cheeks.

"He was a lovely child, Teresa. So kind and caring, not a nasty bone in his body. I can't talk about it."

Teresa handed her mother a tissue and the old woman dabbed at her eyes.

"We've got to, Mum. We've got to try and understand this, why it might have happened. They're saying Mark may have a personality disorder. Don't we owe it to him to try and make some sense out of this?"

"It won't make it right, though, will it? It won't bring those three girls back, will it? It won't help their poor families, will it? How will 'talking about it' help? Saying Mark's got a problem, and that's why he did it...that's not going to help anyone."

"I know that, Mum, of course I do. I'm talking about Mark, our responsibility to him. To find out what made him do it. They say that his disorder may have been triggered by a traumatic event in his childhood. Can you remember if anything happened to him back then?"

The old woman started to cry again.

"So, you think it's our fault. That we made him like this."

Teresa felt guilty, pushing her mother like this, but she knew she had to.

"Not at all, Mum, that's not what I'm saying. You and Dad have been brilliant parents. I'm just trying to understand, that's all. I really didn't mean to upset you, I'm sorry."

She put her arms around her mother and comforted her. The old woman recovered herself a little, dabbed her eyes again with the tissue, and looked at her daughter.

"He was always different to other kids."

"Different in what way, Mum?"

"He wasn't like the other lads in the street. He wouldn't go out and play football with them or ride his bike. He just wasn't interested. He preferred to stay inside with me all the time. Your dad said it wasn't right. We did worry about him, because he was such a loner. Your dad tried to get him to play with the other boys, but he just wasn't interested."

Teresa sat back in the chair. This was the first time she had heard her mother speak about anything for years.

"Your dad worried more about him," she continued. "Said it wasn't right, that Mark should be more boisterous. It didn't bother me so much. I only wanted him to be happy, and he seemed happy. He would help me in the kitchen and around the house, always such a kind and helpful boy. Your dad always said he'd grow up to be a poof if we weren't careful; he didn't want that for his son. Things were different back then, not like now."

"I understand that, Mum, really I do. But do you think Mark is a homosexual? Did he ever have a boyfriend?"

"Not that I know of. He never had any friends really, not boys or girls. Then, when you came along, he changed. He was a lot happier. He loved having a little sister, and your dad softened his attitude towards him too, when he saw how good he was with you."

Her mum dissolved into sobs once more.

"I can't believe it, Teresa. I just can't believe what they're saying about him. A monster that hates all women? That's not my son! I don't understand it at all."

"I know, Mum, I can't believe it either. But they have so much evidence now. I don't think we have any choice but to believe what they're saying. It's out of our hands."

169

Teresa left her mother's bedroom, thinking about their conversation. If Mark had been forced to suppress his personality, for all those years, could that have triggered the emergence of this 'other person' that Sabir had been talking about? If Mark had been born in more enlightened times, if their own father had been more enlightened, would that have made any difference? She didn't know. It was all too much for her to process. She was trying to apply reason to a set of circumstances that didn't conform to any reasoning.

In the kitchen, Samantha and Lily were still eating breakfast.

"Good news, Lily," Teresa greeted her daughter with a smile. "They've found Uncle Mark."

A huge grin came across Lily's face, and she ran to embrace her mother.

"That's brilliant! I knew that they would. I knew they'd find him. There have been lots of people looking for him. When is he coming home?"

"Not yet, sweetheart. He's not very well, so they've taken him to the hospital for now. But all the doctors and nurses are looking after him, and he's not lost anymore."

Lily looked concerned.

"Are we going to see him?"

"Not right now, he's still too poorly for visitors. Maybe in a few days?"

That seemed to placate the child, who looked back to Samantha.

"Does that mean you'll be leaving, now that they've found Uncle Mark?"

"Not just yet," Samantha answered with a smile.

"But you said that all the policemen and the spacemen were here because they were looking for Uncle Mark, and he's not lost anymore, is he?"

"No, he isn't, and that's good news, isn't it? And the spacemen and women have gone now, because they were looking for clues in Uncle Mark's bedroom. But I think me and the policemen will stay a little bit longer, if that's alright with you?"

Lily's face brightened with enthusiasm.

"Of course, it is! You promised we could make a cake together. Can we do that today?"

"Absolutely, we can. I think that's a very good idea, Lily. Let's have a look through this book, and you can decide what sort of cake you'd like to make."

Samantha pulled a cookery book down from the shelf and Lily started to leaf through the pages. Samantha looked over the child's head at Teresa and nodded in approval.

"One step at a time," she encouraged. "We'll get there."

A few moments later, Sabir joined them in the kitchen.

"We've got Doctor Connor here to see you and your mum, Teresa. I know you're not ill, but humour an old man, eh? Let the doctor give you a check-up."

"Okay," replied Teresa.

"He's in the living room, if you'd like to go through?"

Teresa kissed Lily on the forehead and wandered into the other room, where Doctor Connor was waiting for her. He explained to her that, in addition to being a practising GP, he did a lot of work for the police and spent much of his time at the police station, looking after offenders in the custody suite. He told her it made a pleasant change to come out and examine someone who was sober.

Teresa allowed him to take her blood pressure and her temperature. He also looked down her throat and pulled down her eyes to examine them.

"Well, on the face of it, you are very healthy, if a little run-down. How are you sleeping?"

"Not brilliantly," replied Teresa, looking the doctor directly in the eye. "In fits and starts."

"That's understandable. What about your appetite?"

"I really haven't got one at the minute, but I am eating. I don't have much choice with Samantha and Sabir around."

"That's good. Now, I'm going to leave you a prescription for a mild sedative, which you can take at night to help you sleep, if you want to. It's non-addictive and you're completely in control. You don't have to take it, but it might help you to calm your mind and relax. One tablet every night, before you go to bed."

"Thank you, doctor. Are you going up to see Mum?"

"Yes, I'll go now."

When he returned about fifteen minutes later, Doctor Connor handed Teresa two prescriptions.

"This is for you, as we've discussed. This one is for Mrs Applewhite. She doesn't have a problem sleeping, but I am concerned about her weight, she's very frail and undernourished. I've given her a prescription for vitamin and iron supplements, which should hopefully improve her health, and stimulate her appetite.

"Thank you, doctor. I've been worried about her weight for some time, even before all of this started."

"Well, make sure she takes the supplements regularly, three times a day for the vitamins and once for the iron. Avoid giving her big meals, just provide her with small snacks and treats, and plenty of fruit. Her appetite should begin to improve, without her even noticing. If you have any concerns, just speak to the pharmacy."

He closed his bag and Teresa walked with him to the front door, thanking him once again. As the doctor was leaving, a smartly dressed lady appeared in the driveway and walked towards Teresa, carrying a briefcase.

"I'm Janice Porter," she introduced herself to Teresa, extending her hand and smiling broadly. "You must be Teresa? I'm a criminal psychologist, and I'm working on your brothers case. Detective Inspector Sabir asked me to drop by. He said you might find it useful to talk to me."

"Thank you for coming. Please, come in," said Teresa, showing Janice into the living room. "Would you like a drink?"

"No, thank you, that's very kind of you though. Now, I've already had a look through Mark's background and medical history, which is long and complex, and I'm aware of the offences he is currently being accused of. It would be helpful for me to get some family background information from you. But before that, would you like to ask me any questions?"

"I have so many," replied Teresa.

"Well, fire away, I'm here to help. I will do my best."

Teresa began to discuss her jumbled thoughts, trying to be as truthful and candid as she could.

"Mark has had mental health problems for as long as I can remember, but it's always taken the form of depression or self-harm. I just can't seem to get my head around Mark hurting someone else. It seems so out of character…Mark has always been so gentle and kind to everyone, even people that weren't being kind to him. Sabir said that Mark might have a split personality. Even if that is the case, would that 'other person' be the exact opposite of Mark? It just doesn't seem possible."

Janice listened intently to Teresa. She could see the torment that Teresa was going through, and wanted to help her understand, but there was nothing definitive to tell her, and Janice was conscious that she didn't want to add to Teresa's torment any more.

"Personality disorders are very complicated, and I'm not going to tell you that we know exactly what's going on here. We don't have all the answers, but we do have other case studies to refer to. That's one of the reasons criminal psychologists are called in for cases like this, to try and provide insight into the mind of the suspect, and to highlight whether there are similarities between the current case and past cases. It's very much an emerging science."

"So, you don't really know what's going on either?"

"Well, not for sure," admitted Janice. "But there is a lot we do know. For example, there are a series of common factors which contribute to the eventual diagnosis of Dissociative Identity Disorder, one of them being early childhood trauma. Do you know of any distressing events in Mark's childhood?"

"I've asked my mum about this and she can't recall anything. Though we did consider the possibility that he might be gay, and has spent his life hiding it."

"That could have been a trigger, but it's usually something more significant, like an act of physical violence or extreme emotional abuse. The family are often not aware of the incident, as it's usually the act of trying to suppress the event that triggers the disorder. Try not to think of it as one personality splitting, or more than one personality existing inside the same person. We find it more helpful to describe the condition as a disconnection between someone's normal self, the self that they present to the outside world, and their own awareness of self. So it's a sort of letting go or losing touch with someone's usual persona, resulting in that person becoming distant or unfamiliar to others, especially those he is usually close to. There may also be periods of forgetfulness, because the person affected spends increasing amounts of time being disconnected from the everyday things that are happening around them. Does that make any sense?"

"Yes, I think so. And Mark has been very distant lately, I feel like we're not as close as we used to be."

Janice nodded.

"That would definitely fit the pattern. If he has been less aware of who he is, then he will also have become less aware of who you are. It stands to reason that he doesn't feel the same connection to you, but for you, nothing has changed except his behaviour, which is hard to understand. It's particularly difficult for family members, as the relationship between the two of you can change significantly on a day to day basis. This can also then lead to what we call a dissociative fugue, where an individual loses all their memories, often for long periods: weeks, months, and in some cases, years. So, if Mark does wake up, there is no telling whether he will be able to remember the events of the last few days or not. It could also be that he won't understand or recognise the people he knows, either. We won't know any of this until Mark wakes up."

"Oh God, you mean we may never know what happened?"

176

"I'm afraid it's a very strong possibility. That's why this police investigation is so important. Mark may not be able to give us the answers we're looking for, so they need to piece together as much as they can from the evidence they have."

"What about the violence? I just cannot believe that Mark is capable of being violent. I've hardly ever seen him angry, let alone violent."

"This is where it gets interesting," replied Janice. "There is currently no evidence to suggest that people suffering with Dissociative Identity Disorder are any more likely to behave violently when compared to the average person."

"So, what about the girls?"

"The thing about this case, Teresa, is that we don't yet know what happened to the girls. So far, we have no evidence of any violence. There are so many unanswered questions with this case, and we are not yet in a position to link Mark's illness with those events. We can't even diagnose Mark with Dissociative Identity Disorder at this stage. We would need to talk to him and run through some tests. This is still very much a theoretical exercise."

"Is Dissociative Identity Disorder hereditary?"

"Not as far as we know. There have been cases of siblings copying behaviour patterns, as a sort of coping mechanism. Sorry, let me explain that. If someone sees their sibling changing their behaviour, in order to block out a traumatic event, then they may copy that behaviour, in order to cope with the event themselves. With siblings, the source of trauma is

177

often shared or similar, so this copying makes sense. But with regards to the disorder being hereditary, none of our studies suggest that the condition is passed down through families. Is there anything else you want to ask me, Teresa?"

"I don't think so. Thank you for coming, but I think I'm more confused than I was before."

"That's to be expected," replied Janice kindly. "I've given you a lot of information to take in, and this is an extremely complex psychological condition. Even experts in this field struggle to understand these concepts. Don't be hard on yourself, Teresa. You could not have seen this coming, and you couldn't have done anything to stop it. You bear no responsibility for your brother's actions, please remember that."

Teresa was grateful for Janice's kindness and wisdom.

"I will try to."

Janice handed her a contact card.

"If you have any more questions, just give me a call and I will try to help, I promise."

Teresa took the card and shook Janice's hand.

"Thank you."

Chapter 11

"Teresa," Sabir called.

Teresa was sitting on the living room sofa and looked up with a start as he entered. She had clearly been deep in thought.

"Have you got time for a chat? I mentioned earlier about updating you on the case, and we've got some significant new developments I want to go over with you."

He sat on the other end of the sofa.

"I don't really have a choice, do I? I suppose this has to happen at some point."

"Yes, it does, and it might as well be now. We've had some DNA results back."

"I know you have. I heard you all talking this morning on the drive."

Sabir was a more than a little taken aback at Teresa's response. He faltered for a moment.

"I'm really sorry, Teresa. That shouldn't have happened."

"It's okay, Sabir," she sighed with resignation. "What does it matter how I find out? I've just got to accept it now, haven't I? Mark's guilty and that's that."

Sabir looked at her earnestly.

"Still, it's not how I would have liked you to find out. Tell me, what exactly did you hear?"

"I heard the forensics team congratulating themselves, for identifying a link between some of the things they found in Mark's bedroom and the missing girls."

Teresa was visibly crestfallen, and Sabir suddenly felt very uncomfortable talking to her. His professionalism started leaking away as the strong sense of compassion he felt for her became more dominant. This was the part of his job he really didn't like: the collateral damage as he often called it. This young woman had done nothing wrong, but her life was going to be destroyed by this, as were the lives of her whole family.

He had seen it so many times before. Justice would be served, and Mark would get the lifetime in prison that he deserved...but it wouldn't be him that suffered the most. He would be more protected in prison than Teresa, their mother, and Lily would be, in the outside world. Mark wouldn't be hounded by the press for the rest of his life. He wouldn't have to constantly hide from his past, avoid meeting new people, or try to live a normal life while carrying around a huge, ugly secret. How many times had he seen the families suffer more than the criminals? Of course, everybody dealt with difficult situation differently, but looking at this young woman now, so low and so alone, he had no idea how she was going to cope. Would she have the mental strength to survive?

In many ways, Mrs Applewhite was already protected to a degree. She already lived in her own bubble, rarely left the house and had few visitors. It was likely that she could quite happily continue to survive like that. Teresa, on the other hand...she was out there doing her best to make a life for herself and her young daughter. It just wasn't fair on them. He could make sure she received counselling and was given plenty of support, and would offer police protection for as long as he could justify it, but would that be enough?

He remembered a case from a few years before, when the mother of a child rapist had suffered so much with guilt, after discovering her son's crimes, that she had taken her own life. He had known the lady before the crimes came to light; she had been a strong woman, well known and respected in the local community, and had run her own business. But she had not been able to cope with the shame of her son's crimes, and just one day after her son was officially convicted, she had refused to leave the house. Shortly after that, she confined herself to her bedroom, and eventually took an overdose, believing it was the only way she could escape the guilt. The woman had left a long suicide note, apologising to the victims and their parents, and taking full responsibility for the crimes committed by her son, blaming his actions on her poor parenting.

When Sabir looked at Teresa, he felt grave concern for her future. She was young and this was going to be devastating for her. Their lives had already been broken, and who knew what life would look like on the other side of all this. Would Teresa want to live it?

Sabir pulled himself out of his thoughts, returning to his conversation with Teresa.

"We found a hair clip belonging to Maisie Jones, and a bracelet belonging to Claudia in Mark's room. Both girls had been wearing these respective items on the nights they disappeared. The clip and the bracelet both have Mark's fingerprints on them. It's compelling evidence for a jury, Teresa. You should also know that this information has been released to the public today, which will undoubtedly mean increased press activity. They will be pushing for as much information as they can find on Mark, so it's going to be very difficult for anyone who knows him."

Teresa's head dropped.

"It's already awful. How are we going to keep them away from the house? From Lily?"

"I'm not moving our officers anywhere yet. Let's manage this storm first, then we'll see where we are. We can put a statement out on your behalf, if you want us to, informing the public that this has nothing to do with you, and that you don't know anything? We can also appeal to the press and the public, asking them to leave you alone. I can't say how effective it will be, but it's got to be worth a try."

Teresa was too upset to answer, but she nodded, tears falling down her cheeks. Sabir handed her a tissue.

"I've been doing this for a long time, pet, and I like to think that I've got a bit of influence in certain places. The press know that if they want information from me, they're going to have to play ball. I'll lay down some conditions: access to this house, and specifically, access to you, will be strictly prohibited. I know this may seem unbelievable, but you'll be surprised how quickly this case becomes old news and they move on to something else."

Teresa's head was still drooped, and she dabbed her face with the tissue. How could anyone ever move on from this, it was so awful? She was silent. She had no words that made any sense, no words at all.

"Sir, can I borrow you for a minute?"

One of the forensics team, the guy who had taken the mysterious parcel earlier that day, put his head round the door and addressed Sabir. The inspector stepped outside to talk. Teresa could hear their muffled voices in the hallway, but she wasn't listening to them. In truth she didn't really know what she was thinking about. Her head felt light and foggy, like she'd been drinking. A few moments later, Sabir returned.

"There's more news, Teresa."

"I don't think I can take any more news," she whispered into her tissue. "I can't take any more. I really don't want to know."

"I know how hard this is for you, Teresa, but I need to ask you about something. A package came this morning addressed to Mark, containing a lock of blonde hair. We've done some DNA analysis, and established that the hair belongs to Joanna Pinkerton, the young woman who went missing from Stonehenge several days ago, at the solstice event."

"So, that's it then. You've connected Mark to all three girls now. That can't have been much of a surprise to you though, can it? That's what you've thought all along, and you were right." Teresa had quickly resigned herself to this new piece of evidence. Even she had thought that it would only be a matter of time before they found something to connect Mark with the third girl's disappearance, and here it was.

"It's not that simple, Teresa. There were no traces of Mark's DNA on that parcel, and none of his fingerprints. And why would he send himself a lock of Joanna's hair through the post, if he has or had access to Joanna? Why not just take it from her and bring it back to his room? Why post it?" Sabir paused to collect his thoughts. "However, it is not unusual for criminals to take what we call 'trophies' from their victims, to remind themselves of each victim, and to bring back memories."

Teresa shook her head and held up her hand to the inspector, indicating for him to stop. She felt sick.

"I'm sorry, Teresa. I promise I am not trying to upset you. The point I'm trying to make here is that Mark would have found it very difficult to send

184

this parcel to himself, without getting his fingerprints on it."

"He could have been wearing gloves, couldn't he?"

"Yes, he could have been. But the other items have his fingerprints all over them. For him to have worn gloves this time would be odd, considering his usual habits."

"So, what are you saying?"

"I'm saying that I don't think Mark has touched this parcel. We've run some tests and there were some interesting fingerprints, several sets and partial sets, which isn't unusual for something that's been through the mailing system. However, one of the full sets belong to a known offender, who popped up on our database. We thought at first that this person may have handled the package as part of the delivery chain, but his fingerprints have also been found on the inside of the package, so we are now fairly certain that this is the person who sent the parcel to Mark."

Teresa stared at the inspector.

"Who is he?"

"His name is Jason Dale. He has previous convictions for sexual assault and soliciting. I have a picture of him here. Do you recognise him?"

Sabir showed Teresa the image on his phone. She saw a man in his mid-forties with thin, reddish-blonde hair. His skin was weathered and lined, but she could still see freckles splashed across the tops of his cheeks. His build was small but muscular, like he worked out, and he had piercings in both of his ears. He had a distinctive tattoo of a bird, possibly a swallow, at the top of his neck. The expression on his face was stern and angry, and his blue eyes pierced into Teresa from the screen.

"I've never seen him before," she said with conviction.

"You're absolutely sure of that? You've never seen him here, at the house?"

"I'm absolutely sure. Mark didn't have any friends round anyway, but I would definitely remember him if I'd seen him before."

"We also had the forensics team take some swabs from Mark in the hospital. We needed his DNA for comparison, and he wasn't on our system as he's never been arrested before. What we found were traces of DNA, belonging to both Joanna and Jason, under Mark's fingernails. So, we know that Mark has been in contact with them very recently."

Teresa didn't understand.

"I'm not following this. What does that mean?"

"We are not completely sure ourselves, but it's clear that Mark and Jason know each other, and that Mark has been in contact with Jason and Joanna. It seems very likely that all three of them have been together, at some point over the last few days. We think that Mark and Jason may be working as accomplices."

Teresa looked at the inspector in amazement.

"That can't be true. Mark doesn't have any friends. He's always been a loner. And now you're saying that he meets up with some chap and they go off abducting young women together?"

"We haven't got all the answers yet, Teresa, but we're working on it. It could explain the first disappearance, Maisie Jones. As you said, Mark was away with you when that happened. It's possible that Jason was responsible for whatever happened to Maisie, and that Mark played no physical role in her disappearance, but that he did get involved in subsequent cases, and they've been working together ever since. It's actually very difficult to abduct somebody who's resisting. If Jason struggled with Maisie, he may have engaged Mark to help him the next time, to make it quicker and easier, thus reducing the likelihood of him getting caught. Two men would find it much easier to overpower a woman than one man alone. It makes sense."

Teresa was trying to get all this new information straight in her head.

"Where could Mark have possibly met a person like that?"

"Anywhere, these days, most likely on social media. There are all sorts of websites where people discuss their fantasies, deviancies, preferences…maybe they found they had something in common and it's developed from there? I'm going to leave you now, Teresa. I've got lots of officers out looking for Jason Dale right now. I've also got a team looking into his background, so I need to get back to base and oversee things. I'll be in touch when I can."

The inspector left Teresa alone with her thoughts. Every day this whole situation was getting more and more bizarre. Sabir had suggested that Mark may have been 'employed' by this Jason person, to help him abduct young women, and that the two of them got further enjoyment from their unpleasant activities by sending trophies to each other through the post! She couldn't get her head around it. Just what had Mark got himself involved in?

Lily skipped into the living room, followed by Samantha, who was holding a plate with a large cake on it.

"Look what we made, Mummy!"

Teresa looked at her daughter, who had chocolate icing all over her face, hands and clothes.

"Can we eat some now?" Lily pleaded.

The very last thing Teresa felt like doing right now was eating cake, but she couldn't say no to her daughter.

"Of course, love."

The cake was messy and lop-sided, and the icing had been applied very thickly in some places and hardly at all in others. Lily had decorated it with coloured chocolate buttons, which she had arranged in what Teresa was sure the little girl had intended to look like a smiley face. To her surprise, despite the revelations of the last few hours, it did make Teresa smile.

As the three of them sat in the living room, eating cake, Teresa could not help but wonder at the absurdity of the situation. Her brother was lying in a hospital bed, gravely ill; the police were out looking for his partner in crime; three young women were still missing, and yet she was sitting eating cake in her living room!

When they had finished, Samantha took Lily upstairs, to get cleaned up and ready for bed, and Teresa put the news channel on. There was Detective Inspector Sabir, issuing an appeal to help find Jason Dale, and informing the public that this man was wanted in connection with the disappearances of three young women; the pictures of the three girls flashed up onto the screen. The inspector carried on, stating that he wasn't prepared to give any further information at the moment, but asking that if anyone knew Jason, or knew where he was, would they please get in touch, as a matter of urgency. A press conference followed, featuring Joanna's parents, who pleaded for anyone with information to get in touch. They held a different picture of Joanna up, one of her standing between her proud parents, holding a trophy in her hand. It was a picture of a happy, healthy family, now shattered, the parents reduced to tears and desperation, begging the public to help them find their beloved daughter.

Teresa was about to turn the television off, when the news item flashed to the local hospital. A reporter was standing outside, informing the television audience that Mark Applewhite was still inside, seriously ill and on life support. He said that no-one from the hospital was prepared to be interviewed live on camera, but that several of the clinical staff had confirmed Mr Applewhite's critical condition, revealing that the next few hours would determine whether he lived or died. Teresa gulped. She had almost forgotten how ill Mark was; that, all too soon, he might not be alive anymore.

When Samantha came down from putting Lily to bed, she found Teresa sitting quietly, the television still on, but the sound muted.

"Tough day?" she asked softly. "Is there anything I can do?"

Teresa looked up, her eyes red and swollen from crying.

"No, Samantha. Thank you. You've been brilliant with Lily. I just don't know where to begin with anything at the minute. I honestly don't know if I could cope with taking care of Lily and Mum if you weren't here."

Samantha gently touched Teresa's arm.

"That's exactly why I'm here. You are not expected to be able to cope with this on your own, nobody could. I'll be here for as long as you need me. And Lily is a delight. It's no problem at all, spending time with her. She's making my job very easy."

"Has she said anything to you, asked you any questions?

"Not really. She is a lot happier since you told her that Mark has been found. It's amazing how resilient children are, Teresa. We'll find a way of explaining this to her, when the time is right."

"I don't know about that. She shouldn't have to cope with something like this, should she? And then there's Mum…I'm so worried that all this stress will kill her."

"Your mum is getting stronger, Teresa. I've noticed lately that she's been doing more for herself; she's even been helping me out with Lily."

"Really? I hadn't noticed."

But then, Teresa hadn't been noticing much recently. She had barely seen her mum today, since their difficult conversation this morning, but Samantha told her that she had helped Lily to put the cake in the oven, and had spent the afternoon reading to the child. Teresa couldn't understand the drastic change in her mum's behaviour. The doctor had given her some supplements, but surely they wouldn't start to work so quickly? Teresa sighed. She really didn't have the energy to think about her mother right now, she already had far too much on her mind.

"Samantha, you're going to think this a terrible idea, but I really need to go and see Mark again."

Samantha looked at her in disbelief.

"Again? After what happened last time?"

"Yes, I know. But I wasn't expecting it then. I'll know what's coming this time, and I'll be more prepared for it. I won't be so frightened. I saw the report earlier from the hospital. The mob was gone, and there weren't so many reporters either."

Samantha shook her head.

"Once word gets out that you're there, they will be back. It's too dangerous, Teresa, you could get hurt."

"The report said that the next few hours are critical. Mark might not make it through the night. I don't expect you to understand, after everything he's done, but I need to see him. I need him to know I love him. Despite it all, he's my brother, and I love him."

"I don't know about this, Teresa. If I ask Sabir, he will say no, and we can't have you sneaking out on your own like last time. I can't go along with that again, it's far too dangerous."

Samantha stopped suddenly, as though she had thought of something.

"Have you had an idea?" Teresa asked her.

"Maybe. Leave it with me for a while, I'll see if I can sort something out. I'm not making any promises, though. And not a word to Sabir, he'll have my guts if he finds out." She left Teresa in the living room and went off to make some calls.

Teresa went upstairs to check on Lily. As she passed Mark's room, she noticed that the door, which had previously been taken off its hinges and sheeted over, was now back in place. There was no policeman standing guard anymore. She ran her hand across the hollow dent left by the battering ram and sighed heavily. As she turned the handle, the door opened. She stood still for a moment, frozen in time, not knowing whether she should enter the room or not.

Over the years she had tried this handle so many times and it had always been locked, whether Mark was in there or not. So she was somewhat taken aback when the door opened. Of course, the police wouldn't lock it again. Besides, they had damaged the lock when they had forced their way in anyway. For the first time in ten years, Teresa went into her brother's bedroom. It was such a strange feeling. She recognised all the items of furniture: the wardrobe, the dressing table, the bed. It was such a long time since she had seen them, it was like she was in some sort of a dream, remembering her past. She recognised the curtains and the carpet. It was all very, very familiar. Yet, at the same time, it felt very remote. It was so odd, like she was somehow walking through her past. She looked around. The police had left everything very tidy, and had stripped the coverings from the bed, leaving just a bare mattress, with a quilt folded neatly at the end of the bed.

Her mind flashed back to her childhood, when she had run in here every morning and jumped on the bed, to wake Mark up. She saw it all so vividly in front of her now, her adored big brother enveloping her in a big hug. She wanted to keep hold of that feeling, that deep, abiding love for her brother. She wanted to cling on to it so tightly that no-one would be able to separate her from it. She had always adored her brother, and somewhere she still felt that. She couldn't make sense of all the things she had been told today: that Mark was definitely involved in these crimes; that he did have something to do with the disappearances of those three girls; that it might not actually be the Mark she knew but some other persona, existing alongside the Mark she knew, who was capable of evil. She had also learnt that Mark had an accomplice, and that they were working together to carry out these awful crimes. How could she possibly make sense of any of that? It was impossible. Still, in this room, in the here and now, all she could feel for Mark was overwhelming love, and concern for his welfare.

She looked around her. The room was exceedingly tidy. She didn't know if it had been this tidy when Mark had left, and the police had just left it as they found it, or whether it looked this tidy because the police had removed so many of Mark's belongings. On the dresser, there was a photograph of Mark with their mother. Mark must have been around eight years old when it was taken. He was sitting on their mother's knee, with a large fluffy feather boa wrapped loosely around both of their necks. They were both smiling broadly at the camera, and Teresa wondered if it was her father who had taken the picture. Yet another clue, she thought as she looked at the photo. Yet another clue that had been there all the time, but that she had missed.

She opened the wardrobe and saw Mark's usual clothes hanging there: a few pairs of faded jeans, some checked shirts, some t-shirts. She'd seen the police remove several large evidence bags from the room, and she'd guessed that these must have contained the female clothing that Sabir had told her about. She knew that they had kept the pink dress and shoes that he had shown her yesterday, but they had also taken other items: more clothing, wigs, make-up and perfume. Sabir had asked Teresa to sign a release for the items and had told her that she would get them back after the trial. She didn't want them back. Mark had kept all that hidden from her for so long; it seemed wrong, somehow, that she now knew all about it. Mark had not wanted her to know about that part of his life, and she should have respected his privacy, and his right to be the person he wanted to be in his own space, uninterrupted by the judgemental world he lived in. Suddenly, she felt a pang of guilt. This was Mark's space, Mark's private space. She shouldn't be in here. Teresa swiftly left the room, closing the door softly behind her.

Chapter 12

Teresa was just heading back downstairs, after having checked that Lily was asleep, when she heard a soft tapping at the front door.

"Dan?" she exclaimed in surprise, as she opened the door. "You are the last person I expected to see!"

Dan glanced at her momentarily, then looked down at the floor, shuffling from foot to foot. Finally, he looked at her.

"Teresa, how are you?"

Teresa had no idea why he was there, what he wanted from her or how she should react to him. She remembered their acrimonious last meeting and winced, trying desperately to find some suitable words to say to him. But her mind was blank.

"What are you doing here?" she managed eventually, her voice breaking.

"I called him."

Teresa swung round to find Samantha standing behind her.

"What? Why?"

"Well, because I think he may be able to help us get you to the hospital. If we're going to get you out of here, unnoticed, then we're going to need his help."

Teresa was too bewildered to reply, but she opened the door wider and beckoned at Dan. As he walked past, he spoke to Samantha.

"I hope you know what you're doing. We could both get into a lot of trouble over this."

"I know," replied Samantha. "But, as I said on the phone, Mark is really poorly. They say he might not make it through the night, what else can we do?"

The three of them sat together at the kitchen table, and Dan searched Teresa's face for some indication of how she was feeling.

"Teresa…how are you doing?"

Teresa looked straight into Dan's eyes. It felt like a hundred years ago when she had adored this man. Once upon a time, any kind of contact from him: a text, a call, a visit, would have made her heart skip a beat. But now, here, in this moment, she really didn't understand how she felt about Dan. Samantha got up.

"I'll leave you two to talk for a couple of minutes. I've got a few things to organise."

After a few moments of awkward silence, Dan spoke.

"Teresa, I really am sorry. You must believe me. I didn't want any of this to happen. I didn't think for a minute that Mark would genuinely be involved in all of this. I know I put his name forward, but that was just to discount him from the enquiry, and to reassure you that he wasn't involved. I swear, you have to believe me."

Teresa was too weary to argue. It had been another traumatic, emotional day.

"I believe you, Dan."

"You do? But you have been so angry with me."

Teresa sighed heavily and looked at Dan.

"I know I have, but I also know that it's not your fault. You could not have predicted any of this. I just felt so betrayed. I realise now that it's Mark who has betrayed me, not you. I'm sorry. I'm sorry about how I spoke to you."

Dan let out a sigh of relief. He had been unsure about coming over again, but Samantha had persuaded him to help.

"You've been through such a lot, Teresa. It's hardly surprising. Don't worry about it."

Samantha came back, carrying a yellow, high-visibility police jacket, and a police constable's cap, which she held out to Teresa.

"I've borrowed these."

"Oh my God!" exclaimed Teresa. "Don't you think we're in enough trouble, without me impersonating a police officer?"

Dan reached out, placing his hand over Teresa's to reassure her.

"Don't worry, you'll be with me. And you're not impersonating a police officer, just wearing one of our coats, it's totally different. Samantha is right, if I drive you out of here, they will follow us, and we'll be mobbed. We need to be more subtle than that."

Teresa was beginning to understand what they had planned.

"What about when we get to the hospital? They still have reporters stationed outside, I saw them on the news earlier."

"I've thought of that," replied Dan. "I have a contact at the hospital. He'll let us in the back way when we arrive. We should really wait until it's dark, though. We'll leave in about half an hour. Is that okay?"

Teresa nodded.

"Yes, if you think it'll work. I really do want to see Mark. This may be my last chance."

Thirty minutes later, Teresa climbed into the passenger seat of Dan's patrol car.

"Now, get down as far as you can," he instructed. "This lot aren't daft, they'll know I was alone when I arrived. We just have to get past the end of the street and then we should be alright."

Teresa did exactly as he asked. It wasn't hard. The jacket she had been given to wear was huge, swamping her small frame, so when she crouched down in the seat it just looked like a discarded jacket. Dan drove confidently through the small posse of reporters, who were camped out at the end of the street. He even put his hand up in acknowledgement to one or two of them, and they reciprocated the gesture, showing no signs of suspicion at all. After they had turned the next corner, Dan said softly to Teresa,

"That's it, we're through. You can sit normally now. Keep that hat on and nobody will look twice at you."

Teresa sat up in her seat.

"You're not really going to get into trouble over this, Dan, are you?" she asked with concern.

"Well, I hope not. But to be honest, I am sailing very close to the wind. Sabir told me not to get involved, because of our relationship, so he definitely wouldn't like it much."

"Why are you risking it, then?"

"Because I owe you, Teresa. You told me your concerns about Mark in good faith and, despite the way things have turned out, I betrayed that faith. I should have told you what I'd done, and I'm sorry that I didn't. Honesty was the least that you deserved from me."

He looked genuinely sorry, and Teresa was less wary of him than she had been. She was beginning to trust him again.

"Dan," she whispered.

"Yes."

"Do we still have a relationship?"

Dan looked at her, unsure what to say. He felt sorry for her, and the situation she had found herself in, and he honestly and genuinely didn't know how to answer her question. Their relationship had barely begun, but the current circumstances had changed things considerably. He knew that Teresa's life was going to change dramatically from here on in, and although he still had strong feelings for her, he couldn't see how he could fit in to that life. Although she was entirely innocent, she would always be the sister of a serial offender, in one of the worst cases to hit the local area for decades. That would be a heavy burden to carry, especially if he wanted to progress in the force. He was so lost in his thoughts that he hadn't noticed the lights turn green.

"Don't worry," said Teresa softly, bringing him back to the moment. "I think I know the answer."

Dan started to speak, but Teresa put her hand up as though to silence him, and he didn't continue. Besides, he didn't really know what to say to her. They drove the rest of the way in an awkward and deafening silence.

When they arrived at the hospital, Teresa saw some press vans a few yards ahead. She could see members of staff leaving, and being approached by various reporters, but they just shook their heads at the journalists and carried on walking. Dan took a turning off to the right, before they reached the main entrance to the hospital, so they were in no danger of being spotted. The sign read 'Service Entrance – All Deliveries This Way'. They drove down an unlit, narrow road, past various outbuildings and vehicle sheds, pulling to a stop outside a building labelled "Porter's Lodge & Deliveries'. They were both relieved to have something to focus on that wasn't the palpable tension between them.

Dan stopped the car and they both got out, making their way towards a large, blue double door. They rang the bell and waited. Moments later, a short, stocky, middle-aged man appeared, wearing a blue uniform. He was almost completely bald, with just the tiniest patch of grey hair left. The two men clearly knew each other.

"Ah, Dan, there you are. I was starting to wonder whether you were coming or not." The man shot Teresa a quizzical look, and nodded to acknowledge her, but she put her head down to avoid eye contact with him. She did not feel like exchanging niceties with anyone.

"Come through this way, I'll get you to the main corridor."

Dan smiled gratefully at the older man.

"Thanks, Pat, I owe you one."

They followed Pat through the porter's private quarters. In another room, Teresa could hear a television and the voices of several people. Pat sensed Teresa's unease.

"Don't worry about that lot, they're only interested in their tea break."

They continued to follow him through a room full of boxes, a post room, then another two doors, which Pat accessed by swiping his identification card. The final door opened onto the main hospital corridor, which Teresa remembered from her last visit. Pat pointed to a telephone situated on the wall nearby.

"There you go. You can get through to the ward from here. When you're ready to leave, pick up this phone and dial three zeros. It'll put you straight through to me and I'll come and let you out."

"Thanks, Pat, you're a star."

202

"No problem, Dan. It's better for me too if we can keep that lot at bay," he said, gesturing to the press outside. "They've been a right nuisance, trying to get information out of anyone and everyone. I, for one, will be glad when it's all over."

He suddenly realised what he had said and looked shamefully at Teresa. "I'm sorry, Miss, I didn't mean..."

Dan interrupted.

"It's alright, Pat. We'll see you on the way back, we'd better get on."

Pat quickly disappeared and Dan turned to Teresa.

"Sorry about that," he said, as they walked along the corridor.

"It's okay," she replied, quietly. "I guess he's only saying what they are all thinking. It can't be easy for them, can it? They're only trying to do their job."

They soon reached the ward, and one of the nurses buzzed them in.

"Do you know where you're going?" he asked.

"Yes, we know the way."

"Great, I'll leave you to it," replied the nurse, picking up the ringing telephone.

Dan and Teresa walked past the nurses' station and made their way to Mark's room. There was a different policeman stationed outside today.

"Dan, what are you doing here, mate?"

Dan spoke to the officer in a hushed voice and winked at him.

"Just a flying visit, won't be long. And the fewer people that know we're here the better, if you know what I mean."

"No problem, mate. You're secret's safe with me."

He looked at Teresa.

"You can go in if you want to, Miss. They've finished with fingerprints and DNA, so he's cleared now. That is…if you want to, of course."

"Thank you," Teresa replied.

She had not expected to be allowed to enter the room, assuming that she would just have to look through the window, like last time. A nurse was in the room when she entered, writing down some readings from the monitors. Teresa walked to the side of his bed.

"You're Mark's sister, aren't you?" said the nurse.

"Yes, I am," Teresa replied, unsure what the nurse's reaction would be.

"Well, come in. I'm afraid nothing much has changed since you came before, and there's no tangible improvement. Unfortunately, he hasn't responded to the antibiotics we gave him, and the infection has now spread to his bloodstream."

"What does that mean?"

"It means that his organs are in danger of failing. I'm afraid his chances are survival are not good."

Teresa looked at her brother with concern.

"Is he in any pain?"

"No, sweetheart, he isn't. He's been unconscious since he arrived here, and we've been giving him painkillers, so he's not in any pain at all. I'll leave you with him, just press this buzzer here if you need anyone. Speak to him if you like, he might be able to hear you. They always say that hearing is the last sense to go."

Teresa was left alone with her dying brother, unsure what to do. He was still covered in wires and tubes, so she took his hand, careful not to dislodge anything. It was warm, and clammy with sweat.

A wave of immense sadness overcame her. How could this be happening? She still could not believe the events of the past few days. How could this man, the man that she recognised as her loving brother, also be the man that they kept speaking about on the television? A secretive, failure of a man, disconnected from normal society. It still didn't feel real to her. Her confusion prompted a sudden realisation; the idea that two personalities were existing inside this one man suddenly seemed feasible.

She remembered what the nurse had said, and decided to talk to Mark. But she was going to talk to the Mark she knew; not the 'other' Mark, the one she didn't know, the one everyone else was talking about. No, she couldn't talk to him. But she could talk to her brother. She gripped his hand tightly and tenderly stroked his forehead.

"Mark, it's Teresa. You are in hospital, and you're very poorly." She spoke to him softly. "I don't want you to worry about anything. Mum is okay, and Lily is fine too. We all want you to come back to us, Mark, so we can make things right. We love you, Mark, and we want you to get better."

She looked at him, but he showed no sign of being able to hear her. Wherever he was, he couldn't come back to her. In that moment, deep within herself, Teresa knew that all hope was gone. She knew her brother; if he had the capacity to fight his way through this, to find a way to get back to her, then she would have sensed it. They would be in it together, as they always had been. But there was nothing coming back from Mark, no flicker of recognition, no connection...nothing. She didn't even feel like Mark lying there. This was just a shell, an empty body. His spirit was gone.

She kissed him lightly on the cheek. She knew she had to free him from the promise he had made to their father, so many years before.

"Mark, if you have to go, you can, okay? We will be fine, I promise. You have done your job. You've looked after us all, as you promised Dad you would. He would be so proud of you, Mark. Now it's our turn to look after you, and if that means we have to let you go, then I release you, okay? I set you free, Mark, you can go now. Go where you can be who you want to be; where you can be free and happy."

Tears were streaming down her face as she spoke those words, but she knew she needed to say them. She really hoped he could hear them. Despite everything, she still loved him, and she wanted him to feel loved. He must have spent so much of his life feeling wretched and unhappy. He had given up so much of himself for her. This was the least she could do for him.

Dan walked over from where he had been standing in the doorway, and passed her a tissue.

"I'm so sorry, Teresa. I'm sorry it's not better news."

She turned to him, buried her head in his shoulder and sobbed. Dan instinctively wrapped his arms around her to comfort her. He could feel her small, fragile body shaking, and squeezed her tightly. He knew that he really did love this girl. He wanted to protect her, and keep her safe, more than anything in the world. What an absolute mess this whole situation was.

"Let's get you home" he said, gently.

"Yes. I need to talk to Mum; make sure she knows how bad it is."

Teresa squeezed her brother's hand and kissed him once more on the cheek.

"Goodbye, Mark. I love you."

Dan led her away from the ward, back through the route they had come by, and drove her home.

"Are you okay?" he asked gently, as they were driving back to her mother's house.

"I really don't know anymore, Dan. I've lost all sense of who I am, of the person I used to be, of the life I had. None of this feels real. It's like I'm in some sort of awful nightmare that I can't wake up from. I'm never going to lead a normal life again, am I? And poor Lily…I can't begin to explain any of this to Lily."

Dan didn't reply. He felt her torment and put his hand over hers, squeezing it reassuringly. When they got back to the house, there were only a couple of hardy journalists still there. The reporters didn't take any notice of them at all; they probably assumed it was a shift change.

As they entered the house together, Teresa took off the jacket and cap, handing them back to Dan.

"Thank you for doing this, Dan. I know you didn't have to," she said, as she sat wearily on the sofa.

The house was still and quiet, Samantha must have gone to bed, too. Dan left Teresa sitting there, heading into the kitchen to make her a drink. But when he returned, she was curled up on the sofa, fast asleep. Poor thing, he thought to himself, she must be exhausted. He sat on the chair opposite and watched her sleep for some time. She looked beautiful, even now, with all this distress and despair around her. While she was sleeping, she looked a picture of peacefulness, free from worry, like she had when he had first been attracted to her. He missed her. He sighed deeply, imagining what they might have had if things were different.

Eventually, he dragged himself out of his thoughts. He took a throw from the back of the sofa and draped it over her sleeping form, dimming the living room lights and leaving her to rest. Before he left the house, he went upstairs to check on Teresa's mum and Lily, who were both sleeping soundly. Under any other circumstances, he felt this could have become his family. He had really wanted this. He knew that he loved Teresa, and he knew that he could happily take responsibility for Lily, and help with Teresa's mum, too. He felt connected to them all. It was a life he would have loved to have, a ready-made family, perfect.

But that was before he knew about Mark. Could he live his life, in the shadow of what Mark had done? He knew what his family would say. He knew what his colleagues and supervisors would say. And he also knew, when he was thinking with his head and not his heart, that they were all right. He could not afford to get involved in this situation. He should think himself lucky that his relationship with Teresa had only been in its' formative stages when this had come to light. If they had been more established, then he really would be in a difficult situation right now. As it was, he felt that both he and Teresa knew and understood that this was the end of the road for them. It broke his heart to admit it, but he knew that it was the right decision.

He quietly pulled the door shut on his way out of the house, nodded to the police officer guarding the driveway, and took a deep, cleansing lungful of fresh air. He walked away from the house, knowing at that moment that he was walking away from Teresa as well.

Chapter 13

Sabir entered the incident room, full of energy and determination. He was in a good mood. Finally, he felt like he had a lead that made sense in this case.

It was still early, but several of his officers were there, some having come in earlier that morning and a couple who had been working all night, putting together any information they could find pertaining to Jason Dale. One of the officers who had spent the night there was Megan.

"What have we got, Megan?"

The young woman jumped up from her desk as Sabir came in. She was full of energy, despite the long night, and eager to please.

"We've got a lot of background, sir. We're ready to bring you up to speed, as and when you're ready."

He smiled at her. She was young, keen, and a good worker. She was going to go far.

"Ten minutes, in my office. Bring me what you've got. Then I'll brief the team when we're all in."

"Right away, sir," replied Megan, tidying some documents up on her desk.

"No, Megan. Ten minutes. And Megan..."

"Yes, sir?"

"Bring coffee."

Sabir smiled to himself and walked off into his office. He didn't want her getting too far above her station. She would have to learn her trade from the bottom, just as he had done.

Megan, feeling a little deflated, dutifully went off to make the coffee.

Exactly ten minutes later, Sabir, Megan and Colin, who had also been up researching through the night, were in Sabir's office. Sabir took a sip of coffee and nodded at Megan in appreciation.

"So, what do we know about him?"

"Jason Moon Shadows Dale, forty-six years old," Megan began.

Sabir interrupted her immediately.

"Moon Shadows? Is that some kind of nickname?"

"No, sir. That's his given name. We will come to that. His mother is a strange one."

Sabir nodded in acknowledgement.

"Okay, carry on."

"Jason Moon Shadows Dale, forty-six years old. As we were already aware, he has previously been convicted for soliciting, ABH and sexual assault. All these offences took place when he was in his early twenties, but we haven't found anything on our records which post-dates these convictions. However, when he was just thirteen years old, we pulled him in for an assault on his mother. He'd done a good job on her, and she was a bit of a mess according to the report sheet, but she didn't want to press charges. He was a minor, so the whole thing was swept under the carpet."

"Tell me more about his previous convictions," encouraged Sabir. "Was he banged up at any point?"

"In 1994 he was arrested and cautioned, but not charged, with soliciting on West Bank. At the time, it was a rough area, and prostitution was common, though it's more recently been cleaned up and become a desirable area to live. Anyway, the next time we meet Jason Dale is in 1996, when police were called to a disturbance in Fen Lane, not too far from West Bank. Two men were fighting and causing disruption in a block of flats; it was the neighbours who called us. Our man, Jason, and an older man were found beating each other up in the corridor. Officers had to intervene to pull Dale off the other bloke. Dale's story was that the older man had picked him up from West Bank, they had engaged in sexual activity, and then an argument had broken out about payment. Dale punched the man so hard he broke his nose. Under questioning, the victim of the assault also accused Dale of sexual assault. He was found guilty of both grievous bodily harm and serious sexual assault, and sent to Whitemoor, a specialist correctional prison, for four years.

"Nothing since?" asked Sabir.

"No, sir. I spoke to Whitemoor. They say they are a specialist unit, focusing on rehabilitation and resettlement, aiming to reduce the risk of re-offending through work, education and behavioural programmes. They cite Dale as one of their success stories. He walked straight into work when he was released from Whitemoor, with the help of their programme, and he hasn't been in trouble since."

"Until now," said Sabir, nodding his head. "Where did he work?"

"They got him into care work, mainly in residential settings, looking after people with mental health problems."

"Aha," exclaimed Sabir. "The missing link!"

"You got it, sir." Megan was now very animated. "In 2002, Dale was working nights in the same supported living facility where Mark Applewhite spent six months. He has moved around a lot, from job to job, but the dates add up. They were there at the same time, for around four months."

"Great work, Megan. Where is he now?"

"That we don't know, sir. He has a history of moving from place to place, renting, staying six months to one year, and moving on again. We've got a good record of him up to 2010, then the trail goes cold. We've got nothing current on him."

"Okay, I'm sure his whereabouts will reveal themselves. It's very hard to hide yourself these days. What do we know about his background?"

Colin shuffled some papers on his lap.

"Only child to a single mother, sir. She's a bit of a fruit-loop, I'm afraid. She's also been in a few times, but nothing serious; no convictions, just cautions. It's quite a list though: public indecency; petty theft; trespassing; multiple cautions for possessing cannabis, always very small quantities though, so probably just for personal use. She's a bit of a 'free spirit' shall we say? Interestingly, though, two of those cautions were picked up on the night of the summer solstice, at Stonehenge. One in 1972 and the other in '81. Could be that she's a regular visitor to the festival. Oh, coincidently, 1972 was the year Dale was born."

"Well, she sounds an utter delight. I can't wait to make her acquaintance," said Sabir, not even attempting to hide his sarcasm. "Where is his mother now?"

"We've traced her to a multiple occupancy house, the other side of Basingstoke. Some sort of 'hippy commune' community, apparently."

"Really," Sabir sneered. "I thought all the flower children had grown up."

"Nope. Still alive, well, and all living in Basingstoke, sir."

"Anything else to add?"

"I think that covers what we've got so far," replied Megan.

"Great work, you two. I'm briefing the whole team in twenty minutes, and I'd like you both to stay for that, in case there are any questions. After that, you'd better get yourselves off home for some sleep."

"Thank you, sir," they replied in unison, swiftly leaving his office.

An hour later, Sabir was finishing off the team briefing. Over twenty officers of all ranks, uniformed and plain clothes, were assembled in the room, listening to the latest information.

"So, now that you all know as much as I do, listen up," Sabir instructed. "Here's the plan for the next few hours. I want us to spread ourselves out a bit. Go and find out as much as you can about Jason Dale, I want to know the last time he tied his shoelaces, you hear me? Chapter and verse, nothing less! One of you has got a long trek up to Greengates, we need to look at his record, find out why he left. And one of you can contact the tax office, check out his work background. I want to know where it goes cold. Pay a visit to anyone who employed him; see what we can find out. We need home addresses, friends, known associates, everything. Take a couple of uniforms with you, look through everything. Let them know we're not messing about. Get me records of everything they've got. You two,"

He pointed at a couple of uniformed officers at the back of the room.

"Get onto the DVLA record. What's he driving? He's not on foot, that's for sure. He must have a vehicle. Find out what it is, and when you have that information, get it out there with instructions from me not to intercept if traced. Just call it in and keep a safe distance, we don't want him spooked. We need to tread carefully with this one. Whatever you find, I want to be the first to know, you got that?"

The two officers nodded and made their way over to a spare computer screen.

Confident that the team knew what they were doing, Sabir left the incident room and went back to his office. He felt a little more satisfied. This case had been moving far too slowly, he felt like he'd just been waiting around for Mark to wake up, which he had known was unlikely to happen. Then that criminal psychologist, Janice, had told him that even if Mark did wake up he might not remember anything about the events at Stonehenge.

Sabir had plenty of evidence to link Mark to the disappearances, but still had no motive. Something just didn't feel right. Mark wasn't what he had expected to find after all these years of trying to figure out who was responsible for these disappearances. He picked up a photograph of Jason Dale that was lying on his desk. Unlike Mark, this man certainly did fit the mould.

After the disappearance of the second girl, Claudia, and once a clear link had been established between the two Stonehenge disappearances, the investigative team had sought the advice of a criminal profiler. She had put together a unique psychological profile of the person she believed was likely to be responsible for carrying out these crimes. The profiling exercise had identified certain likely character traits of the perpetrator, by looking at how the crime had been carried out and what was known about how the perpetrator had conducted themselves at the crime scene. The exercise had suggested that the culprit was likely to be a single male; probably a loner, with no close family or friends. He would have had a difficult, if not abusive, relationship with his

216

own mother, and few or no female friends, most probably eschewing women completely. He would be of low intelligence, and his behaviour patterns would be subversive, obsessive and secretive. If he was in any kind of relationship with anyone, he would need to be the dominant force within that relationship.

Mark Applewhite fitted some key aspects of this profile: he was a single male, had obsessive and secretive behaviour patterns, and was a loner. But that was where the profiling fell apart. Mark had a close, loving relationship with his three closest female relatives, and Sabir could see no obvious attempts at coercion or control by Mark in those relationships; it also appeared that he loved and respected his mother. It seemed far more likely to Sabir that Jason had managed to rope Mark into this, as a subordinate. Mark was no criminal mastermind. Although Sabir had never once spoken to Mark Applewhite, he knew that much.

As part of the investigation, the psychological profile had been sent round to other forces in the country, and they had been asked to eliminate local suspects who fit the profile. His own force had completed that exercise too, identifying and visiting individuals on the sexual offenders register. Those without a valid alibi for the nights in question had been interrogated, and watched covertly, but no substantial leads had been established.

Sabir was under a lot of pressure. The press were hounding him for progress daily, and the families wanted answers, fast. There was a constant public conversation about how the investigation was going; if someone else would get better results; if Sabir was still up to the job. The top brass were also demanding answers, and there had been a lot of criticism from that direction too. They believed the disappearances of Maisie and Claudia could have been linked earlier, saving valuable police time and resources. They were particularly critical of the time spent on investigating Julian Freeman, the boyfriend of Claudia Merrick, who had since been cleared of any wrongdoing.

Sabir picked up his desk phone and called the Chief Constable.

"Good morning, sir. Sabir, here. I'm on my way over with an update for you. We have some significant findings and a second suspect. I'll be with you in five minutes."

He put the receiver down and left his office.

Later, an interrogation officer, Jack, knocked on Sabir's door.

"Sir, we've got Martina Dale downstairs. She's kicking off mind, not at all happy about being woken up and pulled in."

Sabir was slumped in his chair, drained from the grilling given to him by his superiors. He let out a heavy sigh.

"Great, just what I need right now," he said, pulling himself to his feet. "Let's go and have a word with her, and see what she has to say for herself."

He followed Jack downstairs, into a small interview room, where a female police constable was standing at the door. Martina Dale was sitting in a chair, slumped over the table.

"About bloody time," Martina immediately fired at Sabir, as he entered the room. "If you're gonna get me out of bed at the crack of bloody dawn, the least you can do is get your bleedin' act together when I arrive, you tossers!"

"10.30 am." Jack's response was dry. "It was 10.30am."

Sabir cleared his throat and looked the woman directly in the eye. He was in no mood to be dealing with her.

"Okay, Ms Dale. Now, as much as I realise it was a great inconvenience to you, it was necessary, and we really do appreciate the effort you've made. We have some serious concerns about your son, and we're hoping you may be able to help us with our inquiries."

"Jason, what's he done now?"

"Have you not seen the news, Ms Dale?"

"We don't have a television or radio up at the commune. Too distracting."

Sabir looked at the mess of a woman sitting in front of him. She must be in her sixties now, but wore her hair in dreadlocks, dyed purple and blue, which she had tied up in an orange headscarf. She was of slight build and very thin, emaciated even, and her skin was sallow. She wasn't wearing any make-up, so nothing to hide the dark rings under her eyes, and was fiddling with a chain that ran from a

219

piercing in her nose to one of three piercings in her left ear. She was dressed in faded, blue denim jeans, a thick, green, woollen cardigan and a tie-dye t-shirt, with flip-flops on her feet. Her hands were gnarled and old, her nails were dirty, and on the seat next to her, she had an embroidered bag, with several stitches hanging loose. Sabir didn't imagine she had ever worked, held down a job or assumed any responsibility for anything in her life. She had probably always lived like this, on the outskirts of 'normal' society. It had been a popular way of living in the sixties, but it was much rarer to find people living this way now.

"What do you do all day at the commune, then?" he asked. "High on drugs all day, are you?"

She spat her response at him.

"What if I am? We ain't causing no trouble. It's a friendly place, there ain't no crime. I don't know why I'm here."

"I told you, it's Jason we want. Where is he?"

"Don't know. Don't want to know neither. I told your officer, I ain't seen him for years. We don't get on."

"And why is that?"

"Well, he's not right. I think he's one of them misogynies, you know? Hates women. Hates me, anyway."

"You mean he's a misogynist," encouraged Sabir.

"Yes, that's it," Martina replied. "He's gay of course. Always knew that. But lots of people are gay.

220

Don't mean you have to hate women, does it? But he does. Told me all women are whores."

"When did you last see him?"

"I don't know, years ago. We don't have no phones up at the commune. But even if we did, he wouldn't call. Like I said, hates me."

"What about his father?"

"What about him?"

Sabir was losing his patience. He took a deep breath and continued to press her for details.

"Is Jason in touch with his father?"

Martina threw her head back and laughed.

"You're having a laugh, aren't you? I don't know who his father is. And if I don't know, he certainly don't!"

"Did you ever take Jason to Stonehenge, when he was younger? To the Solstice event?"

"Course I did. We all went. Used to go every year when I was young. Don't go anymore, but some of the younger ones from the commune, they still go."

"And what about Jason, did he used to go too?"

"Yeah, course," Martina replied. "He used to enjoy it when he was little, wandering around with the other kiddies. But when he got older, he'd always be looking for me, trying to stop me having a good time. He was too clingy that boy, a real pain in the arse. He never was right in the head, if you ask me."

"You said he hated women. Was he ever violent towards women?"

"Only me. Used to hit me. But one of the blokes who was bigger than 'im would usually pull him off, give him a good hiding an' all that. I never saw him hit anyone else, though. When he was old enough, he just disappeared one day. Up and left, without a word to no-one. I ain't seen him since."

"And you've never been worried about him?"

"Nah, you have to look out for yourself in this world, don't ya?" Martina said. "No, I can't help you. If you wanna find Jason, you're gonna have to find him yourself."

Sabir had reached his limits. It seemed there was nothing more they could learn from this exasperating woman.

"Jack, we're wasting our time here. Take her home."

"About bloody time, too," said Martina, with a smile.

Sabir returned to the incident room. Two more glass screens had been added to the two existing evidence boards. One showed pictures of Joanna and her family, alongside a written timeline of her movements on the night she disappeared, based on what they had been able to piece together. The other was entitled 'suspects' and exhibited pictures of both Mark and Jason, as well as all the known information about them both. A thick, black line had recently been drawn between the two of them, and someone had written '2002 - Greengates'. That was the year Mark and Jason had met, it had to be. Sabir was convinced that, somehow, their meeting was fundamental to this case, and to understanding what had happened to the three victims.

The screens also featured pictures of Teresa and Lily. They had been discounted as suspects as soon as the enquiry into Mark had started, but they were still there on the board. There was also a picture of Martina Dale, Jason's mother. If you could call her a mother, Sabir thought to himself. She hadn't put a lot of effort into raising her child, as far as he could see. The conversation with her had gone nowhere either, although it had given Sabir a valuable insight into Jason's background, which had clearly been chaotic and disaffected. They needed to find Jason Dale, and fast.

A female officer approached Sabir.

"We know what he's driving, sir. A white Citroen Berlingo. It's a small, three door van, all legal, taxed and had a recent MOT. He is the registered owner."

"Great work, Sammy. There's a couple of free pints available for whoever spots it first."

"I'll get the word around, sir."

The officer grinned as she walked away, leaving Sabir looking at the screens.

"We're coming for you, Jason Dale," Sabir murmured quietly to himself. "Make no mistake."

"How's it going, sir?" Dan asked, approaching Sabir, who was still staring at the screens. "I'd still like to help out, if I can."

"You know that's not possible, Dan. You're too close to it all."

"I don't know Jason Dale at all. Couldn't I help out on that side of things?"

"Dan, I'm sorry. It's not going to happen. Jason is a suspect and we're all out looking for him, but that doesn't mean Mark's off the hook. We've got too much on him to discount him entirely."

"I understand that, sir, but I do feel kind of useless."

"Well, get out on the road and start looking for that van. I don't see any harm in you doing that. CCTV are on the lookout too, so it shouldn't take too long. There's a couple of pints going for the first one to spot it."

Dan smiled at Sabir and nodded, leaving the inspector to his musings. This had been the biggest case in the local area for years, and it looked like it was about to crack. Dan understood why he'd been kept out of it. But, inside, he was kicking himself. After all, it had been his information which had led them to this point, after two years of no leads. He was not coping well with the fact that no-one would talk to him about the case.

He was struggling with his loyalties, too. Despite his best intentions, he still felt some loyalty to Teresa. He felt sorry for her, and the situation she had found herself in, and he knew some of his colleagues saw that as a sign of weakness. They thought he couldn't be trusted, and that frustrated Dan. Surely his colleagues and his superiors knew he was more professional than that? Then he thought about the events of last night. Perhaps it wasn't the wisest thing to have done, escorting Teresa to the hospital…if word got around about that, his colleagues would definitely freeze him out. But he had also wanted to help her, he had a duty of care, didn't he? It was all so unfair. He kicked the waste bin in frustration and left the incident room, feeling lost and rejected.

Sabir went over to one of his officers, who was sitting at a computer screen.

"How's it going, Kate? Have we got a work record?"

"It's very patchy, sir," Kate replied. "Whitemoor got him the placement at Greengates, which is where we think he met Mark Applewhite. They kept him for the period of his probation, about nine months, but he left soon after that, and hasn't worked since by the looks of it."

"So much for Whitemoor's rehabilitation scheme then," said Sabir with a sneer. "No more convictions though?"

"It looks like that's the case. He's certainly been keeping a low profile. We've just been sent his benefits records though, and it looks like he's been moving around a lot. He wasn't staying anywhere for any length of time. Until, that is, a couple of years ago. Out of nowhere he suddenly upgraded his living accommodation, from a long list of bedsits in central town to a suburban semi on the outskirts," she explained, putting a picture of the property up on the screen. "And he's been there ever since. Still not working as far as I can see."

Sabir examined the property. It looked tidy enough, and well maintained.

"Who owns it?" he asked.

"A retired builder. Purchased it twenty plus years ago. He did it up and has been letting it out ever since. He's an old chap now. Managed to have a word with him on the phone and he says that he's never had any problems with Jason. Always pays his rent on time. No complaints from the neighbours, keeps the property in good order. A perfect tenant apparently."

"When did he move in?"

"April 2017, sir."

"April 2017," repeated Sabir. "Just two months before Maisie Jones went missing."

Sabir went over to one of the other officers.

"Jim, we need to stake out this property. No uniforms in sight. I don't want to scare him off. Get two CID over there straight away, in an unmarked car. I want this place watched night and day. I'll get a rota organised and I'll clear it with top brass. But I want it to start now. Get on it."

Jim picked up the phone.

"Yes, sir"

Thirty minutes later, two CID officers, Pete and Marie, were sitting in an ordinary suburban street, opposite the small, innocuous looking semi-detached house. They had earpieces in and were in contact with both the control room and Sabir.

"What can you see?" Sabir asked them over the radio.

"A small, typical looking semi-detached house," replied Marie. "Very small front garden, with a parking space for one vehicle, which is currently empty. There don't appear to be any lights on in the property, though it's probably too bright to tell for sure. Net curtains downstairs so no visibility into the property from here. Upstairs curtains are also drawn. Property does look lived in, though. The front lawn has been mown recently, and everything is in good order."

"Okay, what about the neighbouring properties?"

This time, Pete answered.

"Both sides are occupied. The neighbours on the attached side appear to be at home. A Ford Fiesta is parked on the drive, registered to an elderly man, Mr Simms, who lives at this property with his wife, according to our research. They are both retired teachers, with no convictions. Nobody home on the other side. Should be occupied by a family, with two young children. They are probably still out at work; we are expecting some activity at that property after 5pm."

"Has anyone spotted you?"

"Negative, sir. We are now a few yards up the road on the opposite side, but we have eyeballs on the semi. We have a good vantage point and, so far, have not aroused any suspicion. We've seen a couple of dog walkers who took no notice of us at all."

"Good work. Usual procedure, then. Move the car after an hour, so as not to raise suspicion, then after the second hour we'll change vehicle and personnel. If it goes on any longer than tonight, we'll utilise the observation van. Let's see where we are later this evening. Let me know as soon as there's anything to report, and do not approach the suspect or the property until you've spoken to me. Understood?"

"Got it, sir, over and out," said Pete. He turned to Maire. "He's hoping it'll all be done and dusted tonight."

"Let's hope he's right," she replied, turning the radio on and adjusting the backrest of her seat to a more comfortable position. It was going to be a long wait, might as well make it a comfortable one.

Chapter 14

An hour later, Pete and Marie watched as a white van arrived at the property and parked on the street, right outside the house. Jason Dale jumped down from the driver's side and grabbed two shopping bags from the passenger seat, carrying them into the house. The kitchen light went on, allowing Pete and Marie to see into the house for a brief moment, before Jason Dale pulled the blind down, once again blocking their view. Moments later, a second light went on, this time upstairs. Pete radioed through to the control room and Sabir.

"The suspect, identified as Jason Dale, has entered the premises. He arrived alone and appears to be alone in the property."

"Are you absolutely sure it's Dale?" Sabir radioed back.

"Yes, sir," replied Pete. "He looks a bit older than the pictures we have on file, but there's no doubt. It's a positive identification."

"Right," said Sabir. "His arrest warrant is in place, as is the search warrant for the property. I'm sending back-up. When they arrive, I want you to cover all exits, then go in and get him. We've got enough on him to take him in for questioning, so I see no point in prolonging this."

"Roger that, sir. We're ready whenever you give the word."

"As soon as you've got him in cuffs, I want an initial search of the property. Then, we need you to seal it up and station a guard outside until I can get SOCO on the job first thing tomorrow."

Half an hour later, a squad car and a police van drove quietly up the street, and parked silently a few yards up from the house. Six police officers surrounded the house, covering both front and rear exits. The officers had their radios on silent, and all of them were wearing earpieces, waiting for their next instruction.

"How do you want to do this?" Pete asked his partner.

"Well, I was thinking it might be easier to flush him out, rather than pushing our way in. There's no telling whether he'll even answer the door to us anyway, and we might spook him or give him the upper hand if we let him know we're here. I think we need a plan to get him out of the house."

"Right you are, leave that one with me," said Pete. "I've got an idea. You make sure everyone is ready."

Ten minutes later, Pete was poised and ready. Two burley police officers were standing near the front door with Marie. They had their backs pushed against the wall, being careful to remain unseen by anyone who might be looking out of the windows of the house. Pete knew he had to act fast. He'd been in this situation many times before, and he was acutely aware that he didn't have long before one of them would be spotted. This was exactly the kind of street where somebody was always about.

Pete signalled to the group to be on their guard and murmured into his mouthpiece:

"We are code red, code red, I'm going in now."

He crept to the rear of the van and pulled sharply on the handle. As he had anticipated, the sudden movement set the van's alarm off. At the sound of the alarm, Pete immediately shot round to the far side of the van and crouched very low, well out of sight of the watched house. The alarm wailed loudly, piercing through the peaceful, sleepy, suburban neighbourhood. Jason looked out from an upstairs window. He had a good look up and down the street. He couldn't see anything out of the ordinary. Clearly annoyed at the disturbance, he ran down the stairs and opened the front door. As he stepped through the threshold, the two burly officers grabbed him from either side and forced him to the ground. There was a brief struggle, as the three men tussled around on the floor, but the two police officers soon had control over Jason and quickly managed to get his hands behind his back and put handcuffs on his wrists. While he was still on the floor, Marie bent down and spoke to him in a clear voice.

"Jason Dale, you are under arrest for the suspected abduction of Maisie Jones, Claudia Merrick and Joanna Pinkerton. You have the right to remain silent. If you do say anything, what you say can be used against you in a court of law. You have the right to consult with a legal representative and to have that legal representative present during any questioning. If you cannot afford legal representation, this will be provided for you if you so desire. Have you got anything you wish to say?"

Jason still had his head forced down by one of the officers, but he managed to shake his head. He didn't speak.

Marie addressed the two policemen.

"Take him to the station. We'll follow shortly so that I can book him in with the custody sergeant."

The two officers pulled Jason to his feet and he walked slowly to the police van, climbing in under his own steam. He glanced briefly at the bedroom window of the house, before they closed the door on him.

The police van disappeared up the street. Two more police officers stood guard outside the property, to deter any inquisitors. Pete had already noticed that Mrs Simms was looking through her curtains next door, watching the excitement with interest.

Pete and Marie cautiously entered the property. On first appearance, it looked in good order, neat and tidy. The two shopping bags they had seen Jason bringing into the property had been abandoned on the kitchen counter, but all the other surfaces were clear. They entered the living room together, which again looked clean and presentable.

"Shall we take a look upstairs?"

Upon reaching the top of the stairs, Pete entered the first bedroom, while Marie carried on to the end of the landing, towards a smaller room. As soon as she stepped inside, she called loudly up the landing to her partner.

"Pete, in here. Quick!"

Pete rushed to the other room, and saw Marie bent down over the body of a young woman.

"It's Joanna, call for an ambulance, now."

Pete radioed the control room straight away and requested an ambulance to attend immediately. The young woman was sitting on the floor, with rope tied around her wrists which was attached to the leg of a bed. She was slumped over on her knees, and when Marie lifted her head up, she flinched and pulled herself away.

"It's okay, love, we're the police. You're safe now. We're going to get you out of here."

Joanna lifted her head and looked up, and Marie could see that the young woman had a large plaster placed over her mouth. The girl's eyes were sunken, and she was very pale. Marie held Joanna's head with one hand and quickly removed the plaster with the other. The girl gasped loudly and immediately burst into tears. Marie held her tightly.

"It's okay, you're okay now. It's Joanna, isn't it?"

The young woman nodded and collapsed onto Marie's shoulder, as Pete left the room and radioed through to Sabir.

"You're not going to believe this, sir, but we've got Joanna. She's alive."

The shock in Sabir's voice echoed through Pete's radio.

"Oh my God, I wasn't expecting that, is she hurt?"

"She's been bound and gagged. She looks exhausted and she's extremely traumatised. Marie's with her now, and there's an ambulance on its way."

"Great work, you two. Priority is to check the rest of the house, you never know what might turn up. Tell Marie to accompany the girl to the hospital. I'll meet them both there."

"Yes, sir. I'll conduct a thorough search of the property straight away."

The ambulance arrived moments later, and the crew put a blanket over Joanna, strapping her into a chair to carry her down the stairs. Joanna was still gripping Marie's hand tightly.

"He's gone now, Joanna. We've got him at the police station. He's not coming back, I promise."

In the back of the ambulance, the technician gave Joanna a quick once over.

"How's she doing?" Marie asked.

"I can't see any serious physical injuries," replied the technician. "There is some bruising, and her wrists are raw from where she's been tied up. Mentally, though, she's clearly in a lot of distress and not communicating very well. Let's get her to hospital and make sure there's nothing we've missed."

Marie sat beside Joanna for the journey and Joanna didn't once let go of her hand. On arrival at the hospital, a young nurse rushed over to them.

"My name's Cara. I'm one of the nurses here today, and I'll be looking after you while we wait for a doctor."

Cara prised Joanna's hand gently from Marie's and squeezed it.

"We're going to do a few tests, Joanna, while we're waiting, just to see how you're getting on. Then I'm going to get you something to eat and drink, okay? That should make you feel a bit better. Is that alright?"

Joanna nodded at the young nurse, and Marie was happy to hand her over. She could see Sabir talking to one of the doctors and headed over to join them. As she came nearer, the doctor walked off in the direction of the cubicle Joanna was in.

"Much obliged," shouted Sabir after him.

He greeted Marie.

"Amazing, Marie! I'd given up all hope of finding her alive!"

"Me too, sir. Thank God we did!"

"Yes, thank God indeed. Now, did Dale say anything when he was arrested?"

"No, sir, not a word. I need to get back to the station. I'm the arresting officer, so the custody sergeant won't be able to book him in until I get there."

"Okay, you get back Marie. Joanna's parents are on their way, so I'll stay and speak to them. We'll have to put a statement out, but it can wait until we get a clearer picture of how she is."

Marie thanked Sabir and headed off back to the station.

The doctor called Sabir over.

"We've examined Joanna. Aside from some mild bruising, and chafing to her wrists and ankles, she's not physically hurt. However, we believe she has been drugged; she is very confused. We've sent off some blood and urine samples, which will tell us a lot more, but that's my best guess."

"Thank you, doctor. Please keep me informed of any developments."

The young nurse, Cara, approached the two men.

"Joanna's parents have arrived, doctor. Is it okay for them to see her? They are both very agitated."

The doctor looked at Sabir for guidance.

"Yes, yes. Let them see her. I'm guessing you will be keeping Joanna in overnight?"

The doctor nodded.

"I will come back in the morning and talk to all three of them. I have other patients to see to right now."

'MISSING GIRL FOUND ALIVE AND WELL' Teresa read on the morning news. She called through to the kitchen.

"Samantha, have you seen this?"

Samantha came in and read the headline.

236

"I found out late last night but you had gone to bed, I didn't want to disturb you. They've also picked up Jason Dale. Sabir is going to start questioning him this morning."

"What about the other two girls?" Teresa asked.

"There was no sign of them, but Jason's house is being searched this morning. We should know more soon. The good news, for you, is that the press have gone from the end of the road. It appears they have bigger fish to fry. I see no reason why you couldn't go out today, on your own, if you feel up to it. Maybe for a walk, or a drive to the shop to pick up a few things? It's time to start slowly going back to living life as normal. What about taking Lily to school?"

Teresa looked horrified, and scared.

"I really don't think I can," she stuttered. "And Lily...Lily hasn't been told everything yet. What if she hears something at school?"

Samantha was sympathetic.

"Maybe not today, then, but soon. We need to get her back into a routine. And people are going to talk, that's just natural. We will deal with Lily's questions as she asks them."

"I know you're right. Let me think about it," conceded Teresa. "I could take her out in the car later, to the park maybe. We could both do with some fresh air. But I think it's too soon for school."

Sabir knocked on Jason Dale's neighbour's door. Mrs Simms opened it and greeted him politely.

"Hello, can I help you?"

"Good morning, Mrs Simms," replied Sabir. "My name is Detective Inspector Asrat Sabir. I'd like to come in and ask you and your husband some questions, if that's alright?"

He flashed his identity card at her, and the concern in her face changed immediately to compliance.

"Well, of course, please come in."

Mrs Simms showed the detective into their twee living room, where they found Mr Simms reading the sports pages of the newspaper.

"Arthur, this is Detective Inspector Sabir. He'd like to talk with us both."

"What have you been up to now, Mabel?" joked Arthur Simms, laughing at his own joke. "Take a seat here, can we get you a drink?"

"No, thank you. I'm here to ask you some questions about your neighbour, Jason Dale."

Mr and Mrs Simms exchanged quizzical glances.

"Don't you mean Jamie?" Mrs Simms asked him. "His name is Jamie, not Jason. We don't know his last name though; we've never needed to know. We just call him Jamie."

"Well, I regret to inform you that his name is not Jamie. His name is Jason Dale, and we have him in custody. We have reason to suspect that he may be responsible for the abduction of three girls from Stonehenge."

Mrs Simms gasped audibly.

"You're not serious? I thought you already had the man who did that? I'm sure Jamie can't have been involved. We've never had any trouble from him, have we Arthur?"

She looked over at her husband. Mr Simms shook his head, in agreement with his wife's statement. Sabir continued to question Mr and Mrs Simms for the next hour. When he was ready to leave, Mr Simms showed him to the door.

"You could knock me down with a feather. We didn't have any idea about any of this. We were just really pleased to have a nice, quiet neighbour. We've had all sorts living there over the years, I don't mind telling you. There was this one girl…"

Sabir interrupted and shook Mr Simms hand.

"Thank you, you've both been extremely helpful. Please remember, if you do think of anything else that might be important, please get in touch."

"Yes, we will do," said Mr Simms, as he closed the door.

Sabir walked next door and spoke to one of the forensic investigators.

"What have we got?"

"Nothing yet, sir. The place is very clean, too clean really, which is always suspicious. We've taken lots of samples which have gone off to the lab, and we have some things that appear to belong to Joanna, items she had with her when she went missing. But so far, there's nothing that links this property with the other two girls."

"Okay, keep looking," sighed Sabir, disappointed. "There has to be something. He must be involved in all three crimes. Oh, and have a look in the back garden. The neighbours said it was a right mess out there three years ago, when Dale first moved in. One of the first things he did was lay a new lawn, and he's in the middle of digging a hole for a pond at the bottom of the garden, but he's been hampered by heavy rains. I'm off back to the station to talk to Dale."

"Right you are, sir. As soon as we find anything, you'll be the first to know."

"For the tape, Detective Inspector Sabir has entered the interview room. It is now 10:03 a.m."

"Sir, Mr Dale has confirmed his name and address, but he has stated that he will not be answering any further questions. His solicitor has prepared a written statement that Mr Dale has signed. It reads, 'I, Jason Dale, admit to the abduction of Joanna Pinkerton from Stonehenge, on the night of the solstice event. Since that night, she has been kept at my house against her will. I have not harmed or assaulted her in any way. I do not know anything regarding the disappearances of Maisie Jones or Claudia Merrick."

Sabir looked hard into the face of Jason Dale.

"Do you expect me to believe that? We have you bang to rights for Joanna. Are you telling me that you were not involved in the abduction of Maisie or Claudia?"

Jason looked at Sabir with contempt.

240

"No comment."

Sabir sighed. He was already exasperated.

"We know that you have been working together with Mark Applewhite. We have items from both Maisie and Claudia, linking you and Mark to the disappearances. We know that you're in it together."

Jason smirked at the detective.

"No comment."

"Where did you meet Mark Applewhite?"

Jason fixed his gaze on the detective, speaking slowly and deliberately.

"No comment."

Sabir continued.

"We know that you met Mark at the Greengates facility, in 2002. Did the two of you work together, as accomplices?"

"No comment."

Sabir left the interview room. He'd had enough of Jason Dale already. The man clearly wasn't going to be much help to them. Still, he reasoned, they could keep Jason in custody for a while, and once they had a statement from Joanna, they could charge him. Jason Dale wasn't going anywhere.

Later that day, Sabir returned to the hospital. A huge crowd of reporters had gathered around the main entrance.

"Detective Inspector Sabir, is it true that Joanna has been found alive?"

"Have you got any news about the other two girls?"

"Is it true that you now have a second man in custody?"

"What can you tell us?"

The questions were coming thick and fast.

"I will be making a statement later today, regarding the recent developments in this case. I can confirm that Joanna Pinkerton has been found, safe and well, and that the man suspected of abducting her is in police custody."

"You said previously that Mark Applewhite was responsible. Do you still think that is the case?" persisted one of the reporters.

"Our investigations are ongoing, and it would be wrong to speculate at this time. I will give you a full update later today, when I have more information to share with you."

Sabir pushed his way through the crowd and into the hospital, making his way to the private room where Joanna was staying. He was pleased to see her sitting up in bed, looking quite well. Both her parents were with her.

"Joanna. How are you?" he asked.

Before she had time to reply, her father spoke sharply to the inspector.

"She needs time to rest. Can't this wait?"

Sabir addressed Mr Pinkerton kindly, but very firmly.

"Sadly not, Mr Pinkerton. We are absolutely delighted that Joanna has been found, but I really do need to speak to her. There are still two young women unaccounted for, and their parents remain very worried. I'm sure you can appreciate that."

Mr Pinkerton looked at his daughter.

"It's okay, Dad. I feel a lot better today, and the officer is right, I need to do what I can to help. I want to help."

She looked at Sabir.

"I can't remember much, as he had me drugged most of the time. But I'll answer your questions if I can."

Sabir nodded.

"Have the blood and urine tests come back yet?"

"Yes, he used Rohypnol on me, that's why I felt so awful. But it's wearing off now, and I do feel a lot better. My head is much clearer."

Sabir smiled at the young woman.

"I'm pleased to hear that. We were all very concerned for you. Now, if you don't mind, can you tell me everything you remember?"

Joanna started to tell her story.

"I remember the night it happened. I was dancing with my sister Suzie, and some of our friends. They got tired and wanted a rest, so they went back to where we'd left our things, to have a coffee. I wanted to keep on dancing, and to start off with there was quite a crowd of us, but after a while, the other dancers started to disperse. I noticed that I was on my own so I went to re-join my friends. I started walking towards them, but suddenly this man grabbed my wrist and started dragging me away. I tried to resist but he was so strong. I put my free arm up and waved, trying to attract Suzie's attention. I was shouting to them, to Suzie and the others, but they just couldn't hear me. The man kept pulling and pulling me; I couldn't free myself from his grip. I was terrified, grabbing at people as I was pulled past them, but nobody took any notice."

Mrs Pinkerton started to sob.

"Oh, Joanna, my darling. How awful! Suzie has been distraught. She hasn't slept and won't eat."

"It's not Suzie's fault, Mum, don't blame her. It all happened so quickly. One woman did stop and look at us, but he just told her that I'd had too much to drink and he was taking me home. He carried on dragging me away until we came to this narrow lane. There was a white van parked there. As we approached, I could see another man standing beside the van, waiting for us. I thought the two of them were going to do something awful to me, but the other man challenged Jason and started to attack him. He tried to get between us, and wrestle me away, but Jason was so strong that he somehow managed to throw me into the back of the van while fighting off this man. I heard the two of them outside, still fighting, but Jason must have won because he climbed into the back of the van with me shortly afterwards. I never saw the other man again. I don't know who he was."

"Would you recognise him again, if we showed you a photo?"

"Yes, I think I would."

Sabir looked at the girl kindly.

"I'm sorry to have to ask this, Joanna, but did Jason hurt you?"

Joanna dropped her head and looked down shyly.

"No, I don't think so. The doctors have examined me, and they don't think I've been raped or molested."

"Is there anything else you can remember?"

"One night, Jason brought me some food. He untied one of my hands so that I could eat it. I tried to be really nice to him. He did say that he was sorry about what he'd done to me. He said it wasn't my fault, he just couldn't help himself; that something inside him made him do it; that I was just in the wrong place at the wrong time. He seemed calm when he was talking to me, and I thought he might let me go."

Joanna started to cry and her mother immediately stood up and went to comfort the girl. After a few moments, Joanna continued.

"I promised him that I wouldn't tell anyone about what he'd done, if he would just let me go. But he said that he couldn't. It was too late. I was sure he was going to kill me."

Sabir looked at the girl sympathetically.

"You've been through a terrible ordeal, pet. But you're safe now. We've got him in the cells, and I promise you, we're not letting him go. Did he tell you anything about the other two girls?"

Joanna recovered herself a little.

"Yes. He said that the first girl, Maisie, had put up a hell of a fight. She had punched him; kicked him; bitten him. He had struggled to manage her. He said he hadn't planned that one properly, and she had taken him by surprise by fighting back. He told me that he had killed her, but that it was accidental; he hadn't meant for it to end that way. But when he had put her in the van, she was hysterical, and had lashed out at him. He hadn't been able to calm her down, so he hit her, to make her stop. She was dead before he even left Stonehenge. He said that's why he used the drugs on me, because he couldn't risk that happening again."

"Did he say what happened to Claudia?"

"Not really, but he did tell me that she was really pretty and kind. I could tell from the way he was talking that he really liked her, but he didn't tell me what happened to her. Do you think he killed her too?"

"We don't know, pet. There's no trace of her at his house. Did anyone else come to the house while you were there? The other man, perhaps?"

"I don't think so, but it's possible. I was drugged for most of the time."

"Okay. That's enough for today. You have been a fantastic help Joanna. I'm going to leave you here now, with your mum and dad. When you're feeling a bit better, I'll send someone down to take a formal statement from you. But for now, you get some rest."

As Sabir walked through the hospital, after leaving the Pinkertons, he made a call to the forensics team.

"We have at least one body, possibly two. I want you to start with the garden. Get the dogs up there, and take the GPR equipment too, see if it picks up anything unusual underground. If nothing shows up, just dig up the whole garden. I want those girls found."

He drove back to the station with the radio turned off, mentally preparing to update his boss on the events of the last twenty-four hours, and considering what information he was going to release at the press conference. He also despatched two pairs of officers to visit the families of Maisie and Claudia. He needed to give them a formal update before it hit the news.

Chapter 15

Samantha sat in the living room, with Teresa and Mrs Applewhite, watching the early evening news. The knots in her stomach were so tight that she had to sit bolt upright. They had been warned to expect a report of some new developments, regarding the Stonehenge case, and were all eagerly awaiting further details. Teresa was fidgeting, trying to find a comfortable way to sit, and wringing her hands, as she always did when she felt anxious. She felt sick, nervous about what else she was going to learn about her brother, and worried about what her mother's reaction would be.

The newsreader's face and tone were serious. He announced that the police had found and arrested another man, a known associate of Mark Applewhite, who was believed to have been involved in the abduction of the girls from the Stonehenge festival. The last girl to be taken, Joanna Pinkerton, had been found alive, and was recovering from her ordeal in hospital. Teresa was absolutely delighted to hear the news about Joanna, but she was also worried about what this girl would have to say about Mark and his involvement. Finally, she was going to know the full extent of what Mark had been doing. There would be no conjecture or theories from experts, no opinion or supposition from the police,

248

and no speculation or sensationalism from the press. This was going to be fact and truth, and she wasn't sure how she was going to react to that.

The news bulletin cut from the studio to some photographs of a very ordinary looking house, in a very ordinary looking street. This was where, the reporter said, Jason Dale had been living and where they had found Joanna, a prisoner in the house since the night of her disappearance. The bulletin showed clips of sniffer dogs, with their handlers, being taken into the property, and footage of a small digger arriving and being lifted by crane over the house, into the back garden. The house had been cordoned off and was guarded by police officers, exactly as their own house had been until yesterday.

A photograph of a smiling Joanna Pinkerton flashed up, with a strapline announcing 'FOUND', followed by photographs of Maisie and Claudia, side by side, with the word 'MISSING' underneath, in big red letters. Teresa was relieved to hear that Joanna had only minor injuries and was expected to make a full recovery. It was clearly stated that she hadn't been sexually abused or violated, which was very good news, but Teresa was confused as to what the motive for taking these girls was, if it wasn't sexual. She asked Samantha what other motives there might be. Samantha was as engrossed and intrigued by the news bulletin as the other two women.

"In my experience, it's always sexual," she replied. "Whether that be for the sexual pleasure of the abductor himself, or whether that be for some sort of trafficking, and therefore the sexual pleasure of someone else, the answer is always sex. This is very unusual. To keep a girl for several days and not to harm her is very, odd. I have never come across a case like this before. I don't think we know the full story yet."

For the rest of the evening, Teresa could think of little else. Samantha was right, it was odd. Why would two gay men, as she now believed them both to be, kidnap three young women? Why had they taken an interest in them? Surely, it would have made more sense for them to kidnap young men? Then again, if the motive wasn't sexual, that wouldn't have made any sense either. It was all very confusing.

Sabir's phone buzzed.

"We've got human bones, sir. One complete skeleton, under the lawn. Female and young by the looks of it. We're excavating now and will let you know as soon as it's confirmed, but items buried with the body have been identified as belonging to Maisie Jones, and the pathologist's initial findings substantiate that. It's likely that the remains are hers."

Sabir's heart sank. Yesterday, finding Joanna alive and unharmed, had been unexpected and encouraging. But now…he exhaled sharply, opening his office door and shouting to the officers in the next room.

"Get Dale back in the interview room, now. I'm just in the mood for him!"

Twenty minutes later, Sabir sat opposite Jason Dale and his solicitor.

The solicitor spoke first.

"Inspector Sabir, I am at a loss as to why you have called my client for a second interview, when he made it perfectly clear yesterday that he has no comment to make, and has given you a written statement. This is harassment."

Sabir did not reply to the solicitor, or even make eye contact with him. He fixed his gaze firmly on Jason Dale and spoke directly to him.

"We've found Maisie's body buried in your back garden."

At once, Jason's face and demeanour changed. Gone was his cocky, smirking grin, and unhelpful attitude. His face paled as Sabir continued to stare at him, and when Jason finally spoke, his voice was shaky and quiet.

"I...I didn't think you'd find her."

His solicitor leant across and whispered something. Jason replied to him.

"No, it's over. If they've found her, they'll find everything."

"Yes, Jason. We found Maisie, and it's my guess that Joanna was going to end up under the pond; she would already be there if there hadn't been so much rain this summer. So, that just leaves Claudia. What have you done with Claudia?"

Jason put his head in his hands.

"You won't find her at the house, she's not there."

"We will find her, if she's there, so there's no use trying to hide it. We're taking the whole place to pieces, brick by brick. Whatever it takes," said Sabir with authority.

Jason looked down, thinking hard. He knew there was no point in continuing to be uncooperative.

"She's not there. I couldn't do that to her. I buried her properly, in the woods. Wickden Woods."

"You killed her?"

"Yes, I killed her. I didn't want to, but I had to."

"Why?"

"It was the first one's fault, Maisie. I took her for a laugh, just to see if I could do it. I wasn't going to hurt her, just frighten her a bit and drop her off up the road. I didn't plan to kill her. But she kicked off badly and started attacking me. She was strong too. I was trying to control her, but she left me no choice. I had to fight her off and before I knew what had happened, I'd killed her. I just wanted her to settle down, but she kept lashing out. In the end, I suffocated her. She was dead. I'd killed her."

"If that's true, why didn't you come to us then, and explain that it was an accident?"

"I expected you lot round when I'd killed Maisie, but you didn't come. You didn't have any idea what had happened to her. I'd got away with it. So I thought, why not do it again? I enjoyed seeing it on the news every day; it felt good knowing what had happened and knowing where she was, when nobody else had a clue. It made me feel important."

Sabir shook his head in disbelief.

"And Claudia, what happened to Claudia?"

"I had gone prepared that time, it was much easier. I got her in the back of the van easy enough and forced her to drink some water that I'd laced with a knock-out drug. Once she was out cold, I was able to tie her hands together and then carry her into the house when we got back."

"Is that what you did with Joanna?"

"Yes, it worked well with Claudia, so why mess with it?"

"How long did you keep Claudia alive?" asked Sabir.

Jason became upset at this question. He ran his fingers nervously through his hair and shuffled in his seat.

"Nearly a week, in the end. It was odd because she started talking to me. She was nice, really kind and sweet; I began to like her a bit. I'd never spoken to a woman like that before, properly. Usually, women stay away from me and don't want to talk to me, but Claudia was different. She asked me questions, she tried to understand me…nobody's ever done that before."

"Why did you kill her, then, if you liked her so much?"

"I had to. Me and Claudia were talking one day, and I told her about Maisie; that I'd killed her. I told her how it happened and that it was a mistake, but she knew I'd killed her. Claudia said that, if I explained, people would understand. She even said that if I let her go, she'd speak up for me, and say that I'd treated her well. She said that they'd be lenient with me. I thought about it. I really did. But in the end, I couldn't risk it. I had to kill her. She was probably lying anyway. Women always lie."

"Why did you take her to Wickden Woods?" asked Sabir. "She could have been found at any time. Why not just put her in the garden, like you did with Maisie?"

Jason wrung his hands; he was visibly upset.

"Claudia deserved a proper burial. I said prayers for her, and planted a tree to mark the spot. I've been there several times and taken flowers for her. It's a proper grave, in a beautiful place. I thought she'd be happy there."

"Were you going to kill Joanna?"

Jason buried his head and pushed it further into his folded arms on the table.

"Yes, tonight. She thought she was talking me round, but I knew I had to do it. I knew it was time. I didn't want her getting under my skin, like Claudia. They're all the same, women. They'll tell you anything to get what they want."

Sabir sighed heavily.

"What about Mark Applewhite? What was his role in all of this? Did he help you take the girls?"

Jason looked up at Sabir and smirked.

"Don't be daft. He hasn't got it in him. Mark's as soft as anything. He's the reason I started all this. I was teasing him; it worked too, it was so easy to do."

Sabir looked puzzled.

"I don't understand. Explain what Mark Applewhite has got to do with all of this."

Guilt spread across Jason's face.

"I just told you, he hasn't got anything to do with it. You may as well know everything, it's not going to make any difference now, is it? It was all my doing. Mark was trying to stop me."

Jason went on to explain that he and Mark had a fling at Greengates. They had become close when Jason had been working nights and Mark was an inpatient. They would often sit up together at night, talking, and Jason had told Mark all about his chaotic upbringing and his feckless mother, whom he hated. He told Mark about how she would always hook up with lots of different men, especially at Stonehenge on Solstice night, and how he'd had to watch her parade herself around and get-off with all these men. Mark and Jason had become close, and they had eventually started a relationship, which Mark had regretted and pulled away from almost immediately. He couldn't face anyone at all knowing he was gay. Jason had felt rejected all over again, and had been angry with Mark for treating him so badly. He had felt pushed out of Mark's life, just like he had felt pushed out of his mother's life.

Jason knew that when he took Maisie, and sent Mark her hair clip, Mark would know who was responsible. The girl wasn't supposed to die, but she had, and suddenly the situation had become a lot more serious. But Jason had felt he had nothing to lose. He had expected Mark to go straight to the police, when he received the hairclip, and tell them what he knew. Jason had sat at home for three days, waiting for the knock on the door. But when that didn't happen, Jason thought that meant Mark must still like him and have some loyalty to him. He had felt that they still had something in common. A shared secret. He had felt connected to Mark again.

Sabir was shocked. Two young women were dead, and this was why?

"So, what you're saying is that you were doing all this to test Mark, and to mess with his head? Was Mark involved in any of the kidnappings?"

"No," replied Jason. "But he knew that I was responsible."

"How can you know that?"

"After I took Claudia, he saw me in town one day, and chased after me. I really wanted to stop and talk to him, but I saw how angry he was with me. So I just ran. He chased me for ages, but eventually I lost him. He knew it was me, else why would he have been so angry? He didn't go to the police though. I never understood why."

"Are you aware that Mark is still in the hospital? He hasn't regained consciousness, and it looks unlikely that he ever will. So, there's no point hiding anything. You see, there's still one thing that doesn't add up, Jason. We found both yours and Joanna's DNA under Mark's fingernails, so he must have been there with you both. I'm not sure you're telling the complete truth. Are you protecting him?"

Jason sighed.

"Mark came looking for me this year, at Stonehenge, didn't he? And he found me, with Joanna. He tried to play the superhero and rescue the girl, but I fought him off. He put up a bloody good fight, but I kicked him in the ribs. Then, while he was doubled over in pain, I drove off. I saw on the news that you lot had pinned it all on him. He's an idiot for getting involved, but I thought that if you lot thought it was him, then I'd be in the clear. And it didn't look like he'd be able to tell you any different. I'd decided that I wouldn't go to Stonehenge again. Then he'd go down in history as the guilty party, and I'd be the only person in the world that knew the truth"

"Are you telling me that Mark was trying to stop you taking Joanna?"

"Yeah, the bloody fool. He said he'd been there last year as well, looking for me. But he couldn't find me. He told me that, as soon as he received the hair clip, he knew it was me, like I thought he would. He hadn't forgotten about me after all. I wanted to make him think about me, and I did. But it turned out that he was just angry with me. I thought he'd understand. When I used to talk to him about my problems, he always understood me, even when I told him about hitting my mother. I missed that."

Sabir shook his head in disbelief. He'd heard enough.

"Jason Dale, I am arresting you for the abduction and murder of Maisie Jones and Claudia Merrick; for the abduction and confinement of Joanna Pinkerton, and for the grievous bodily harm and attempted murder of Mark Applewhite. You will appear in a magistrates court in the morning, where you will be remanded in custody until your trial. Do you understand?"

"Yes, I do."

Sabir left the interview room and sighed heavily. Two innocent young girls had lost their lives, because of some silly mind games Jason Dale had decided to play with Mark Applewhite. He hadn't raped or molested any of the girls, because they weren't what he'd wanted. It had never been about them. He had just taken them to exert control over Mark, and to get his attention. Mark was innocent in all this. Or was he? He had known when the first girl went missing that Jason was responsible, but he had decided to say nothing, which had to make him culpable too, surely? Sabir wondered if Mark had thought that no-one would believe him…or could it have been the shame of having his homosexuality discovered that had stopped him going to the police? Sabir shook his head. This job, this bloody job! Just when you thought it couldn't surprise or disturb you anymore; just when you believed that you'd seen everything there was to see, it would throw something else at you, something challenging and monumental that made you question everything that had gone before. He shook his head again. Maybe that's why he kept doing it?

Teresa opened the door to Sabir. She wasn't pleased to see him.

"I've been expecting you. I suppose this Jason has blamed everything on Mark; said he was the mastermind behind the whole thing? That's what any sane person would do, wouldn't they? Since Mark's not in any fit state to dispute any of it, or give his side of the story."

"He has been talking, Teresa, and we know a lot more than we did previously. I think we ought to sit down with your mum, and I'll tell you both what we know so far."

Ten minutes later, the three of them were seated in the living room, while Samantha distracted Lily in the back garden.

"Are you alright, Mum? You don't have to listen to this if you don't want to. I can deal with it."

"No, Teresa" replied her mother firmly. "Mark is my son. I need to hear this."

Teresa looked over at her mother. She had coped with all of this remarkably well. In fact, Teresa felt that her mum seemed to be getting stronger. She was doing more things for herself and around the house, and she seemed more alive than she had been in years. It was almost like the shock of the situation had forced her out of her own world, and into the real one. Maybe it was because of the constant stream of strangers passing through the house: police, investigators, forensics, doctors, psychologists? Maybe, all these people being here had forced her to acknowledge that the wider world was there? Instead of her just existing on her own, she had been forced to meet and interact with all of these people, and Teresa had to admit that it seemed to have done her some good.

Samantha had been a good influence on her too. She didn't just do everything for her, as Teresa and Mark had done. She encouraged her to look after herself more and had gently pushed her to take a more active role in caring for Lily. Teresa had noticed, over the past few days, that her mum was moving around more easily. She was sprightlier than Teresa ever remembered seeing her. She seemed to interact more with people now and had stopped staring off into space. But despite this improvement, Teresa was still worried that whatever Sabir was about to tell them could be devastating for her, and might set her back to square one again.

Sabir cleared his throat and began to speak.

"As you are already aware, we have Jason Dale in custody, and after interviewing him we have found out a lot more about him. He has a criminal past and has previously been employed in care work, which is how he met Mark. Mark was sectioned voluntarily in 2002, as you know, and spent time at Greengates Residential Establishment. Jason was also at Greengates in 2002, on a back-to-work placement scheme for offenders, after serving time for sexual assault. It appears that the two of them struck up some kind of intimate relationship with each other, while they were there. Obviously, we only have Jason's account that this was the case, though we have spoken to other staff members who recall that the two of them seemed close and spent a lot of time together."

Teresa looked over at her mother, who was close to tears.

"Go on," Teresa encouraged Sabir.

"It seems that, when they both left Greengates, Jason would have liked to pursue a relationship with Mark. But Mark rejected him, which frustrated Jason. He felt that Mark had abandoned him."

"What has this got to do with the girls at Stonehenge?" Teresa asked.

Sabir continued.

"Well, during their relationship at Greengates, Jason confided in Mark about his upbringing, which was certainly unusual. His past appears to have had a disastrous and devastating effect on Jason, in particular his perception and treatment of women. He told our psychologist that he didn't ever want to be a homosexual, but when he was younger and approached women, they ridiculed and rejected him. This, along with his complicated relationship with his mother, made him develop and nurture a strong hatred for women, so much so that he couldn't bear to be in their company, and instead sought out the company of men."

"Mark knew all this?" asked Teresa.

"Mark certainly knew about Jason's dislike for women, and about his disastrous early life. He also knew that Jason's mother had taken him to Stonehenge every year as a child, and that he had spent each year watching her get-off with various men. This appears to have had a profound effect on Jason, instigating a mistrust and hatred of women which he has carried into adulthood."

Teresa was confused.

"So, he and Mark cooked up a plan to kidnap women from Stonehenge, as some sort of payback, because this Jason had a terrible mother and wasn't popular with women?"

"Well, no. Not Mark," replied Sabir. "We're fairly confident that Jason Dale was working on his own when he abducted all three of the girls."

Teresa looked at him in astonishment.

"Mark wasn't involved? I don't understand. You found so much evidence. The things belonging to the girls in his bedroom, and Joanna's DNA on Mark...how could that have happened if he wasn't involved?"

Sabir sighed sadly.

"Although he wasn't involved in, or party to, any of the abductions, it seems that Mark was aware from very early on that Jason was responsible for those acts. As you told us, Teresa, Mark was miles away when the first incident happened. But it does seem that he knew Jason was responsible immediately, from the very first abduction."

"Why didn't he say anything?" she asked.

"I'm not sure we are ever going to know the answer to that one, Teresa. Jason was taunting Mark, by sending him things through the post, trying to exert control over him and get his attention. Mark went to Stonehenge in 2018, to search for Jason, but he couldn't find him. Then, this year, he went back again, and he found Jason. Mark intercepted him as he was trying to force Joanna into his van, and tried to pull the girl away from Jason, which would explain why he had Joanna's DNA on him. However, he was unsuccessful; he and Jason ended up in a fight, where Mark sustained his injuries, and

Mark lost, leaving Jason free to make off with the girl."

Mrs Applewhite, who had been listening intently to the conversation between her daughter and the inspector, gasped from the other side of the room.

"Oh, my word. Poor Mark."

"Yes, Mum. It looks like he was trying to handle this whole situation by himself. That would explain his erratic behaviour, and mood swings. I wonder why he didn't just tell somebody about it? He hadn't done anything wrong. He could have stopped all this."

"Don't be too hard on him, Teresa," said Sabir. "It's not a situation that any of us have ever found ourselves in, so none of us really know how we would react if we were put under that amount of pressure. I think Mark was probably completely overwhelmed by it all. And let's not forget his past. He has a deep-seated mistrust of the police, and authority figures generally. Maybe he thought that the only way to resolve it was to try and fix it himself, and that's what he tried to do. If Mark regains consciousness, we may charge him, but with a much lesser crime of withholding and obstructing information."

"Teresa, I want to go and see him," said her mum, suddenly.

Teresa smiled. This was the first time since Mark had been found that her mother had asked to see him.

"I'll take you, Mum, let's go now."

Sabir got up to leave.

"Would you like me to arrange a lift for you both?"

"No, thank you, Inspector," said Teresa straightening herself. "I think it's about time we raised our heads and started living our lives independently again. My brother is not a murderer, or a kidnapper. He just came up against a problem that he couldn't fix, that's all."

Sabir nodded in agreement.

"The press are now aware that Jason Dale is in the frame, so you shouldn't have any more trouble from them. But they may still try and get you to speak about Mark. I would advise you not to speak to anyone until after the court case. The families of the girls have also been informed of the facts, as we currently know them. I will remove the officer from the front of the house today and hopefully things can start to get back to normal around here."

He left the two women together. Teresa hugged her mother tightly; they were both crying tears of relief.

"I told you Mark couldn't do anything bad. He's never done anything bad. He's always been such a lovely boy."

"I know he has, Mum. You were right all along. Now, let's go and see him, shall we?"

As Sabir left the Applewhite's house, his phone buzzed again. Sniffer dogs had found Claudia Merrick's body, in an unmarked grave in Wickden Woods. It was exactly where Jason Dale had told them it was. Two detectives were on their way to the Merrick family home, to break the news to her parents. It looked like the case was solved. All three girls had been accounted for, one way or another.

Teresa and her mum stood at Mark's bedside, each of them holding one of his hands. Mrs Applewhite spoke to her son.

"We love you, Mark, and we know you didn't hurt those girls. We know you tried to protect them, to stop him from hurting them. We know everything."

If Mark could hear those words, he didn't respond to them. The doctor entered the room and looked gravely at the two women standing over the young man's bed.

"I'm glad you're both here, I need to discuss Mark's condition with you. I'm afraid we've reached a point where there is nothing more we can do for Mark. He hasn't responded to any treatment, and now his major organs are failing. He is unable to breathe for himself; he is only alive because we are keeping him alive artificially. We feel that it is time to switch off the machines and let Mark go. Perhaps you would both like some time to think about it?"

"I don't need any time," said Teresa's mum. "He has been through so much. It's the right decision. We need to let him go."

The doctor nodded and left the room. Teresa and her mum stood there, on either side of Mark, with tears streaming down their faces.

"Goodbye, Mark," Teresa managed through her tears. "Goodbye to the best brother and uncle that there ever was. I will miss you forever."

The doctor came back in, with a nurse by his side.

"Are you ready?"

Mrs Applewhite took charge of the situation.

"Yes. We're ready."

She walked round to Teresa and held her hand. The doctor and nurse methodically turned off the machines, which stopped beeping. They removed the tube from his mouth and took down the drips attached to his arms. Then they pulled a sheet up to his shoulders, adjusted his arms, and smoothed his bedclothes.

"It's all done," the doctor said, looking at them with sympathy. "I'm very sorry for your loss. Please stay here as long as you like; take your time."

"Thank you for everything that you tried to do," Mrs Applewhite said to the doctor, as he left the three of them alone in the room.

"It's just us now, Teresa. Just you, me and Lily. Let's go home, shall we? Let's go and see Lily."

They both kissed Mark on the cheek and walked away, hand in hand, back to the car.

Later that evening, Teresa held Lily in her arms; the child shook and sobbed, small quiet sobs. Uncle Mark wasn't coming home anymore. Teresa had told her daughter that he had gone to heaven, because they needed someone to look after their garden.

A week later, Teresa and Mrs Applewhite stood at the front door of their home and watched as the hearse arrived outside. As it pulled up in the street, they looked at each other and smiled. They had chosen a bright pink coffin, and had it adorned with the most enormous wreath, made up of blue and white sweet peas, Mark's favourite. In death, if not in life, Mark could be the person that he had always wanted to be.

The service was short, and Teresa read a poem. There were only a few people in the small church, but outside a small group had gathered. A young woman approached Teresa and she recognised her immediately.

"Hello, Teresa, I hope you don't mind me being here. I wanted to say thank you to Mark, for what he tried to do, but I can't now. So I wanted to say it to you."

Teresa hugged her tightly and they both cried, holding each other close. When they eventually pulled away from their embrace, Teresa wiped her tears and put her hands on the girl's shoulders.

"Joanna, thank you so much for coming. It means so much to me. It must have been so hard for you. Some of the things that have been said in the press…that if Mark had told the police earlier, you would have never been taken…"

"It's okay, Teresa. I'm okay. I was lucky, very lucky. I understand what Mark tried to do. I was there. I know how hard he tried to stop it happening.

He lost his life trying to save mine and I will be forever grateful to him."

Joanna's father approached the pair. He didn't speak to Teresa.

"Come on, Joanna. Let's get you back home. You're still recovering, and I don't want you to overdo it. Let's get you away from prying eyes."

The young woman waved to Teresa and turned away, holding onto her father as he led her through the small group of onlookers.

Teresa turned to Sabir.

"Would you take Mum home for me, please? I need to go for a walk by myself for a while, to clear my head."

Sabir gripped Teresa's hand tightly and squeezed it.

"Of course, I will."

Moments later, Teresa watched him guide her mum into his car and drive away. Teresa walked away from the chapel. She took a deep breath of fresh air, enjoying the freedom of walking along the street alone. The phone in her pocket rang. Dan.

"Dan, hi. Yes, I'd love to meet you for a coffee. Where are you? Right, I'm on my way."

BV - #0048 - 261120 - C0 - 197/132/16 - PB - 9781912964437